Jaxon

with an

X

JAXON WITH AN X

A NOVEL

D. K. WALL

Conjuring
Reality

All inquiries should be addressed to:

Conjuring Reality Media
65 Merrimon Avenue #1053
Asheville NC 28801

ISBN 978-1-950293-03-2 (Paperback)
ISBN 978-1-950293-04-9 (eBook)

Library of Congress Control Number: 2020912270

This book is a work of fiction. The story incorporates real locations and entities, but all are used in a fictitious manner. The events of the story, the characters, and the communities of Millerton and Wattsville are products of the author's imagination and purely fictional. Any resemblance to actual persons, living or dead, is coincidental.

Cover designed by Glendon S. Haddix of Streetlight Graphics

ALSO BY D. K. WALL

1

———

I never knew the world could be so damned cold.

Back there, where I'm from, the stone walls chilled bones, the broken windows let rain puddle, and the uneven floor tripped feet and invited stubbed toes. But at least those walls provided protection from biting winds, pelting sleet, and piles of snow and ice.

Out here, though, I'm exposed. The wind whips through the holes in my clothing. The icy snow slips under my shirt and slides down my back. The sleet stings my face.

But I'm free.

A fair trade as far as I'm concerned.

My numb ears pick up the sound of car tires hissing through the snow. I turn and squint against the storm. A glow of headlights grows from beyond the curve in the mountains. A car is coming down the desolate highway.

I curse under my breath. I've got to keep my mind from wandering off. In my inattention, I almost violated his first rule: *Never let them see you.*

A rush of adrenaline courses through my exhausted body, providing the boost of energy I need to scramble over the guardrail. I wriggle into a crevice and deep into the shadows between the icy boulders lining the edge of the highway.

The car comes into view. Heavy snowflakes glitter in the beams of light arcing over my head. I cower until the car sloshes past, praying the driver is unaware that I'm hunkering just feet away. The whine of the engine drops and fades into the distance.

I smile despite the frigid weather. For the first time in my sheltered life, *Doppler effect* is more than words I read in a dictionary.

Doppler effect—the change in the frequency of sound waves as an object moves closer or further from a listener.

It's real, not some concept I've only read about. The approaching roar of a car. The swoosh of its pass. The drop in frequency. The dwindling drone as it drives into the distance.

I never knew the world could be so magical.

In our isolation, we spent hours quizzing each other from the dictionary, one of the few books other than the little kids' picture books we had hidden away. We could only read the tongue twisters of Dr. Seuss and look at the stunning images of *Where the Wild Things Are* so many times before we memorized them. New books arrived infrequently. Not every kid came to us with a backpack.

The dictionary, which we'd found hidden in a blue satchel with pens, notebooks, and a ruler, enlarged our little world, revealing something new every time we opened it. We struggled to pronounce words correctly and erupted in muffled laughter at our mangled attempts. Each unraveled definition compelled us to look up more words. We had little practical experience to understand anything we learned, but the word games helped us pass the time, which felt interminable.

Interminable—having or seeming to have no end.

Unlike the *Doppler effect*, we experienced *interminable*. Day after day after day, we wondered when the end would come.

From my perch behind the protective rocks, I watch the taillights dwindle into the fog. The fear of being spotted subsides. My heart slows its pounding inside my thin chest. I'm grateful for an unexpected bonus—my hiding place shelters me from the fierce winds. I sit in relative comfort and watch the ruts created by the car turn white as the falling snow fills the void.

I cup my hands and blow warmth across my fingers, silently begging the feeling to come back. A shrill pain lights them up as the numbness fades, stabbing to the bone as I wriggle my digits to get the blood flowing. Though they don't feel anything close to normal, I take it as a sign to resume my march down the road.

I clamber back onto the pavement. The wind beats my back and blows ice crystals from my shaggy hair. I wrap my arms around my thin shirt, shivering against the air rippling through the holes of my jeans and stinging the bare skin below. I tighten the rope threaded through the belt loops, cinching the pants to my waist. Hunched against the weather, I force my burlap-wrapped feet to shuffle through the snow and into the blackness that once again envelops the canyon and hides my presence.

I haven't been as lucky hiding all night. My mind wanders down tangents and I drop my guard. A few hours ago, a guy in a dress shirt and loosened tie spotted me and slowed his car. He gawked at me, his eyes popped wide in surprise as I disappeared into the shadows off the side of the road.

Later, a trucker stopped his giant rig, a vehicle so large I had never imagined such a thing even existed. At first, I was startled by the rumbling engine and the hiss of the air brakes, a dragon exhaling its threat. The driver pushed open his door and climbed down the ladder of his cab as I scrambled into the brush. He stood in front of his growling beast and yelled into the wind for me to come to him. I stayed low, hidden away as he paced, shining a flashlight in hopes of spotting me. He meant no harm, he claimed. He said he wouldn't hurt me and only wanted to get me somewhere safe and warm, but I knew he was a threat. All strangers are.

I remained tucked away, shivering but silent, until he finally surrendered his search with a shrug. With a last look over his shoulder, he climbed back into his warm cab. The gears ground, and he drove away, leaving a cloud of diesel exhaust.

Perhaps they wondered why I didn't accept their offers of help.

The answer is simple. The first rule:

Never let them see you.

I wonder how many more times I'll have the energy to pull myself back out of the shadows and onto this road. Another car will inevitably pass my hiding spot and, from sheer exhaustion, I'll resign myself to my fate and refuse to move again. I'll lower my head onto a granite pillow, the desire to close my eyes and rest outweighing the pull of moving farther down the road. I'll drift into an eternal sleep, my heart slowing until it surrenders and ceases beating. My life will end as I have lived it, hidden from the world.

Even nature will conspire against me then, as it is doing now. He taught us that bodies needed to be buried deep to keep the animals from ravaging them. If I die out here with no one to tend to my remains and hide them out of reach of nature's creatures, then the coyotes will emerge from the canyon, sniff my lifeless body, and drag it away. No one will ever find me. It'll be a fitting end to my invisible life.

My foot hits a patch of ice and I tumble to the ground. The pain rattling my body saves me, breaking my wandering mind from its morbid reflections and forcing me back to cold reality. Horrified by my thoughts, I push myself to my feet, brush the snow off my body, and carry on. As bad as the odds are against me, I refuse to quit.

In all these years, I never have. I've watched others surrender and fade, their hope gone as their lives slip from their grasp, but something inside me kept pushing to live just one more damned day.

Not because I had anything to live for. There was no future back there. I just didn't want to die in that dank, dark place.

I won. I didn't die there. I made it out into the larger world —a much colder and snowier world than I expected, but I'm in it. And that's a good thing. But now I need a new goal.

I pause and look around the dark canyon. A river runs loudly somewhere far below. Forested walls rise high on either side. The stars are obliterated by thick cloud cover and falling snow.

I'm tired of living in darkness, so I set myself a new goal— to see a sunrise. I've never seen one, but I know what others have told me. The brilliant pink and red hues shimmering against the dark blue sky. The magical light peeking over the horizon and extinguishing the stars one by one. The warmth of the sun on their skin. That warmth would feel great right now.

So that's it. I want to experience a sunrise before I die.

Energized with a new goal in mind, I map the process in my mind. Step one—live through the night. It won't be easy, but nothing ever has been.

I look to the east. At least, I think it's east. This road has so many twists and turns as it follows the canyon carved out by the ancient river that I don't know which way I'm facing. When I walked up to this big highway on the two-lane road from deep in the mountains, the red-and-blue signs had said east to the right and west to the left.

I'd taken the access ramp to the right—not because I'd thought of sunrises yet, but because it was closer than crossing under the bridge to turn left. Maybe it was fate that I'd turned in the direction of a sunrise. But a quick glance tells me the sky in front of me is still dark. There's no hopeful, faint glow teasing a brighter day ahead.

I have no choice but to keep moving—to keep living—at least through the night if I want to see a sunrise. Then I can die happy.

Or maybe I'll set a new goal and try to live another day.

I lower my head, lean against the wind, and trudge through the snow, hoping to survive until the sky in front of me brightens.

I never knew the world could be so damned cold.

2

Deputy Jon Patterson slowed his cruiser on Interstate 40, his headlights illuminating the "Welcome to Tennessee" sign through the swirling snow. He followed a pair of snowplows U-turning via a short, paved access road connecting the westbound lanes to the east. The plows, fighting a losing battle against the falling flakes, dropped their blades to the pavement and roared back into North Carolina.

He brought his car to a stop beside a black-and-cream Tennessee highway patrol car facing the other direction in the median. With a tap of the button on his armrest, the driver's window opened. The trooper balanced a steaming cup of coffee in the glow of his dashboard lights and nodded a hello. "Haven't seen a Miller County deputy out this far in a long time."

Patterson couldn't dispute that. The sheriff's department had only six deputies patrolling the sprawling mountainous county at any given time. They had little time or reason to venture into its remote northwestern corner when so little of it was under their jurisdiction.

Over two million acres of undeveloped federal lands—the

Great Smoky Mountains National Park and the Pisgah and Cherokee National Forests—straddled the state line and fell under the control of the federal park and forest rangers. The two states' highway patrols handled their respective portion of the interstate winding through the Pigeon River Gorge, which bisected the parks.

Only a few hardy souls lived in the remote wilderness outside of the federal or state lands and were subject to the sheriff department's jurisdiction—independent-minded people who prided themselves on self-sufficiency. They resented any government interference, particularly from someone wearing a badge and intent on telling them how to live. Little crime happened outside of brewing homemade whiskey, fishing for dinner without a license, or hunting out of season. Violence was unheard of or at least unreported. Disputes were settled without calling the law.

They responded to any reported crime in the remote district, of course, not that any reports were ever made. They also quickly backed up any ranger or trooper requesting assistance, but that was rare. Patterson had never been out there in his year of being a deputy—not even with his training officer. The deputies' routine patrol time was better spent in the eastern portion of the county, among the smaller tourist towns closer to Asheville.

Off-duty, he joined others coming to the area seeking a great place to hike and camp. Even then, he didn't encounter the reclusive people who lived there. They wanted to be left alone.

"The roads are a mess down around Asheville. The troopers on our side of the line are swamped with fender benders." Patterson watched the snow dance in front of his car. "If there is a kid out here…"

The trooper nodded and sipped coffee as he studied the dark road. Few cars traveled that stretch of interstate at two a.m. on a normal night, but the snow had reduced the number to almost none. Without any approaching cars to monitor, the dash-mounted speed detector remained blank. After a long pause, he asked, "Think he's really out here?"

The soft hiss of falling snow filled the silence of their halting conversation. "Doesn't make sense. I haven't seen any sign of him, that's for sure. I can't imagine anyone walking down the highway in this weather. If it was someone with a stalled car or who'd been in a wreck, they wouldn't hide from people offering help."

The trooper snorted. "Which means *if* they exist, they are up to no good and don't want to get caught."

"How much trouble could a boy"—Patterson glanced at his glowing laptop screen mounted on the dash—"between ten and thirteen years old cause out here?"

A chuckle floated from the highway patrol car. "Bad news. One of our callers said girl."

"Great. We don't even know what we are looking for." The deputy ran his finger down the lists of descriptions received from the various reporting parties. "RPs say between four-and-a-half and five-and-a-half feet tall, with shaggy black, brown, or blond hair. Most say wearing jeans and a flannel shirt, but they can't even agree if he's wearing a hat and a coat. And all sorts of conflicting reports of where they saw him"—he paused and looked over at the trooper—"or her..." Getting a smile in return, Patterson continued reading aloud. "...Along a thirty-mile stretch of highway running through the gorge. They can't even decide if he's on your side or our side of the state line. Damn needle in a haystack."

The trooper settled his coffee cup back in its holder. He peered into the darkness surrounding them, stretching his back and shifting his bulletproof vest. "Still, if it's true, he isn't going to last long out here. I've stopped and checked a dozen drifts, just in case."

The deputy nodded quietly in agreement. He knew he got the call because he was the least experienced deputy on the shift—no longer classified as a rookie, but barely. Still, he would rather have wasted his time driving up and down the snow-covered interstate than fail to find some poor kid before he froze to death. As hardened as officers became dealing with the tragedies they saw every day, they all shared a soft spot for innocent kids caught up in bad situations. Besides, if he hadn't been sent out, he would have been handling some drunken domestic disturbance in town.

Thinking out loud more than talking, he mumbled, "Who the hell leaves a little kid alone on a highway? Especially in this weather."

"Scum."

The two men sat in their respective cars, warm and comfortable but thinking of how cold and lonely it would be walking these mountainous roads.

3

I slap my hands on my thighs, willing my frozen muscles to move. As I take a step forward, a scraping sound—metal dragging across pavement—comes from behind me, accompanied by the roar of heavy engines. The rock canyon walls reflect strobing yellow lights. I turn as a pair of snowplows round the bend, their blades scooping snow off the pavement and throwing it in a high arc to the side of the road.

Never let them see you.

Especially them.

Government people. The worst kind of humans. They have all these rules telling people what they can and can't do, even on their own land. And they'll take that land if they want to, just like they took his grandpappy's land and made him poor. Government people can't be trusted, so *never, never, never let government people see you.*

Government people drive those big snowplows roaring down the highway, so I have to hide.

I turn to the side of the road in a feeble attempt to run for the camouflage of shadows, but my feet, numb from walking in the freezing snow, slip from under me. I slam to the ground on my belly, knocking the air from my lungs. The world goes gray, and the guardrail slips in and out of focus. I suck the frigid air into my lungs, desperate for strength, struggling to push myself up onto my hands and knees. Too cold, hungry, and weak, I collapse onto the ground and gasp for air. The bright lights of the approaching vehicles haven't reached me, but my shadow is coming into focus on the boulders in front of me. I have to hurry. His command echoes in my brain:

Never let them see you.

I wriggle my fingers through the frozen layers of snow and ice to gain purchase on the asphalt below. Inch by inch, I drag my body forward. A nail rips off the middle finger of my left hand. I hold my arm up in the growing light, startled to see fresh blood dripping around the dangling nail. For seconds I feel nothing, my frozen body refusing to acknowledge the loss until a searing pain flashes up my arm. I wince against the agony, but it shocks my body into action and gives me the strength I need.

Kicking with my feet, I slide on my belly across the ground and under the guardrail. I roll into the weeds and land in a pile of discarded trash. Curling into a small ball and cradling my injured hand, I hide in the shadows and pray that the drivers of those roaring machines didn't notice my escape.

The front-mounted plow scrapes across the road and clears a path, allowing the chains on the giant tires to clatter against the newly bare pavement. The sounds echo off the walls around me. The first truck roars past in the far lane, the ground vibrating as its blade rakes across the asphalt, hurling the offending snow into the near lane. It rattles off the metal guardrail with a deafening sound as the ice pings the metal.

I try to roll away from the falling debris, but my movement must have caught the attention of the driver of the second plow. We lock eyes, and his head swivels to keep me in his sight as he passes. His mouth forms a shocked O, and then I am pummeled with the slush falling around me. Chunks of ice ricochet off of the rocky cliff. A mixture of freezing cold water, ice, snow, and salt hammer my aching body and soak my clothes.

The truck brakes hard, stopping the small cluster of cars following him in the safety of the freshly exposed pavement. The driver jumps out of the cab and runs alongside the road, shouting and searching, but he can't see me buried under the piles of snow. He and the driver of the other plow argue, but I can't hear their words over the roar of the wind.

One of them grabs an orange cone off the back of his plow and settles it over the guardrail post. He then climbs back into his vehicle. I hear the air brakes and the grind of gears, the plows resuming their clearing of the road.

As the noise fades, I raise my head, snow sliding down the neck of my shirt, and watch the last of the taillights disappear around the next curve. Shivering, I slide back under the rail and onto the pavement. I stagger to my feet and stand, weaving in the wind. The sky remains pitch-black with no hint of a coming sunrise. I doubt I will live long enough to see it.

I wrap my arms around my body, my drenched clothing already freezing against my skin, and take another step down the road.

4

Patterson's radio crackled, the warm, soothing voice of the dispatcher muffled by static in the remote location. "A snowplow operator says he saw the boy on the side of the eastbound lanes a quarter mile beyond mile marker three. White male, approximately twelve years old, five-foot-two, one hundred pounds, shaggy dark hair, flannel shirt, blue jeans."

The trooper and deputy exchanged glances as Patterson picked up his microphone. "Do they have him?"

"Negative. He scrambled under the guardrail, toward the river. They looked for him. Couldn't locate but marked the exact spot with an orange cone."

"Bunch of orange cones in the gorge, dispatch." Construction repairs were a constant hazard, thanks to the numerous mudslides.

"Yes, but they said they put it on the guardrail support itself. Said it would be obvious."

"HP Notified?"

"Highway Patrol ETA is thirty minutes. Closest is down near Asheville."

"Ten-four. Responding."

As Patterson shifted his vehicle into gear, the trooper called out, "Snowplow operators. Good sighting."

"Best we've had since that trucker."

"Good luck. Call if you need me."

With a nod to the Tennessee trooper, Patterson rolled his window up and maneuvered his cruiser through the accumulating snow back onto the deserted highway and reentered North Carolina. He accelerated and pushed the car as hard as he dared around the sharp curves as the chains on his tires clacked against the pavement. He struggled to keep his car between the lane markers disappearing from view in the drifting snow, but he didn't want to miss the golden opportunity provided by the best lead of the night.

Snowplow operators memorized every curve and pothole from their regular sweeps for snow removal. They knew where ice and snow accumulate, where a dip in the road could catch the blade and twist the steering wheel from the impact. If they said just east of mile marker three, that's where the boy was. Patterson thought the long, cold night might end on a good note yet.

The deputy's spirits rose as the mile marker glowed in his headlights, its "3" barely visible under the crusting ice. A few hundred yards later, a reflective orange cone perched atop the guardrail. He scanned the shadows for any movement as his wipers clunked back and forth, shoveling the accumulating powder off the windshield. The boy had to be close.

He slowed the car to a crawl, rubbed his tired eyes, and cursed the lack of visibility. The defroster ran full blast, pumping warm air but struggling to stay ahead of the encroaching haze building on the inside of the glass. The wipers fought against the accumulating snow outside. He peered along the beam of his headlights and scanned the sides of the road, but the snowflakes swirled in a blinding fury and obscured his view.

He swiveled his bright searchlight and strained to see anything in the dark gloom. The brilliant beam illuminated the edge of the road, but his spirits sank as he continued to see nothing. The blowing snow erased any signs of footprints. The plows had piled snow several feet deep along the edge of the highway, deep enough to hide the giant boulders. They certainly could have hidden the body of a child.

5

I stagger down the side of the road, my arms wrapped around my body, trying to preserve any heat left inside my ice-encrusted clothes. I have been cold before, but never like this. But I haven't been warm much either.

Sometimes, back there, I was allowed outside. I would swing the ax, splitting logs, pile firewood, cut brush away from the house with a sling, or dig holes as deep as he demanded, spending every minute under his critical eye as he sat in the shadows, caressing his shotgun, silent except for hurled criticisms.

Those are the best memories I have. Working, moving my muscles, and taking pride in my accomplishments felt good. His harsh words would ring in my ears—I was too slow or doing it wrong—but they were simply the price I paid to be out in the midst of the hottest summer day. Suffocating humidity cloaked the still air, but the shade and altitude kept the temperatures cool. Beams of sunlight penetrated the thick canopy of leaves wriggling their way to the moist ground and dancing among the detritus from rotting trees and vegetation.

Detritus. That's a good one. *Loose material such as rock fragments or organic particles that results directly from disintegration.* It felt good between my bare toes, a welcome respite to the hard-packed floor of the basement. I savored the time outdoors, as rare as it was.

Soon enough, though, he tired of watching me work. I stored the tools under his incessant gaze, which prevented me from smuggling even the smallest implement. Then he marched me back inside the gloomy house, where the air sat stuffy and still. The grimy windows filtered the indirect light. No electric lights illuminated the interior, so the house was always cloaked in thick, cool shadows.

While being outside was a delight, being inside was not. I never wanted to linger, praying under my breath that he wanted nothing else until he extracted his keys, unlocked the padlock, and opened the cellar door. Lest he changed his mind, I moved quickly down the creaky steps and into the dank room below.

Only a little light slipped through the few small, rectangular windows of broken glass high above our heads. I knew from my time outdoors that the portals were mere inches above ground level, hidden behind the weeds and brush growing against the house, but inside, they were out of our reach, just below the floor joists.

A hint of sunlight but nothing more leached through to us below. The stone walls and dirt floor kept the temperatures cool through the day. At night, in the darkness, the room chilled, and we shivered in our sleep. Still, the summer was more tolerable than the rest of the year.

Spring brought torrential rains. Another terrific word: *torrent*—a *violent stream of a liquid.*

Violent was right. The temperature plummeted. Lightning flashed through the sky, briefly illuminating our world below. The crashing of thunder followed, felt through the trembling walls as it rattled the windowpanes. And then the water would fall in waves. It seeped underground and through the walls of the basement, leaving slick, slimy layers of mold on the exposed fieldstone, chilling our bodies if we dared lean against them. We huddled in the center of the dark room, wrapped in threadbare blankets, shivering and hoping to steal body heat from each other. We warmed our hands from a flickering candle or a smoking oil lamp when we were lucky enough to have those, which was only when he forgot and left them behind.

Despite the frigid nights, at least spring brought the promise of summer. The falling temperatures and shortening days of autumn, however, hinted at the misery of the winter to come. The leaves fell from the trees outside, so more sunlight hit our sparse windows, but that only teased us as the days grew shorter and the nights longer. We would wake most mornings to our own breath forming fog in the air.

The winters were the worst of all. Fierce winds whipped over the mountain ridges, rattling the denuded tree branches before whistling into our confines through the gaps of those meager windows. Snow trickled through the shattered glass and piled into drifts on the dirt floor, creating yet another obstacle for our bare feet. We wrapped them in the burlap sacks we used as blankets. We weren't allowed shoes.

The temperatures dropped so much on the worst days that the moisture accumulating on those stone walls froze into sheets of thin ice, removing even the slight comfort of being able to recline against that support. The chill pooled and extended its icy tentacles throughout our dungeon, making escape from its arctic grip nearly impossible.

Upstairs, the logs I had carefully gathered and stacked during the warmer months blazed in the old stone fireplace. Plastic taped over the frosty windows trapped the radiant heat and kept the temperature inside his little den tolerable, though the rest of the drafty house was barely better than being outside.

The crumbling chimney restricted the escaping smoke, so some of it curled through the room and streaked the walls with soot. The fumes slipped under the cellar door and crept down the steps, taunting us with the scent of heat without giving us any of its comfort.

But not even the chance to warm ourselves in front of those flames made any trip upstairs worthwhile. There are things worse than being cold. Much worse.

When he opened the door and stood at the top of those stairs, scanning us as we cowered in the shadows, we always prayed the same thing—*Pick someone else. Not me. Please, not me.*

He would indicate his selection with a gesture or a mumbled name. Those of us unchosen would cast our eyes down at the ground, silently whispering our gratitude. The poor boy selected would look to us with wide, begging eyes, knowing in his heart that we were doing what he would have done if one of us had been selected but begging and praying this time would be different.

It never was.

We never revolted. None of us except the selectee wanted the man to change his mind and pick someone else instead. I didn't want to hear my name. No one else did either. The condemned, knowing we were not going to rise up to defend him, would trudge up the stairs, resigned to his fate.

Hours later, the door would open, and the boy would slink back downstairs, curl in a corner, and cry until exhaustion brought sleep. When he finally awoke, we carried on as if nothing had happened. Some topics were better not discussed. We all knew what went on upstairs.

We also knew that sometimes the door never reopened to return the chosen one. We never discussed that, either, mostly because we couldn't decide whether it was better to return or not.

But now I know the answer. Anywhere, even freezing to death in a snowstorm, was better than there.

The chilly basement, even with its ice-covered walls and drafty windows, afforded some protection from winter's assault. Out here, I have nothing to block the howling wind and blowing snow. But I never plan to return, even if the only alternative is that the cold kills me.

I am here, wherever here is. That's an improvement.

Back there, death was certain.

Out here, it's only likely.

6

Dispirited, Deputy Patterson reached for the microphone to report his lack of success when a shadow a hundred feet up the road stood out from the others. Training his searchlight down the road, he watched a figure stumbling along the edge. He closed the gap with his car, balancing his fear that the boy would bolt over the guardrail against his desire to be as close as possible before getting out on foot. His luck held. The boy didn't break his stumbling stride.

As the boy's shadow took shape, Patterson assessed his target. He was barely over five feet tall and maybe one hundred pounds. His shaggy hair was coated in snow. But it was his clothing that shocked the deputy the most. A tattered flannel shirt flapped in the wind. Baggy jeans were cinched around his waist with a hemp rope threaded through the belt loops and knotted in the front. He didn't have visible boots or shoes. Instead, what appeared to be burlap seed bags were wrapped around his feet and tied with twine. No coat, hat, or gloves protected him from the storm. With so little protection and the first report hours earlier, he should have been dead under a drift of snow.

Patterson pulled his patrol car into the breakdown lane a few feet behind the boy and shifted the car into park. He pushed open the driver's door and stepped into the howling storm. He tried to shout a friendly hello, but the wind whipped across his face and ripped the words away.

The boy paused, appearing to have heard him, and slowly turned his head. His ice-crusted eyebrows glinted in the lights as he faced the deputy. Patterson held his breath, watching the boy debate his options, knowing he was too far away to stop him if he decided to scramble over the cliffs. After several agonizing seconds of indecision, the boy shrugged and swayed in the wind.

Maybe, Patterson thought, he was too exhausted to continue to hide. He pulled his own padded coat tight against his body and stepped around the open door and in front of the idling car. The lights stretched his shadow down the road beyond the approaching boy as he called out, "Son, are you okay?"

In the bright lights, Patterson could see the boy's eyes widen in fear. He hesitated for a second as their gazes locked. To the deputy's surprise, the boy turned and bolted toward the edge of the road.

The boy's sudden movement caught Patterson flat-footed. He watched the boy pivot and race toward the guardrail and the boulders beyond. The burlap on the fleeing kid's feet slipped and slid on the snow-covered road, slowing his escape.

With the deputy's heavy shoes gripping the slick ground, he closed the gap between them. He reached out and snagged the kid's shirt collar. They stumbled together, lost their footing, and crashed hard to the pavement, the boy's chin plowing through the snow. The deputy planted his hand firmly on the boy's back, pinning him to the ground. The kid's quivering body recoiled from the touch, and he struggled wildly to escape. A high-pitched whine escaped his lips. Blood dripped from his scraped chin and dotted the white ground. He pushed his hands into the snow and strained to work his legs underneath him. His attempt to stand failed. The boy was too weak to overcome the deputy's advantage in size and strength.

With his other hand, the deputy gripped the rope threaded through the boy's belt loops and waited for the fight to melt out of him. His stringy back muscles relaxed. The boy's trembling body surrendered, and he collapsed into the snow. Unable to escape, the boy turned his head to look back at the deputy with wide eyes. He whimpered, "Please don't hurt me."

Patterson recoiled at the words. His bulletproof vest offered no protection from the pain in those terrified eyes. He loved police work but hated domestic-violence calls because of the kids cowering in the corner of a house, desperately wanting things to be better but not wanting to tell on Mom or Dad. Even in only the light from his car, he could see the kid was in worse shape than anyone he had seen before.

Leaving his hand resting on the boy's back in case he tried to flee again, the deputy leaned back on his haunches and stared into his face. "Son, I'm not going to hurt you. I want to help."

The boy's blue lips moved rhythmically as he recited a mantra over and over as if he was praying. Patterson struggled to understand, but the voice was too soft, and the wind was blowing too hard. He leaned over to hear the words.

"Never let them see you. Never let them see you. Never let them see you."

"Never let who see you? Who are you afraid of?"

The boy didn't answer but continued his recitation. His eyes darted about, searching for an escape. Patterson slipped his arms under the boy's body, balanced in a crouch, and stood, easily lifting the kid into the air. He was paper-light, with bone-thin arms and legs and protruding ribs. The boy didn't resist, but nor did he help or wrap his arms around the deputy's neck. His body slackened in total surrender. He shivered uncontrollably as he repeatedly muttered, "Never let them see you. Never let them see you. Never let them see you."

Patterson carried the light load cradled in his arms to the rear of his cruiser and balanced him while opening the back door. As easily as he would a bag of groceries, he laid him across the plastic backseat then closed the door. He extracted a bright-yellow emergency blanket from the trunk of his car and reopened the back door. The dome light went on, and the boy scrambled across the seat to the other side of the car, curled into a tight ball, and quaked in fear. Careful not to move too quickly, the deputy unfolded the blanket, leaned into the car, and stretched it across his shivering body.

With his charge safely stowed in the backseat, Patterson returned to the driver's seat and cranked the heat. Through the rearview mirror, he watched the boy clutch the blanket across his body. Their eyes met, and the boy began franticly clacking the door handles. "They only open from the outside, son."

The boy slumped and returned the deputy's stare with wide, fearful eyes hidden under frozen locks of shaggy brown hair. "Oh."

Patterson didn't have kids and wasn't even married, but he had a nephew he adored. The boy was eleven. Healthy. Athletic. They spent hours in the river together, trout fishing, telling jokes, and laughing with each other. The kid in the backseat didn't look anything like that—he was more like an injured animal, cornered and scared. "You thirsty?"

The boy shrugged.

Patterson removed a water bottle from the small cooler on the floorboard of the passenger side of the cruiser. He cracked open the lid and held the bottle through the cage.

The boy eyed it and licked his lips.

"Go ahead, son. You can have it."

A bloodied hand shot forward, grabbed the bottle, and

pulled it back into the shadows. He tilted it upwards and guzzled the liquid, water sloshing across his chin and dribbling on his shirt.

"You're okay, son. Just relax."

The boy's hand wiped the dripping water from his chin. His eyes flicked across the steel cage separating the backseat from the front before looking outside into the storm.

"Son, I'm not gonna hurt you. Whatever is wrong, I can help."

The boy curled back into a tight ball against the far door and wrapped the blanket firmly around himself. To Patterson, he appeared to be attempting to vanish into the corner. The melting snow and ice clung to his stringy hair, partially hiding his gaunt face. His fear-filled eyes were cold, gray, and lifeless. A strong stench of body odor emanated from him and filled the car. His teeth were crooked and dirty. Worse, Patterson noted, several teeth were missing. A jagged scar stretched from his right ear to his mouth. His lips were cracked and bleeding. Blood dripped from his chin and stained his left hand.

"Were you in an accident?"

A shake of the head.

"Are your parents okay?"

A pause followed by a small shrug.

Patterson opened the paper sack sitting on the passenger seat and extracted half a sandwich. He unwrapped the plastic and slipped the food through a slot in the mesh. "You hungry?"

The boy eyed the sandwich warily. With the same sudden swiftness used to retrieve the water, his hand shot forward, grabbed the bread, and yanked it back. He stuffed it inside his mouth and devoured the food as if he didn't remember his last meal or know when the next was coming.

"Slow down. There's plenty more food where that came from."

The boy gagged and coughed but swallowed as quickly as he could. He didn't appear to believe in endless food supplies.

"Where are your parents? How do I get in touch with them?"

The boy shrugged again and licked the crumbs from his fingers. Patterson grabbed another bottle of water from the seat beside him and offered it through the cage. Again, the boy eyed him closely before snatching the bottle and retreating into his corner. His frozen fingers fumbled with the cap before spinning it off. He drank deeply, but more slowly and controlled than before.

"Did you run away? Don't you think they're worried about you?"

The boy glanced up into the rearview mirror and locked eyes with the deputy before shaking his head.

"Look, kid, if you're running from something, I can help. Just tell me what's going on."

The boy shrugged his scrawny shoulders.

Patterson sucked on his lower lip. "Okay, let's back up and start with an easy question. My name's Jon. What should I call you? Can you give me a name?"

A *name? Sorry, Deputy, but that's not an easy question.*

He called me Teddy. If he was in a good mood, it might be T-Dog. If he was being sarcastic, I got called Terrible Ted. If he was pissed off about something, which was often, he had more colorful labels for me—Dipshit, Asshole, Dufus, Dumbass, or other derogatory monikers. Lots of times, he didn't bother with a name at all and just called me "boy" or even "Hey, you."

It wasn't just me. He did things like that to everyone.

I replied no matter what he called me because not answering resulted in beatings. The name didn't matter when his fists flew.

But now, I'm away from him. My name matters. It matters a lot. I don't want to be Teddy anymore, the name he gave me, because it's not really my name.

Every kid got a new name on their first day.

Sometimes, when that door to the cellar opened and we cowered, praying, *not me. Please don't pick me*, he wasn't there to call one of us upstairs. Instead, he would shove some new kid down that flight of steps, watch him tumble head over heels, and then shout, "This is Joey. Welcome him to our family." Or Chad or Mike or Steve or Dave or whatever.

Joey would be bruised, beaten, bleeding, and worse. And he would be crying for Mommy and Daddy, telling us over and over his name wasn't Joey.

We comforted him and told him it would be okay. It wouldn't, but it would have done no good to tell him that.

And we would tell him to get used to being called Joey. Get used to it real quick. We didn't want the man to overhear the new kid's protest, rip that door open, and storm down the steps to teach the kid a lesson about living in his brand-new home. Not that we cared much about the new kid, but those things tended to get out of hand. We didn't want to be collateral damage.

Besides, beatings would happen soon enough, so there was no need for Joey to rush things.

He gave us new names because, he said, old names reminded us of old things. Our pasts. Our friends. Our families. Things that were gone and never coming back. The past didn't belong to us anymore, so no good could come from remembering it. We each got a new name suitable for our new home with a new family and new friends.

The sooner Joey figured that out and accepted his fate, the easier things would be, for him and for the rest of us. So we called him Joey. Loudly. We wanted him to know we understood the rule and embraced the names he had given us.

Some kids accepted it quickly. Some were slower. I don't know how long it took me. I can't remember my first day. I've been Teddy forever.

Sometimes, when we thought he couldn't hear, we rebelled in our own little way. The upstairs door closed, the lock snapped shut, darkness descended on us, and we couldn't hear him stomping around upstairs. Then—and only then—some of us, the braver ones, rolled out past names and told stories about past lives. A little bit of resistance, even though it was done quietly and hidden from him, freed our imprisoned souls.

Kevin did that. He was my best friend, the boy closest to my age, and we both had been there for a long time. The new kids, the Joeys, came and went, but Kevin and I remained. We huddled together for warmth and whispered tales of our previous lives. He told me about his old friends and the games they used to play. He spun tales about his family and told funny stories about his brother and the stupid things they used to do. Sitting shoulder to shoulder, swapping fables about past lives, kept us sane.

As much as we hated the suffering a new person faced, we also rejoiced that a newbie livened things up because their stories were new. We would coax them into whispering all about their previous life—family, friends, siblings. The new stories enlivened our little world for a while, but once we tired of them, we resorted to retelling ours again and again.

For those who never returned from a final trip upstairs, we honored their memory by sharing their stories and weaving them into our own. Sometimes, we told it as their story, and sometimes, we told it as our own. We didn't mean to lie, but our histories became so intertwined that it became difficult to remember whose past was whose. Our personal histories grew foggy with the mingling of fact and fiction.

We made up nicknames for each other too. We called one kid Digger because he was convinced he could tunnel out of the cellar, though he never made it past the stone walls. Another went by Mad Dog because he yelled at one kid for trying to eat more than his fair share of our meager rations. We had a Twinkletoes because, weak from hunger, he fainted and busted his lip on the stone floor. Bucky earned his nickname after the man upstairs said he was bucking his rules, though he didn't learn of the new name until he regained consciousness. Someone was Spidermonkey because he had long arms and legs on a skinny body. I remember a kid called Biscuit, though I can't remember why.

So, Deputy, what's my name is a tough question. In the telling and retelling of our stories, in the myth-making and bullshitting, in all of the years of living in that hellhole, I've heard many names.

I wade through them one by one and discard them. I reach back through my memories to an ancient time, a time I can remember only through a haze. The day before the day I arrived. Back in history when life was lived outside, happy and away from the awful place. Back to when the warm sun shined on my face and I had a family who loved me and cared for me and wanted the best for me.

I reach back through my memories for that warm embrace, for a real name, not a made-up one. Not one given to forget, but one given to remember. I open my mouth, my voice cracks, and I say words I haven't uttered in a very long time.

"Jaxon. With an X."

8

Coincidence, thought Sheriff David Newman. Many people were called Jack or some variation like Jackson. Many parents wanted unusual names for their kids, so spelling it "Jaxon" wasn't that strange. If he'd called the principal down at the high school, she probably would have told him of others.

Just because the name was spelled the same didn't mean it was *his* Jaxon. Besides, *his* Jaxon would be sixteen years old, not twelve.

"Stop seeing ghosts," he muttered to himself as he parked his unmarked black SUV in a reserved-for-law-enforcement space beside an ambulance at the emergency-room entrance. He waved to the maintenance workers salting the sidewalks and nodded a good morning to a paramedic pushing an empty stretcher out of the building.

Voters loved a sheriff who was another down-to-earth, working-class guy, same as them, not too full of himself to say hello. He made a point to smile and shake hands wherever he went. It had to be done. The key to being reelected time after time was being both likable and tough.

All it took, though, was some particularly heinous unsolved

crime, a deputy captured on a cell phone being overzealous during an arrest, or some other ridiculous scandal to push open the door for some ambitious person to emerge and challenge him for the office.

The former sheriff had certainly understood that, if too late to save his job. The disappearance of Jaxon Lathan a decade earlier had brought hordes of national media to their small town. Unaccustomed to the limelight, he'd tried to explain how thoroughly they were checking every lead—knocking on doors of all known sex offenders, interviewing every neighbor, questioning teachers. The reporters who'd wanted a simple story and a bad guy to pursue portrayed him as indecisive and weak. His statement that they had no suspects and no leads was played over and over, even becoming the headline of the local weekly paper.

Wanting to take the heat off himself, the sheriff had invited his lead investigator to handle the press. David knew what the sheriff told the reporters was truthful and accurate. They were following every possible angle, even if none of them looked particularly promising. But having learned from his boss's mistakes, David had stood shoulder to shoulder with the FBI agents in front of a swarm of cameras, confidently describing their desire to locate the ex-husband as a person of interest. Not a suspect, oh no, but he had disappeared at the same time as the missing child. They just wanted to talk to him, to find out what he knew. And that gave the media horde and the public someone else to focus on.

By the time Harold Lathan was found days later, drunk and high in a motel room with a hooker, the public was convinced he was guilty. The citizens of Miller County clamored for his head on a stake. Without any other viable suspects, David dragged him into an interrogation room and leaned on him hard, but Harold refused to confess. He couldn't—or wouldn't —explain where he had been or what he had been doing during the days following the boy's disappearance. He couldn't even remember if he had shown up to watch his sons that day like he was supposed to. Still, he steadfastly denied abducting or harming Jaxon. He would never have hurt him, he protested.

Armed with search warrants, they combed Harold's few possessions for clues. Jaxon's prized baseball cap was tucked under the front seat of his car. The boy was rarely seen without it, and his older brother, Connor, was sure—pretty sure—well, maybe—that Jaxon had worn it that fateful morning. When pressed, though, Connor really couldn't remember whether he had been wearing the hat or not. Maybe it had been the day before or the day before that.

A pair of Jaxon's underwear was found in Harold's mobile home along with other clothes. Some of Connor's clothes were in the trailer too. Harold admitted the boys often visited, despite the custody agreement forbidding either of them from being at his place or in his car. Connor backed him up, saying the boys often snuck over there during the day.

They needed a body. Without forensic evidence from a corpse, they didn't have a case. Despite days of searching with dogs, they never found it.

Frustrated by the lack of evidence and needing to respond to the citizens' cry for justice, David and the district attorney did the only thing they could do—they charged Harold with unrelated but provable crimes. Enough drugs to charge him with intent to distribute had been found in his car and home. Given his previous convictions and the suspicions of worse crimes, he went to prison.

The community became convinced that justice had been served. The district attorney became a law-and-order congressman. David ousted the former sheriff at the next election. No one other than Harold questioned the outcome.

Ten years later, a boy with the same first name with the

same unusual spelling was found wandering in a snowstorm along the interstate. *What if it's his Jaxon? Where had he been? Who took him? Did Harold Lathan have nothing to do with his son's disappearance? Were the man's professions of innocence real? And, if so, had the real kidnapper slipped away undetected?*

Stop it. This kid isn't the same Jaxon, so think of the upside. Finding a lost kid could be a boon in an election year.

A heroic sheriff's department rescue of a little boy during a snowstorm—a story like that could go a long way in solidifying political support. Even the television station down in Asheville would love an image of the thankful waif sitting in his hospital bed, smiling his gratitude while the sheriff modestly stated in a photogenic aw-shucks way, "Just doing our jobs." The citizens of Miller County deserved to see an ever-vigilant, professional, and highly reelectable sheriff on their TV screens, describing the successful search and rescue.

He marched through a pair of sliding glass doors, paused to say hello to a maintenance worker mopping the hall—barely spoke English so probably wasn't even a voter, but one never could be sure—and entered the large rectangular room housing the hospital's emergency department. At that early-morning hour, most of the patient cubicles ringing the outer wall were empty, their privacy curtains pulled open to expose vacant beds and clean sheets waiting for the inevitable patients a snowy day would bring. Cars would collide on slippery roads, feet would slip on icy sidewalks, kids would crash sleds into trees, and people would have heart attacks shoveling snow, but the carnage wouldn't begin until after breakfast.

Closed curtains indicated five occupied beds. A young couple in neighboring units ached from minor bumps and bruises after their car had slipped on the icy roads and into a ditch. One man loudly proclaimed he had chest pains, *damn it*, and he was going to sue everybody if they didn't take care of him *right now*. A lady who had avoided going to her doctor three days earlier because of a lack of insurance had flu symptoms that had morphed into pneumonia, and she now faced a much larger emergency room bill.

But the fifth curtain held David's focus. It hid a boy named Jaxon.

A waist-high counter separated the corridor from the open workspace in the center of the emergency department. Computer terminals glowed, awaiting data entry, and a bank of video screens—most connected to vacant beds and dark at the moment—displayed patient statistics. Coffeepots percolated their energy-giving substances, files sat neatly in wire racks, telephones blinked with waiting calls, and a half-eaten sandwich waited on a paper plate for its hungry owner's return. The complainer's voice—"I'm going to die in here of a heart attack, and none of you care!"—elicited eye rolls from a pair of nurses as it carried over the soft beeps of the few operating monitors.

A uniformed deputy leaned over the counter with his back to the entrance, talking with a young nurse. Based on her smile and twinkling eyes, David guessed she found the uniformed officer entertaining. Enthralled in the conversation, the young man didn't seem to notice the approach of the six-foot-four-inch sheriff until he stepped behind him and cleared his throat. "Can I interrupt your chat?"

Deputy Patterson straightened and spun, his equipment belt jangling. His face blushed as he stammered, "Sir, I didn't know you were coming here."

Chatting with a nurse was hardly an unprofessional act, so David smiled at the young man's flustered response to let him know he was fine. He had been young once, long ago, and would have been attracted to the nurse, too, if she hadn't been young enough to be his daughter. Not that he saw his kids much anymore. His ex-wife and children lived in Charlotte with a new husband-slash-dad who kept steady banker's hours and earned a salary that could pay for college tuition.

Patterson was proving to be a great young deputy with a lot of potential. His training officer had bragged about his rookie performance and recommended him, based on his military experience, for a trainee role with the SWAT team. In a small department, David knew all of his deputies and wanted to develop Patterson. "Tell me what you know."

The deputy pulled a small notepad from his shirt pocket, flipped it open, and stared at it. He closed it again and sheepishly shrugged as his face turned red. "Not much yet. The boy was exhausted and fell asleep in my car before he could answer many of my questions. All I got out of him was his first name."

"Jaxon? X and not J-A-C-K-S-O-N?"

"Yes, sir. 'Jaxon with an x.' The kid said it just like that."

Just like my Jaxon told his first-grade teacher. But don't get ahead of yourself. It's just a coincidence. With a clenched stomach, David asked, "No last name?"

"No, sir. He didn't say anything else at all. And he didn't have any identification in his pockets, so no last name and no address." The deputy paused, and his face scrunched in puzzlement. "The really weird part is I didn't find anything at all in his pockets. No keys, cell phone, wallet, money. Nothing. My nephew always has crap in his pockets. What boy doesn't?"

The sheriff waved away the question with a flick of his hand. "Walking barefoot in the snow? Did I hear that right?"

"No, sir, not exactly. No shoes or socks, but he had burlap sacks wrapped around his feet and tied with twine. He was wearing jeans and a flannel shirt. No coat, gloves, or hat. Hell, sir, the docs found he wasn't even wearing underwear. It's amazing he didn't freeze his nuts off."

David chewed on his lip. A quick check with his office during the drive over confirmed none of the neighboring states had issued Amber Alerts. No recent missing-children reports matched or even came close. Twelve-year-old kids didn't just walk away unnoticed, but until someone reported him missing, they had few clues to his identity except what the boy told them. For the time being, that was almost nothing.

"You confirmed with highway patrol no reported wrecks in the area?"

"Yes, sir, I checked. HP handled a few fender benders in the gorge overnight, but nothing serious. No one unconscious or anything like that. No one saying they were missing a boy. Same thing on the Tennessee side. I checked with a trooper I know over there." The man's face reddened further as he floundered in front of the sheriff. "Well, I mean, I kind of met him last night."

"Good thinking to reach out to him." *A young deputy,* David thought, *but thorough.* He kept his tone gentle. *Encourage, don't discourage.* "Maybe a car over the railing that hasn't been reported?"

"I was up and down that stretch of road several times last night. Never saw a guardrail torn up or any other sign of anything like that. HP said the same thing. And the snowplow guys would have noticed."

"Get day shift to make one more pass on the interstate to be sure. Maybe he was a hitchhiker who had to get out of a car quick. Once we can talk to him, we'll figure out how he got there."

"I'll do one more sweep myself if you want before I go off shift."

The beeping monitors counted the seconds as David shifted the conversation where he needed—to confirm it wasn't his Jaxon and then focus on the poor kid. "Let's get a good description prepared to send out. You say he's around twelve?"

"I doubt that, Sheriff," a voice called from behind. "That boy is older than twelve."

9

M y first morning away from there has been *surreal—marked by the intense irrational reality of a dream.*

Just a few hours ago, I sat in the back of that deputy's car as he asked his questions, but I didn't trust him enough to answer. Why should I? He's from the government. A cop, no less. All I've ever heard is never to trust government people, and certainly not cops, with their cages inside their cars and back doors that only open from the outside.

I shouldn't even have given him a name. Should've refused to say anything at all. But I did eat his sandwich, drink his water, and enjoy the warmth of his car as the feeling returned to my numbed body. I was warmer than I could ever remember being. I was so comfortable, so full, so warm. I couldn't help it—I fell asleep.

Next sound I hear is the car door opening. I pretend to stay asleep, a trick I learned years ago, and smell the deputy's sweat mingled with a fragrant smell—*cologne—a perfumed liquid—*as he leans into the car and scoops me up in his arms. He settles me into a wheelchair while I keep my eyes closed. I feel the cold air swirl around me and hear the chatter of others joining him. I wait until he steps back then jump up and run.

I make it five steps. He and this big black guy grab me and sit me back down. I've never seen anyone with dark skin like that, though others have told me and the dictionary alluded to it. Fascinating how people can be different.

The deputy curses under his breath—nothing I haven't heard before—and calls me slippery, though I don't know if he means *tending to slip from the grasp* or *one not to be trusted*. I guess both definitions fit.

Once they have me reseated, the deputy says, "Jaxon, we're gonna help you. I promise. But you have to stay put, or I have to handcuff you to the chair."

The other guy defends me. "Come on, Jon. That ain't no way to treat a kid."

"Kid? Jackrabbit's more like it, Horace, so you better watch him, or you'll be chasing him down the halls."

"He's scared. That's it. We're good, right, Jaxon?"

He's right, I'm scared. I don't know if Horace is a regular them or a government them, but I'm supposed to hide from him either way. I can't figure out how, though, because he's bigger and faster than me. He chatters away as he rolls me through glass doors that swoosh open without anyone touching them then swoosh back closed as soon as we're inside. I don't know what made them open and close, so I am trapped again until I can figure it out.

I decide to bide my time and watch for another chance to escape. I can do that. I've waited ours before. I can do it again.

We roll up beside a bed, and a nurse is standing there in colorful blue scrubs with cartoon characters all over. She smiles at me and says, "Good morning, Jaxon, my name's Carla. You doing okay?"

I nod while she draws the curtain closed around us and

looks at my clothes. My shirt and jeans are ripped in several places, caked in mud, and covered in blood stains. My feet are still wrapped in burlap. "Would you be okay slipping out of those clothes and putting on this gown instead? It's clean, you'll be more comfortable, and it'll make it easier for us too."

I reach for the ropes holding the burlap to my ankles but hit the finger with the ripped nail. I wince, and Horace drops down to his knees and tsks. He loosens the knots for me and unwraps my feet. They both grimace and shake their heads when he reveals cuts, bruises, and open sores.

Horace drops the burlap and ropes into a plastic bag while I slip off my shirt and hand it to him. I reach for my pants, but he hands me the gown first and helps me get into it.

Modesty—propriety in dress. It isn't something I've ever had the privilege of, but apparently, it matters to them.

Once the gown is secured, he has me slip off my pants and add them to the bag. He waits while I stand there and then says, "Underwear too."

I shake my head.

"It's okay. The gown will keep you covered."

I shake my head again and speak for the first time since giving my name to the deputy. "I don't have any."

They exchange glances, but Horace seals up my bag of clothes. He helps me get into bed, and I savor how nice it is. It's warm, dry, comfortable, and has clean sheets. My head rests on pillows. Actual pillows. As many as I want, Horace says. I've never rested my head on anything other than the floor, my arm, or someone else. It's heaven.

Horace and Carla leave and pull the curtains that surround my bed closed. As I listen to their shoes squeak away, I debate getting up and trying to run again, but I don't know how to get those glass doors to open for me. Besides, I saw that deputy leaning against the counter right outside the curtain, his hand outstretched to take my bag of clothes from Horace. I have almost worked up the nerve to try anyway when the curtain pulls back and Carla returns.

"I'm gonna get an IV going—it's just a saline solution for now until the doc comes in—and I'm gonna take some blood just like a Cullen, okay?"

I have no idea what she's talking about. Blood I understand, and it scares me that she wants to take some, but what's a Cullen?

"You know, *Twilight*? The movies? The books?"

I stare at her.

"Edward Cullen. Sparkly and moody." When I don't answer, she continues, "Or maybe you're more of a Stephen King fan... Barlow... *Salem's Lot*."

I shrug.

"Count Dracula? A vampire?"

That one's in the dictionary. I gasp and ask, "Are you really *a reanimated body of a dead person who sucks blood from his victims*?"

Her eyes grow big, and her smile falters. "Oh, no, honey, it's just a little joke I tell. It makes... well, usually, it makes people laugh. Don't worry, though. I just need to draw some blood for tests."

She reaches forward and gently holds my wrist. She swabs the skin with a cool liquid and then picks up a needle off a tray she has wheeled in. "This might hurt a little bit, but it will be over real quick."

She runs her gloved finger along my veins and lines the needle up with it. I watch it pierce the skin and slide smoothly into the vein. Blood flows into the connected vial. She replaces that vial with another, fills it, and then another vial. Once she has drawn enough, she slips the needle back out of me, caps it, and disposes of it in a red plastic box. "There. That didn't hurt too bad, did it?"

That seems to be a harmless question, and answering it doesn't break any rules of giving away information. "Nah, not at all. Kinda like a bug bite or a bee sting. Not near as bad as a rat chomping on your finger."

Her eyes widen again, and her face pales. She pats my arm and mutters, "Poor baby."

She flips my hand over, sterilizes the back of it, and slips another needle into a different vein. Instead of drawing blood, she tapes it into place then connects a clear plastic bag of fluid to it. "Don't worry, just saline. It'll rehydrate you, which will make you feel better and help your body fight off infection."

I can't imagine feeling better than I am, being all warm and cozy, so I don't even think much about escaping when she steps out of the room again. Besides, I can see the deputy still standing out there, so there's no point in trying.

Carla returns with a thin man in blue scrubs and a stethoscope draped around his neck. He appears to be in charge. "Good morning, Jaxon, I'm Dr. Queen. How are you feeling?"

I shrug.

"Any pain? Discomfort?"

What else can I do but shrug?

"I'm told you have quite the collection of cuts and scars. Do you mind if I look?"

I don't understand why he would ask permission. I've always been told what to do. Saying no has never been an option.

His hands are warm and gentle as he inspects me, pausing before each step to tell me what he is going to do. Then he leaves as abruptly as he arrived.

A few minutes later, a heavyset guy with a beard comes into the room. "Hey, Jaxon, I'm Bert. Doc said he wants to see your insides. Is that cool with you?"

Not really, Bert. That sounds like it's going to hurt, but it's not like I can refuse. As he and Carla help me into the wheelchair, I think about running, but then they pull the curtain back, and the deputy is still standing there. Maybe he's never leaving. We go through a pair of doors and into a room with equipment mounted to the ceiling.

"Okay, buddy, let's get you up on this table."

I do as I'm told. He positions me on the table and moves equipment around. "Okay. Lie still for me, buddy."

I tense as he steps from the room. Clicking and buzzing sounds fill the air. When they stop, Bert comes back in. "Okay, now flat on your back." He rotates equipment, aims, and says, "Stay still again, buddy." He steps from the room. Click, buzz.

I'm waiting for pain, but it doesn't seem to be coming. After several more repositions, exits, clicks, buzzes, and reentries, he helps me settle back into the wheelchair. Confused, I ask, "So when you going to cut me?"

He stops. "What?"

"To see my insides."

"No, buddy, that's not how this works." He runs his hand through his beard and glances toward the empty doorway. "Come on, let me show you."

He wheels me into a room next door and turns a big screen to face me so I can see it. He taps away on a keyboard, and a picture pops up on the screen. "See, that's your rib cage."

I've seen bones, so I know a rib cage, but mine? "That's me?"

"Yeah, that's you."

I lean forward and follow the bones as they branch off from the sternum. I point toward a bright, white line on one of the ribs. "Why does that look different?"

"Rules are, only the docs are supposed to diagnose things." Bert looks over his shoulder again. He turns back to me and lowers his voice. "But I don't see any harm in telling you that's an old fracture. You can see several of them."

Fracture—the act or process of breaking.

"So that's where the bone's broken?"

"Well, more like used to be broken. Your body has healed it as well as it can."

"So anywhere I've had a broken bone, you can tell?"

"Yeah, sure." He presses a button, and the photos slide by on the screen. "Like here on your arm. You can see a couple of old breaks."

"And they've all healed?"

He stared at the screen. "Well, some have healed better than others, but yes."

"So you're done taking pictures?"

"For now, yes. The doc will probably order a CT, too, to get an even better look."

"A CT?"

"Don't worry, buddy, it doesn't hurt either. I promise."

He rolls me back to my cubicle in the emergency room and helps me settle into my bed. As he departs, he leaves the curtain open a bit. It's my chance to escape, except I can see the deputy talking to a tall man in the same uniform. The doctor walks over and joins them. There's no way I can slip away unnoticed, so I settle back to wait.

10

D avid watched out of the corner of his eye as the boy was rolled back into his emergency-room cubicle. Like his deputy, he would have guessed the boy's age around twelve, given his short stature and thin frame. But if the doctor was right, if he was older, then he might have been... *Not my Jaxon. Couldn't be.*

Dr. Gregory Queen slipped a folder into the holder on the counter and poured himself a cup of coffee. In Millerton, most residents could trace their family back several generations. The doctor, however, was a rare outsider. He had arrived at the hospital two years earlier, fresh out of residency and a new employee of the outsourcing company operating the small-town emergency room. He had never settled into small-town life, so he didn't attend the usual functions with the sheriff— Rotary, Kiwanis, the big churches—anywhere the town leaders were. The man wasn't trying to put down roots in Millerton, the sheriff thought. Probably waiting on a chance at a bigger city hospital.

Impatient, Deputy Patterson protested, "But from his size... I mean, I picked him up in my arms like he was nothing.

My nephew is eleven and weighs more than he does. No way that kid is older than twelve."

The doctor sipped his coffee. "Based on his weight and height, twelve would be a reasonable guess... if he were healthy, which he's not. This boy's been subjected to years of malnutrition stunting his growth. Properly fed, I expect he would be several inches taller and thirty to forty pounds heavier."

"So he's thin, but that doesn't mean he's older, though, right?"

"We see other signs."

The sheriff asked, "Like what?"

"For one, Sheriff, he's well through puberty."

"But some kids do start early, right?"

"Sure, some kids. A kid with a healthy diet in a conducive environment. But not one as malnourished as our patient. His poor nutrition levels would have delayed puberty's onset." The doctor fiddled with his stethoscope. "Besides, we also see signs in his bone structure and muscle development, what muscle there is. And, very importantly, his teeth."

"Teeth?"

"He has all of his adult teeth." The doctor crinkled his face in disgust. "At least he had them all. The kid hasn't seen a dentist in years, if ever, and is missing several teeth, either knocked out or fallen out from lack of care. Anyway, they all come in by twelve or thirteen, and they have been in for a while, so he's certainly older."

"So he's at least thirteen, maybe fourteen."

The doctor crossed his arms. "There's more, Sheriff. What is really notable is his wisdom teeth are starting to come in. That rarely happens until at least fifteen or sixteen years old."

The pen in David's hand shook as his hands trembled. He whispered, "Fifteen or sixteen? Are you sure?"

"Can't pinpoint it exactly, and the boy isn't talking, but, yes,

I'm reasonably sure he's in his mid-to-late teens. My best guess is fifteen to seventeen."

David leaned against the counter and stared up into the ceiling lights. *Did I screw up all those years ago?* He forced himself to focus on the case. "How bad of shape is he in?"

"He's not in immediate physical danger, if that's what you want to know." Dr. Queen motioned for the sheriff and deputy to follow him into one of the examination cubicles and continued in a hushed tone. "Hypothermia and frostbite presented as his biggest acute problems upon arrival. I thought he was going to lose some toes or fingers, but circulation is improving, so I think we can save them. We're still cleaning his feet from lacerations and abrasions, a direct impact of walking so far without shoes. Several other injuries, but nothing life-threatening. Minor cuts, which he appeared to sustain crossing through the woods. His hands are bruised. He has broken fingers and a sprained wrist. A couple of fingernails have been ripped out, which certainly creates additional infection risk. I've seen guys in here after bar fights with less damage to their hands."

"You think he fought with someone?"

"More like with some*thing*. His hands are full of splinters, as if he was hitting something wooden. And those missing fingernails suggest clawing at something."

The sheriff curled and flexed his fingers, imagining the pain. "Perhaps like he escaped from somewhere?"

The doctor flinched, his already pale skin going even whiter. "Possibly. Certainly would explain some of the injuries. Wherever he was, it's good he got away from it. His long-term injuries suggest a quite abusive background. He's got dozens of scars on his arms, legs, back, chest, face... everywhere, really. We're still cataloging them. Burn marks on his chest and arms consistent with cigarettes. Multiple cuts never healed correctly, including a nasty jagged one on his face that should have had stitches but never did. X-rays have revealed multiple old broken bones that never healed properly. Cracked ribs. His jaw and nose were broken at some point, probably more than once. And a spiral fracture of the left arm indicates being yanked around by the arm. And, of course, the missing teeth I've already mentioned. This kid has been subjected to physical abuse in the worst way imaginable. Not just once, Sheriff. Repeatedly and over many years."

David scribbled the list in his notepad, his pen bearing down harder and harder on the pad as anger welled up inside him. Like most police officers, child abuse cases bothered him more than almost any other crime. He really didn't want to hear the answer, but he had to ask the hardest question. "Molestation?"

"I've only done a cursory exam so far, but no obvious physical signs of recent sexual abuse. Even with a more extensive exam, though, anything less than recent would be hard to spot physically. That information, unfortunately, will come once he starts talking to us." The doctor shook his head and sighed. "Hate to sound like a cheap TV commercial, but wait—there's more."

"What else?"

"When I said 'malnourished' earlier, I wasn't specific enough. We're talking severe malnutrition. In the immediate past, this kid hasn't eaten in days. I mean, absolutely nothing is in his stomach other than what your deputy gave him. We can get plenty of food in him here, and we're adding supplements through IV's, but I'm more concerned about the very long-term deficit we have to overcome." Dr. Queen looked toward the closed curtain surrounding the boy's bed. "I don't mean a kid living on chips, candy, and colas like we see a lot here in the county. I'm talking a long-term deprivation—a total lack of food. I haven't seen anything like it since dealing with famines in the Peace Corps."

Just like this doctor to do something goody-two-shoes like volunteering in the Peace Corps, the sheriff thought. Maybe his volunteer work earned him some student loan forgiveness. At least, he believed that's how that worked. Maybe that's why he was in Millerton, too, to work in rural America like it was the same as some third-world country. He chased the thoughts out of his head and said, "The kid's lucky to be alive."

The doctor pursed his lips and nodded. "Now, Sheriff, I've told you everything I know. What am I missing? I get it you have a mystery to solve, but why are you so hung up on the kid's age?"

David tucked his notebook away and leaned against the counter. There was no point in avoiding the question and not telling the doctor. Millerton was a small town. He wasn't the only person who was going to make the connection. Better to be forthright. "It's probably not him, but the name's the same."

"As who?"

He lowered his voice. "Ten years ago, we had a six-year-old boy disappear. Absolutely no trace whatsoever, no witnesses, nothing particularly concrete."

"And you think this is him?"

David paused. "No, not really, because it doesn't make sense. But..."

"But?"

"The name, Jaxon. One of the first writing assignments kids have in school is to print their name, and Jaxon did it with flying colors. He was quite proud of it. And he knew the spelling was a little different, so he was always telling people how to do it... Jaxon with an x. People remembered how he said it. So when this kid used that exact phrase with my deputy..."

The deputy's skin paled while listening. "I remember that case. I was in middle school, so I didn't know him or anything, but everyone talked about it. My parents wouldn't let me out of their sight for weeks. But I thought that kid had been killed."

The sheriff grimaced. "We thought so, too, but only because we found no evidence he was alive."

The doctor set his coffee cup on the counter. "You suspected kidnapping?"

"We suspected everything. At first, we thought he had wandered off and gotten lost. We searched around the city park, near the trails, and up into the mountains, but not a clue. We searched ravines and creeks, thinking maybe he had fallen and been hurt. Without any clues, not even torn clothing on brush, it became more likely something heinous had happened. We interrogated sex offenders and searched their homes. We questioned everyone the kid knew, including teachers, his minister, friends."

Deputy Patterson said, "I thought his dad did it?"

David grimaced. Of course the deputy believed that. Everyone in town did. *Because I believed it.* "He became our prime suspect. No alibi. Claimed he couldn't even remember where he had been. A long history of drug and alcohol abuse. Found evidence the kid had been in his trailer and car, but that only proved he violated his custody agreement."

"I thought he went to prison for it."

"He went to prison for drug charges." David crossed his arms. "The fact is, we didn't have enough of a case other than circumstantial evidence. But if that is the same Jaxon in there…"

Dr. Queen finished the thought. "He might be able to tell you what really happened."

11

The smell hits me and makes my mouth water. A warm, salty-broth aroma wafts through the air, overpowering the chemical smells of the emergency room.

The curtain pulls back, and a new person waltzes in with a glowing smile. "Good morning, young Mr. Jaxon. Everyone calls me Nurse Sheila."

Reticent—inclined to be silent or uncommunicative in speech.

It's another good word, and my reticence crumbles in the face of her cheerfulness. She's a larger woman in outlandishly colorful scrubs. Her voice is warm and cheerful, wrapped with an infectious laugh. I can stay silent against the deputy and the doctor, but I can't resist her. "You're another nurse?"

"Why, yes, sir. Or at least I was. Or maybe I still am. Oh, I don't know. I retired and stayed home all of about three weeks and was bored out of my mind, so I came back here as a volunteer. When I heard a young man had been in this emergency room all morning and hadn't eaten because they were waiting on the cafeteria to open up, I knew where I was needed. So call me whatever you like, but I've got food."

She places a steaming hot bowl, the source of that mouthwatering smell, in front of me. "This here is my chicken-noodle soup. None of that store-bought stuff for you. No, sir. Vegetables from my garden, canned for the winter months. Chickens that hunt and peck in my backyard until they stop producing enough eggs. Even the noodles, I make by hand. My grandchildren"— she says "gran-chitlin"—"beg for this when they come visit."

I inhale deeply as I reach forward to grab the bowl.

"Careful, honey, or you'll burn yourself. Can you handle the spoon with that IV? Or are you left-handed?"

I study my bandaged left hand and the IV line snaking out of my right hand. "I don't really know if I'm left-handed."

She cocks her head. "Which hand do you usually hold your spoon with?"

"I've never held a spoon. We didn't have them."

"Lordy." She sits in the chair and slaps her hands on her meaty thighs. "Forks neither?"

I shook my head.

"Lordy," she repeats, wrapping her fingers around my spoon. "Well, I don't want you hurting that hand no more, so whatcha say I feed ya?"

I can only nod in confusion as she fills the spoon, holds it in the air, then leans forward to let me sip it. When the liquid flows into my mouth, the flavors explode. I close my eyes and hum in satisfaction. The broth is rich and salty, filled with shredded chicken, thick egg noodles, and chopped carrots, celery, and onion. I've never tasted anything so wonderful.

Within minutes, I hear the clank of the spoon on the bottom of the empty bowl. I flop back against my pillow and smile. "That was delicious. Thank you."

"Why, you're welcome, young Mr. Jaxon. You still hungry?"

I can't remember anyone ever asking me that question, at least not anybody who could actually do anything about it. He certainly never cared or asked. No way can I get more. "I'm okay."

She squints then bursts into her big smile. "You just being polite, ain't ya, boy? You just give me five minutes, and I'll be back with something else. And you're gonna love it."

I lie on my pillow with my eyes closed and listen to my stomach gurgle. The deputy's sandwiches were good, but that soup was heaven. I can't imagine what other delicacies await.

The curtain swoops open again, and Nurse Sheila reenters with a steaming sandwich on a paper towel. She sets it down in front of me, and a rich buttery smell fills the air. "Now it ain't much, but my grandchildren"—"granchitlins" is a word I've really got to look up in a dictionary—"love my grilled-cheese sandwiches. Lordy, my own kids are grown, and they love my grilled cheese. Ain't no slices, neither, because it's all shredded to make it melt nice and smooth. Extra-sharp cheddar for flavor, American for that gooeyness to hold it all together, and just a touch of mozzarella for stringiness. And, of course, a good swipe of mayonnaise—gotta be Duke's, cause there ain't no other kind. And a thick slab of butter on the outside of the bread before throwing it all in a cast iron skillet. And yes, sir, I keep all those supplies down in the volunteer break room."

I barely know anything she's saying since we never had cheese, much less types of cheese. If he couldn't grow it, harvest it, or hunt it, we didn't have it. But when I bite into that steaming sandwich, the rich, melty goo explodes in a rainbow of taste. I close my eyes and chew slowly, both wanting to swallow to fill my grumbling belly and not wanting to swallow so I can keep that enchanting flavor on my tongue.

"Do you like it?"

"Oh yes, ma'am. It's… it's… I don't want it to end."

"No hurry here, Mr. Jaxon. You just take your time. Best part of being retired is I ain't got nowhere to be." She settles into the chair and begins humming. She isn't going to try to take my food if I don't finish it quickly. No rats poke their heads up, hoping to steal some crumbs. I bet I could even set the sandwich down on my tray, and it would stay there, waiting for me to pick it up again. Pure luxury. With each bite, I close my eyes and feel deliciousness engulf my mouth.

All too soon, only crumbs remain on the napkin. I pick up as many as I can with the fingers of my good hand and swallow them. I never know when the next meal will come.

"I take it you liked it, young Mr. Jaxon?"

"Yes, ma'am, best meal I've ever had."

"Oh, honey. That's just a simple sandwich. We'll get you a real breakfast shortly, as soon as the cafeteria opens up."

Startled, I look at her in surprise. "Another grilled cheese?"

"Well, no, a man can't live on grilled cheese alone, though I guess he could try. How about some scrambled eggs and bacon and grits and toast all whipped up special for you? Then maybe I'll make you another grilled cheese for lunch. How does that sound to ya?"

"Wow." I lie down on the pillow and smile. "I've never had such good food."

"What about your mama? Didn't she cook for you?"

I roll my head so I can see her. "I don't remember."

She clasps her hands together. "You don't remember what she used to cook for you?"

"No, ma'am." I shake my head. "I don't remember her at all."

She turns her head away from me, but not before I see tears fill her eyes.

12

"Doc, I need to see the kid."

The doctor looked over at the closed curtains sheltering Jaxon's bed. "He's scared and in pain. I've given him a sedative, so he's probably going to be out for a while. Maybe if we give him a little time."

"We don't have time."

"Why not?"

David held his hand out with a single finger in the air. "First of all, if that is the same Jaxon, that means he's been held somewhere for the last decade. Anyone who did that could easily have other kids. What do you think he would do to them once he figures out Jaxon is gone?"

The doctor blanched. "I didn't think about that."

David raised a second finger. "The second problem is the rumor mill. Small towns know everything. The kid's name was broadcast over the police radio, and someone with a scanner heard it. I'm not the only one who is going to make the connection. The last thing we want is for his family to hear from someone else." He added a third finger. "Which brings me to a problem very close to you. The Jaxon who disappeared ten years ago? His mother is a nurse at this hospital."

"A nurse here?"

"Yes. Heather Lathan. You know her?"

"It's a small hospital, Sheriff. We all know each other. Night shift in surgical recovery on the third floor."

"How long do you think it's going to be until she hears about who you have here in the emergency department?"

The doctor raised both his hands. "Got it. But I'm still not sure he's going to speak to you."

"Maybe not, but he'll talk to her." David motioned to a heavyset woman in colorful scrubs who had been going in and out of the boy's room.

Dr. Queen pursed his lips. "If anyone can win him over, it's Sheila."

When Sheila joined them, she wasn't as enthusiastic. The warm, jovial caretaker morphed into a staunch protector of her young charge. She crossed her arms and studied the sheriff with an icy look. "The last thing that boy needs is a bunch of police questions. He needs time to heal."

"Agreed. But I need to figure out where he came from so I can make sure no other kids are in trouble. That's it."

Sheila squinted and studied the sheriff before spinning on her heels. She took off at a brisk walk toward the curtained room. David followed on her heels, but she stopped him just outside the curtain and held up her hand. "Wait," she commanded then slipped inside.

He stewed in the corridor, frustrated to be kept outside when he needed—*needed*—some information, but he reminded himself to be patient. He could hear Sheila whispering to the boy, too quietly to be understood out in the corridor on the other side of the curtain. The boy's mumbled replies were equally impossible to decipher.

Fortunately, Dr. Queen had gone to handle the heart-attack

patient, whose loud protests continued to rattle the room. David hoped the doc would be held up for a while and stay out of his way. Nurse Sheila was enough of an impediment.

After several excruciating moments, Sheila pulled back the curtain and invited David to join them with the admonition, "If you upset Jaxon, I will toss you out. Understand?"

He opened his mouth to respond but froze when he saw the kid on the bed. He had never met Jaxon Lathan in person before he was kidnapped, at least not that he remembered, though it was always possible in a small county, but the face looking back at him looked startlingly like the photographs clipped to the front of the case file.

Shaggy, matted hair hung long over his bare, bony shoulders, only a hint of the original dark brown sheen coming through the filth. His dull gray eyes no longer held the brilliant, shimmering blue captured in a photo of him with a birthday cake. His face was gaunt and drawn around the cheekbones and had lost the long-ago innocence of the six-year-old child. An ugly, purple scar snaked from his ear across his cheek, marring that once-smooth skin.

Despite the differences, David's disbelief dwindled. He had stared at the kid's photo too many times, haunted by his mischievous little grin. Despite the changes wreaked by years of abuse, Jaxon Lathan, missing for a decade, sat in front of the sheriff. He knew that what little doubt danced around the back of his mind could be eliminated with a few simple questions.

Sheila settled into a chair beside the head of the bed. She enveloped the boy's thin hand within her grasp and spoke quietly. "Honey, this is David here. He's here to help, and I'm going to stay with you while he's here. Would you answer a few questions for him?"

The boy's eyes darted back and forth between the sheriff and the nurse, and he gripped her hand. David tucked himself into a chair at the foot of the bed, making himself appear as small and nonthreatening as possible, which wasn't an easy task with his tall frame or something he usually did. Being an imposing figure was usually a strength in law enforcement.

With a soft voice, he asked, "Can you tell me your last name, Jaxon?"

The boy looked at Sheila, his eyes wide and uncertain. She smiled and brushed his long bangs out of his eyes. When he turned back to face David, his hands were trembling, and his voice shook. "We weren't allowed to use our last names. He told us to forget them."

"He?"

"The man." The boy looked confused as he searched for words. "His house. His rules. That's what he always said."

"Tell me about him."

The boy drew his legs up against his chest like a turtle withdrawing into his shell. His face drained of color, and his eyes spread wide in fear. He mumbled, "I don't want to talk about him."

David decided to circle back to identifying the boy. "He isn't here, and it's okay to use last names here in the hospital. For example, my last name is Newman. Can you tell me yours?"

The boy's breath rasped. "I don't remember it."

The answer startled the sheriff. "You don't remember it? Or you aren't allowed to say it?"

"Well, it was against the rules to say it. But it doesn't matter, because I don't remember it, either."

He sat back in his chair. "If I said it, would it ring a bell?"

The boy shrugged.

"For example, if I said Smith, would that mean anything?"

The boy shrugged again, his eyes darting around the room. David swallowed, puzzled about how to proceed. He wasn't getting anywhere and didn't see any risk to going straight to what he wanted to know. He plunged ahead. "What about Lathan?"

The boy's eyes stopped and focused on the sheriff. Barely perceptibly, his lips moved in a soft whisper. "Lathan."

"Is that your last name, son?"

The boy glanced nervously at the nurse, seeking reassurance.

"Jaxon, please look at me. Do you remember that last name, son?"

The boy kept his eyes down, avoiding the sheriff's gaze, but he nodded ever so slightly. He whispered, "Jaxon Lathan."

David clasped his hands together to hide the trembling. *Be sure,* he reminded himself. *Be sure.* "Can you spell it?"

More confidently, the boy spelled, "L-A-T-H-A-N."

Two common names with unusual spellings. The last shreds of doubt were dissipating.

More unsettling, though, was the reaction of the nurse. She clearly hadn't made the connection earlier, but a missing child in a place as small as Millerton would have been remembered, even years later. Her response to the uttered name told him it had sunk into her and wrenched open the memories of the town in shock over the disappearance of one of their own. David knew others would remember as quickly—and many of them would also remember the investigator who had so confidently told everyone the father had been suspected of murdering his own child. But if the boy sat there, living and breathing, he had to wonder what else the investigation had been wrong about.

He needed to be one hundred percent sure. "I want to talk about before you went to that place. Do you remember where you lived before? The address?"

The boy looked puzzled and shook his head. "I don't remember before. It was a long time ago."

"Do you remember how old you were when you left where you lived before?"

The boy glanced nervously at the nurse, who squeezed his hand in comfort. He turned back to the sheriff but kept his eyes lowered as he whispered. "Six. I think. I'm pretty sure."

"What happened that morning? Can you tell me what happened to you?"

Jaxon's voice sounded more confident. "Connor was a really cool big brother and played games and stuff. We were supposed to stay at the house until Dad got there, but he was late like always. Rode bikes to the park so Connor could see his friends. He went riding on the trails around the park. Said he would be back. Don't tell Mom he left. Don't leave the playground. Don't go home. Stay right here."

David considered the story told in such a choppy, hesitant manner. The mention of Connor's name horrified him because he remembered the kid crying incessantly as he confessed to leaving his brother alone while he rode off with his friends. They never published those details because they didn't want to traumatize him.

He knew he should stop asking questions, but the cop in him persisted. Acid spread through his stomach as he was taken back to that day. He swallowed hard but asked the question because he had to know what he had missed that day. "And...?"

Jaxon leaned against Sheila, who shot the sheriff a warning look. But the story up to that point was one David already knew. Who the little boy had left the park with had always been the question. "Just a little more, Jaxon. What happened next?"

The boy hung his head and whispered, "A man asked for help."

"Your... father?"

David's last hope that the investigation had at least pointed in the right direction evaporated as the boy shook his head vigorously. "No. The man."

"What did he say?"

"He'd lost his puppy and needed help finding it. He had a leash in his hand. No one else was around to help. He was nice at first. His van was parked there. Offered a Coke from the cooler in his van for helping him. The door slammed shut. Duct tape on mouth. Duct tape around wrists and ankles. Can't scream. Can't run. Hurt. Can't fight 'cause he's bigger."

David sat back in his chair, horrified at the simple story. "What did the van look like?"

The boy closed his eyes. His answer was monotone, a voice of surrender. "Two-tone brown. Kinda old. The back had boxes and stuff. Smelled funny. Drove a long time."

"You're doing good, Jaxon. What was the man like?"

"There wasn't a puppy. He lied. He smelled and was really mean. He hit and… uh… does stuff. Doesn't care if you cry. Slapped really, really hard if you talked back or tried to stop him." Tears welled up in Jaxon's eyes. He turned to Sheila, who gathered him in her arms. She shook her head at the sheriff as the boy cried, "I don't want to talk about him."

"The place. Can you talk about the place? Tell me where it was?"

But the boy could only sob.

13

Heather Lathan's change-of-shift report to the incoming nursing team was mostly uneventful news about the patients convalescing in the third-floor surgical-recovery wing. All but one had spent the night peacefully, in a happy state of pain-medicated sleep. "But then there's Boris Pavlovich."

Tonya Jackson rolled her eyes. "I thought Mr. Big Shot New York City was being discharged yesterday. If I have to listen to any more stories about the restaurants he could get into, the theater tickets he commanded, the Knicks seats on the floor right near Spike Lee…"

Heather smiled. "The doctor doesn't think he's healing fast enough and said he had to spend another two nights. Of course, that sent Pavlovich into a rant about small-town hick doctors and their incompetence."

"Oh, please. It's his own fault. He should've stayed down there in Florida all winter rather than coming up here to check on his house. Then he wouldn't have wrecked his car and broken his leg. And we wouldn't have to hear how miserable it is here and in Florida and how bloody high the taxes are in

New Yawk." Tonya emphasized the last two words with a mock accent, making both ladies chuckle.

Second homes dotted the ridges of the mountains of Miller County, closed for the winters and used as summer retreats. Many of them were owned by people who had made their careers in the northeastern U.S. and then retired to Florida to avoid income taxes. They quickly tired of the heat and humidity, and so they escaped to their massive homes in the relatively cool Appalachian Mountains. They were commonly known as "halfbacks"—halfway back to New York or wherever.

Heather chuckled. "That's not his fault, don't you know? Last night, he told me he knew how to drive in the snow, much better than we do, and it was only because we don't know how to plow roads down here that he wrecked."

Tonya let loose an exasperated sigh and pointed at a blinking call light at the nurse's station. "Oh, he's already started. Wonder if the room is too hot or too cold? Or maybe the blankets are itchy or the room's too dirty."

"I bet he starts with 'What took you so long? Don't you know who I am?'"

Heather smiled as she watched Tonya walk down the hall and push open the door. "Good morning, Mr. Pavlovich. How are you feeling this morning?" she asked pleasantly.

"What the hell took you so long? I could've died in here waiting on you to—" The door clicked shut, cutting off the rest of the conversation as Heather slipped on her coat. She whistled a tune as she walked to the elevator, ready for a day of peace. The happiness faded when a page requested her to report to the emergency department. They should be asking for one of the day shift nurses—she had already clocked out. She planned breakfast with her son, a soak in a steaming hot tub, and then climbing into bed for eight hours of sleep. She almost walked out to her car, prepared to pretend she never heard it, but then thought maybe it wasn't work related. Maybe Connor had wrecked his car or had been hurt.

She scurried to the emergency room. When she rounded the corner, she saw who was waiting for her.

No, no. What is he doing here?

"Good morning, Heather."

She glared at the sheriff standing in front of her, his hat in his hands. They had talked often over the years, less and less lately, and he never brought good news. "Is Connor okay? What happened?"

"Connor's fine," he hesitated. "At least to the best of my knowledge. I haven't seen him in a long time. But he's not why I asked them to call you."

"Harold?" She clenched her fist. "Damn it, what did he do? Wreck a car again? Drunk driving? You have him here for a BAT?" Uncooperative suspects were sometimes brought by law enforcement to the emergency room for blood alcohol tests. Her ex-husband was the definition of uncooperative, particularly when it came to the sheriff.

"I thought Harold had been sober for a few months. Has he fallen off the wagon again?"

"I don't think so. He always tells me—a hundred fifty or sixty or whatever days since his last drink." She looked around the emergency room at the closed curtains. "So he isn't here?"

"No."

"So…" She squeezed her eyes shut and felt the world sway. If it wasn't Connor and it wasn't Harold, there was only one other reason the sheriff would want to talk to her. "Did you find… his body?"

He gently took her arm and guided her into an empty station. "Heather, listen to me. We brought a patient in this morning. I want you to look at him."

She glanced toward the other nurses for guidance—nurses

always knew everything happening in their department—but they were busily looking anywhere else, avoiding her eyes, and pretending not to eavesdrop. "Why? Sheriff, what's going on?"

"We found a teenage boy, about sixteen, walking along the side of the interstate early this morning. He's got lots of minor injuries—well, not really minor but nothing life-threatening. The thing is…" He looked very uncomfortable and struggled with his words. "He says his name is Jaxon Lathan."

A buzzing filled Heather's ears. Her pulse quickened. *Am I already home in bed and dreaming this nonsense?* "That's ridiculous."

"I agree. I thought the same thing. But"—he lowered his voice—"I've seen him. Talked to him."

Her knees felt weak. "Are you saying it's him?"

"No. I mean, I don't know. It looks like him, at least sort of, to me. And his story matches up. We'll send his blood off for DNA testing, of course, to be sure, but I didn't want to…. I mean, if it's him, and I didn't tell you…. Oh, hell, Heather, it might be him, but I don't know. Tell me I'm crazy. I hate doing this to you, but I don't know what else to do."

She leaned against the wall and closed her eyes. Her hands were trembling, and sweat rolled down her back. "What do you want?"

"Just look at him. He doesn't have to know anything at all. Let him think you're just another nurse."

"Unless he recognizes me…"

The sheriff put his hand on her shoulder and squeezed gently. "Wouldn't that be a good thing?"

She shook his hand off with a shrug. "And if he doesn't…"

"Heather, it's been years. Even if it is him, maybe he still won't recognize you. And it's probably not him. But I think you should look. Just in case."

She took several deep breaths to steady her nerves before laying her coat across a chair. He led the way down the corridor to a closed curtain. She felt the eyes of the other nurses on her back and knew they were all trying to give her space but also wondering what was about to happen.

When they reached the cubicle, the sheriff grabbed the hanging curtain and turned to look at her. He waited for her subtle nod of approval before drawing the covering back to reveal the occupied bed, the hooks clanging against the metal rod.

The boy's appearance in the bed shocked her. Her vision of Jaxon remained what she had last seen, a small six-year-old, but a teenager stared back at her. The strangeness of him frightened her.

He was grotesquely malnourished. The hospital gown hung loosely on his skeletal frame, a thin rag propped up on scarecrow sticks. His sunken cheeks accented the sharp outline of his skull under stretched, pale skin. His reedy arms poked out of the sides and were covered in scars and scratches.

An IV line snaked along the side of the bed to one hand. The other was wrapped in gauze. A scar, puckered and dark against his pale skin, ran in a jagged line across his right cheek. Splotches of red skin from frostbite speckled his cheeks and nose. His chapped lips were raw and peeling with bright-red splits.

Despite the gentle washing by the hospital staff she knew he had to have been given, his hair was ragged and dull. His bangs were shaggy and unevenly cut, as if he had used scissors himself without a mirror.

Heather stood quietly, inventorying the plethora of changes until her gaze settled on the boy's eyes. Six-year-old Jaxon's eyes had shimmered a brilliant sheen of blue, startling in their color and glowing with life. The brilliance in his eyes had faded, much as his once-shiny hair had dulled. The irises were more gray than blue, tired and wary rather than playful and excited.

But those eyes had been the focus of her dreams over the

years. She had missed them more than she had really known. Giving a quiet prayer of thanks, she rejoiced.

My baby boy is back. How is that even possible?

14

Jaxon Lathan.

I hadn't heard or said that name aloud in years. We had whispered it, in the dark, hiding in that cellar and keeping our voices low so *he* wouldn't hear us.

And now, here, I can say it. No one will hit me for it. No one will tell me I can't.

The memories come rushing back. The man. The stench of his sweat. The rotting smell of his teeth. The sting of the back of his hand or the crunch of his fist. We all suffered from his anger. And his appetites.

From the basement, we could hear the van when it arrived or left. Usually, it was empty, at least of anything other than boxes or bags or whatever else he hauled in it. But sometimes, it came back with human cargo. At some point after it returned, I would find myself outside, under his close supervision, hosing out the blood splattered inside. Necessary, he said, to get the attention of the boy.

I would pick up scraps of duct tape and hang up the dog leash, a strip of leather that probably had never been near a dog. He had enticed more than a few boys into his vehicle with his silly story. Silly, except it worked. The tale was the same for everyone, with only minor exceptions. How he would appear, leash in hand, looking around. His actions seemed innocent enough that he could easily disappear again into anonymity if someone else showed up and asked questions.

And every boy, every one, would be the first to ask, "Whatcha looking for?"

"A dog," he said. "I lost my dog. The leash broke. He's a little guy with short brown fur. I'm so worried he's scared or hurt."

And every boy, every one, would think how awful it was to lose your dog or to be the poor lost dog.

Oh sure, you didn't talk to strangers. We all knew that. But you helped those in need. Like a little dog, lost and scared. And so you'd help search.

The man would spot something. "Is that it? Over there?"

And every boy, every one, would wander over, out of sight of others, not even aware they had been separated.

And no one could say what would have happened if someone, say an adult, had come along right then. Probably nothing, right, because the man would keep looking and wander away, and the boy would go home, never aware how close he'd come.

But the boys there, the ones I shared the cellar with… No one had intervened. No one prevented their fate. They searched for the lost dog until they ended up outside the van, where the man offered a Coke as a thank-you for helping.

And every boy, every one, went to the cooler inside the van and opened it. They reached for a Coke as the van door slid closed behind them.

And then it was too late. He was too big. Too powerful.

And every boy, every one, found the life he had known before was now gone. A new life was beginning.

And what a miserable thing that was.

15

Connor laughed as he watched Trigger romp through the fresh snow. The dog slung the white powder into the air with each twist and spin. Startled by the noise, a bird rose from a frozen tree branch, squawking in irritation as Trigger chased it across the yard. Yapping in joyous celebration, he searched for another bird to pursue. To the dog, the morning's wintry weather was sheer magic.

More yellow lab than anything, Trigger exuded pent-up energy every morning, but the cold, wintry air and fresh snow amped him further. He raced in circles with abandon, hopping from drift to drift, lowering his head, and bulldozing the snow with his nose. Reaching the fence, he raised his head and stood still, as if surprised to find his snout caked in the powder. He shook enthusiastically, turned with his tail wagging ferociously, and grinned in doggy delight.

Connor scooped a mound of the powder, packed it into a snowball, and threw it high into the air. Trigger raced under its arc and waited for the descent. With expert timing honed by hours of chasing Frisbees and tennis balls, he leapt and snapped his mouth around the falling snowball, clearly surprising himself with the explosion of icy chunks. Trigger barked at the shower of debris as his object of fetch disintegrated. Laughter from his boy made him wag his tail even faster.

With ice glistening off the fur around the frosty smile on his face, he looked back up at his human and waited for the next game. When one didn't immediately come, he tore across the yard and leapt into the air, planting his big paws on the teenager's chest and knocking them both sprawling into piles of snow.

Laughing, Connor sat up as Trigger raced in circles around him. *Dogs never lose their sense of wonder,* he thought. Or maybe Trigger still celebrated, even five years later, having been adopted out of that crowded shelter where his previous family had abandoned him. Connor had sat on that shelter floor, laughing as the dog danced around him, understanding exactly how he felt. While his freshest wound back then was the death of Duke, the canine who had been his constant companion since he was an infant, Connor's scars included an often-absent father, an overworked mother, and a long-missing younger brother. Boy and dog bonded instantly in their desire to heal each other.

Trigger froze in the middle of his snow dance, stared at the front of the house, and chuffed softly, a warning that interruption to their play approached. The crunch of tires through the snow on the driveway reached Connor's ears long after the dog had detected them. His mother should have been getting home soon from her third-shift job at the hospital, but the dog would have reacted happily to her arrival, not warily.

The boy stood, brushed the snow off his jeans, and walked from the backyard to the front with the dog dancing around him. When he rounded the corner, he halted at the sight of the black SUV. Trigger sensed his master's concern and leaned his body against the boy's legs, his vigorous tail wagging slowing to a gentle swoosh.

"Good morning, Connor." The sheriff unfolded his tall frame from the driver's seat and walked toward them. "Guess you're happy to have a snow day off from school."

Connor shook his head and absentmindedly rubbed the whining dog's ears. "Graduated last year. Guess you could say every day is off from school now. I'm working second shift— part-time until something permanent opens up."

"Out of high school already? How time flies."

Connor's heart pounded, and his palms sweated despite the cold air. When his little brother disappeared, the sheriff—then a detective for the department—had been a regular fixture at the house. At first, he'd seemed to be an ally, leading the pack of police officers searching for Jaxon. But as the hunt stretched into days and seemed to be increasingly focused on their absent father, things grew tense. Connor knew his father couldn't have harmed either of them, at least not on purpose, even if he did lots of stupid things. His mother had protested the same, though less enthusiastically and with some hints of doubt.

When Harold Lathan had been found and arrested, things got worse. David Newman was sure he had his man and only needed to break him. Officially, he told the media "no comment," but the same reporters said over and over that "unnamed sources inside the investigation" expected Harold to confess and lead them to Jaxon's body. And when that never happened, he was still charged and convicted under a litany of other charges, with numerous allusions to the heinous crime. It was bad enough to have had a father who couldn't be relied on to show up when he was supposed to. But after the trial, the man had been totally absent, doing his time in a state prison down east.

With the case all but closed, the sheriff had few reasons to visit. The rare times he did stop by were tense, since he was never very welcome in the Lathan house. Heather doubted Harold's involvement. Connor knew it wasn't true.

When they did see the sheriff's car pull in their driveway, they both braced themselves for the worst news possible—the discovery of a body. By the time months had become years, their resistance morphed into a reluctant acceptance of the loss. Ultimately, they began to secretly wish, though they never discussed it aloud, that his younger brother's body would be found so they could stop wondering. Closure seemed merciful as the years passed. No matter how much they hoped the doubts would end, though, each official visit started with a jolt of fear—that day could be the day.

Connor bristled at the sheriff's presence. The man had never found his brother and had tagged his father as a murderer. He hadn't come out for a social call, so he needed to end the stall tactics and move along. "Mom's still at work. Do you have news I need to tell her?"

"Sorry, it's hard for me not to think of you as the little kid I first met. I guess you're all grown up now."

"Sheriff, I grew up that day. Now tell me whatever you've got to say."

The sheriff glanced again down the road and sighed, his breath forming a big cloud. He returned his look to Connor and nodded. "We think we found Jaxon."

Connor's breath caught as he heard the words they had been expecting for nearly a decade. "When? Where?"

"Last night, along I-40 in the gorge."

Connor looked down at the dog to hide the tears in his eyes. Trigger looked back at him, tail swishing slowly in the snow. "Last night? How would you know it was him? Doesn't it take time to get DNA results back once you found his…"

David stepped forward and rested his hand on the boy's shoulder. "We didn't find his body. We found him. Alive."

Connor shook off the sheriff's hand and stepped back. Confusion swept over him as he let the words soak in. Trigger whined and licked his hand. His voice cracked as he struggled to speak. "Alive?"

"Yes, alive. He's pretty banged up but able to answer some questions. He told us his name, told us about the day he went missing."

"You've seen him?"

"More than seen him. I've talked to him. I wanted to make sure I did that myself before I came out here and raised your hopes. He's sitting in a bed at Millerton Community Hospital with your mom."

Connor's hand gripped the dog's neck to balance himself. The world felt like it was tipping. "Mom's with him?"

"Yes. Talking to him. Catching up."

"He's really alive?" Connor dropped to his knees and buried his face in Trigger's fur. The dog wriggled in delight under his arms. "How's it possible? Where's he been?"

He listened as the sheriff explained about the search, the treatment at the hospital, the questions he had answered so far. "We don't have all the details yet. Wherever he was wasn't good, but he survived it."

Connor sniffled and tried to focus on the sheriff through teary eyes. For years, he had been prepared to hear his brother was dead, a confirmation of something he always suspected. And he tried praying late at night—alone, without raising his mother's own hopes—that maybe, just maybe, Jaxon might come home alive. But he struggled to accept that his prayers had been answered. "So he's really okay?"

"Put Duke in the house and get in my car. I'll take you down to see for yourself. He's been through a lot and is going to need a lot of time and help, but yeah, he seems like he's doing okay."

Connor looked down at the dog. "Trigger."

"Huh?"

"Duke died years ago. This is Trigger."

The sheriff looked perplexed and then shrugged. "Okay. Sorry. Put Trigger up, then."

An airplane buzzed through the sky as Connor struggled with the news. As much as he wanted it to be true, he couldn't wrap his head around it. But he did as he was told.

16

After dropping Connor off at the hospital, David drove to Shawn's Trailer Court, a ragtag collection of faded single-wide trailers wedged tightly onto tiny lots. He inched his SUV through the muddy ruts of the road circling the park. Overturned children's tricycles, rusted cars on blocks, and old dogs on chains dotted the landscape. A heavy woman in a ragged pink robe stood on a set of wooden steps, puffing away on her morning cigarette.

When David had notified Heather and Connor of Jaxon's return, neither of them pointed out the disconnect between the boy being alive and David's theory of Harold's involvement in the crime. Harold, however, would go straight there, at least if he really hadn't had anything to do with it.

Then again, Jaxon's reappearance didn't prove Harold wasn't involved, David reminded himself. It only proved that the theory of the eventual discovery of a hidden body wasn't going to come true.

As he shifted his SUV into park, the trailer door in front of him ripped open. Dressed in work boots, blue jeans, and a sweatshirt, Harold Lathan leaned against the frame, crossed his arms, and did his best go-to-hell look. "What are you doing here?"

David stepped out into the sunshine and faced the man. "I have some news for you. Can I come in for a minute?"

Without budging from the doorway, Harold growled, "Whatever you think I did, I was at work all night. Fifty people can tell you that. So go to hell and let me sleep."

"I'm not here to accuse you of anything."

"Well, that would be a new approach for you, Sheriff."

David looked around at the neighboring trailers—he could almost touch the closest ones. The woman in the pink robe watched as she lit another cigarette, clearly having decided to stay outside in the cold for the show. He didn't want to have the conversation in front of her, knowing full well it would feed the small-town rumor mill, but he didn't have much choice. He turned back to the figure in the doorway. "We found Jaxon last night."

Harold sucked in his breath. A startled look covered his face. He uncrossed his arms, and his features softened. "Have you told Heather yet?"

"Yes, caught her coming off her shift. And I went to the house and told Connor. Took him to the hospital to be with her."

Harold blinked, absorbing the words. "Hospital? She took the news that hard? They sedate her or something?"

David studied the man. He had been so convinced Harold had caused his youngest boy's disappearance, even if by accident. On the way over, he kept thinking he must have been involved—maybe even sold the boy for drug debts or something like that. But the confusion on the man's face said he was as startled by the boy's reappearance as the rest of them. "She's with Jaxon. He's alive. If you'll let me in, I'll tell you what I know."

Harold stood still in the doorway with a blank look on his

face before waving the sheriff inside. He drifted back into the shadows of the trailer as the woman in pink snuffed out her cigarette in disappointment. David stepped up onto the concrete blocks that served as a front porch and then inside. The threadbare curtains let the morning light seep in. On the counter in front of a small microwave, steam curled from a bowl of instant oatmeal. A half-empty cup of coffee sat beside it.

Harold pointed to a ratty couch in front of the TV and leaned against the kitchen counter. The sheriff removed his hat, settled onto the couch, and related all that had happened overnight. Once the story was complete, he fell silent and waited.

Harold's hand shook, the coffee sloshing in the cup. He wasn't just unnerved by the news, David thought—that was an alkie's shake. Despite the early hour, the man craved a drink. A beer, whiskey, anything. His Adam's apple bobbed as he swallowed, a clicking sound evident in the room. "What's he saying?"

David cocked his head. That was a weird question, not the first thought he expected to hear from a concerned father who had just learned his missing son had been found. *Why would he be worried about what the boy said unless he'd been involved?* "Nothing yet. But he will. He'll tell us exactly what happened that morning."

"Good. I hope you catch the son of a bitch who took my son." Harold picked up his coffee cup, hand still trembling, and slurped. "So where's he been?"

David held onto his suspicions. "He hasn't said… yet."

Harold set the mug on the counter and looked out the window. "Can I see him?"

Another thick pause filled the room until the sheriff slowly nodded. "That's up to Heather, of course."

"I just want to see my son, Sheriff."

"We'll have a deputy on the door all the time even if Heather says you can see him. Until we know what happened and who took him. You understand that?"

David watched Harold clench his hands into fists, his forearms rippling the tattoos under his pushed-up sleeves. The man's lips moved as though he was counting off his anger. When he spoke, his voice was controlled and clipped. "I know you don't believe me. Never have. But I didn't have a damn thing to do with Jaxon's disappearance. And I want as much as anyone to see that whoever took him gets caught and punished. I'd love to find him myself before you do, so I can deliver the punishment personally. Then I'll gladly let you arrest me for something I actually did do."

Harold gripped the counter and leaned forward, his head down and eyes hidden. David listened to him sucking in deep breaths and blowing them out slowly. Once calmed, the man looked back up. "I'm good with a deputy on the door keeping him safe. Just make sure he's keeping his eyes open for anyone, not just me."

"We'll be watching. Closely. Trust me on that one." The sheriff leaned back on the sofa. When he resumed talking, his voice was lower and calmer. "Come to the hospital. I'll convince Heather to let you see him as long as somebody else is in the room."

Harold grunted and looked out the window at the snow melting off the branches. "Fine. I can live with that. All I want is for that boy to be safe."

The sheriff stood and dusted off his hat. "I'll give you a ride."

"With you?" Harold snorted and reached behind him for his own car keys. "No thanks. I prefer fresh air."

17

On his return to the hospital, David stopped by Abe's Market for a fresh biscuit and a cup of the best coffee in town, heaps better than the lukewarm, watery-brown liquid the hospital served in its cafeteria. The primary draw of Abe's, however, was a healthy dose of local gossip, courtesy of the regulars swapping tall tales at the Liars' Table.

Abe's son, Danny, had taken over running the market, freeing the older man to hold court at the table with the rest of the retired men. They were all members of the volunteer fire department, though they had long since left the smoke eating and dangerous rescues to the younger men in town. They kept scanners running to stay up to date on what little action Miller County saw, mostly accidents out on the interstate as tourists and truckers misjudged the sharp, winding curves.

Abe called out, "Sheriff, figured you'd be too busy to come in here, what with all the excitement out on the highway last night."

David paid Danny for his order then sauntered over to the table. "Yep, a few wrecks on a snowy night. Y'all know how that goes."

Abe exchanged sly smiles with the men around the table. David understood as well as they did that part of the game was them drawing the details out of him. "True, true, but I meant the boy you found."

"Oh yeah, that too."

"Heard his name was Jaxon. 'With an x' is how the deputy said it." Abe gestured toward the scanner propped up on the table.

"Yep, so the boy said."

"Quite a coincidence, considering that missing Lathan kid all those years ago."

"Yep."

"So is it him?"

"We're looking at all possibilities, just like we always do. But of course we would tell the family before we made anything like that public."

Abe sipped his coffee, his eyes focused on the sheriff through the steam. "If it was that boy, makes you wonder what really happened way back then. You know, with his father and all."

Danny called out that his order was ready, so David went back up to the counter and took the coffee and the small bag with his fresh biscuit. He turned back to the men, measuring his words carefully, knowing they would be repeated throughout the day. "We always wondered what really happened back then, which is why no one was ever charged. Unfortunately, we can't always control the rumors."

The men exchanged startled glances. "But…"

"Y'all have a great day. Give Marge my best, will ya, Abe?" David left them buzzing and headed out to the parking lot. He settled into the driver's seat and looked through the plate-glass window. The men were huddled together, probably feverishly rehashing the conversation.

Of course, the whole town thought Harold Lathan had

kidnapped his own son. The sheriff's department had never said otherwise. But it was also true that he had never been charged, a fact that had probably grown fuzzy over the years. David had planted a seed of clarity with them, giving himself some maneuvering room no matter the outcome.

18

Half of Connor's life had happened after his little brother disappeared. Jaxon was as much myth as memory, snippets of images. Birthday cakes. Shared toys. Sibling fights. Fleeting visions that felt more like dream than reality.

The boy in the bed didn't match those visions. He didn't seem like Jaxon at all. If the sheriff and his mother hadn't told him, Connor would have assumed he was nothing but a stranger.

Too timid to interfere after entering the cubicle, Connor stood with his back against the curtain, watching his mother and younger brother. Heather sobbed uncontrollably with joy in one moment then paced around the room, jabbering nonsensically in the next. But no matter how much she moved and what she said, Jaxon lay still—a cheerless, bony shadow with his arms around his mother's neck when she sat beside him. His eyes darted around the room like a wild, trapped animal when she paced.

Connor wondered how the boy had lost the vibrancy, the giggle, the gleam of a kid who had delighted in both antagonizing and worshiping his older brother, sneaking around their shared room and absconding with his toys. Back then, he had bubbled with laughter at the silliest things—a fart joke, burping the alphabet, blowing bubbles in cereal milk. This joyless boy didn't seem to know how to laugh at all.

Connor's memories were of their similarities, how much they liked each other, and how often they hung around together. But he was suddenly confronted with all of their differences. His own hair was a reddish-brown, unmanageable mop that never responded well to brushes and combs, not something anyone wanted to run their fingers through to relish its silkiness. Heather brushed Jaxon's thick hair out of his eyes and tucked it behind his ears. Even dirty and matted, it hinted at its lushness.

The laughing little boy of the past had smooth, lightly tanned skin that highlighted his constant smile, unlike his older brother's freckled white face. Jaxon probably would never have the pimples that Connor had fought since the beginning of puberty. His skin had turned pale and cracked from the cold and wind. A scar rippled across the cheek, masking the angelic face from the past.

But mostly, Connor realized, it was the eyes that had changed. He couldn't count the number of times he had stared at his own brown eyes in a mirror, wishing he had Jaxon's twinkling blues, which sparkled with mischief. So many people had remarked about how stunning his eyes were. But they had been replaced with dull gray, washed-out shadows of the past—eyes that spoke of defeat, loss, and grief.

In that moment, he understood how much he had been bottling up over the years, pretending they had been perfectly matched siblings. He hadn't wanted to admit how much they competed with each other. Jaxon was smart, reading before he was in kindergarten. He blinked those baby blues and twinkled a smile, and adults smiled back. He made friends quickly and easily, no matter where they went.

Connor had always felt less sure of himself, hesitant in social settings, and slower to make friends. School was drudgery and homework a chore. He never liked reading assignments and hated making presentations in class. He acted out and played the role of class clown to hide his insecurities.

And, truth be told, he hadn't left Jaxon alone that morning because he wanted to be with his friends. They hadn't threatened to leave if they had to hang around the younger boy, a story he had told dozens of times. They liked Jaxon, thought he was cool "for a little kid." Connor had ridden off with them because he wanted to shed himself of his brother, if only for a while.

Blame for the tragedy of that day could only be placed in one spot, Connor knew—on himself. On a selfish kid who wanted to ride bikes with his friends more than he wanted to babysit his little brother. On the impatient kid who couldn't wait for his father to show up—if he ever did—and take them to the park. On the scared little kid who took hours to admit to his mother he had returned to find the swing set empty, Jaxon's bicycle leaning against the tree right where he had left it.

If only I had stayed with him that day. Then I would have my little brother and not this stranger in a hospital bed.

Nurse Sheila, dabbing her own eyes with a tissue as she watched the mother-son interaction, glanced toward Connor. Jaxon followed her gaze and stiffened at the sight of the older boy. Heather smiled through her tears. "Oh, Jaxon, honey, I'm sorry. It's been so long, and I never really thought… I know lots of changes have happened, but that's your brother."

With wary eyes, Jaxon scanned the young man from feet to head, sizing him up. He whispered in a hoarse voice, "Connor?"

The voice was deeper, rougher than the higher-pitched little boy's voice Connor remembered. He heard himself whimper, a choked sound hinting of the tears he fought so hard to contain. "Yeah, Jax, it's me."

"You're…" Jaxon looked at Heather then back to his brother. "You're bigger than I thought."

The words stabbed. He had been inventorying all of the changes in his sibling without thinking of how strange he must seem to Jaxon. The last time they had seen each other, Connor had been a foot-and-a-half shorter and half his weight. He tried to smile but failed and choked on his words instead. "Yeah… You've changed too, lil' bro."

Jaxon lay back on the pillow and stared at the ceiling. He muttered as if he was talking to an apparition floating above his head. "I don't know what's real."

Confused, Connor took a hesitant step forward. "What do you mean? This is real."

"No, not now. The past." Jaxon closed his eyes. "We told each other stories. About our families. About things we did."

"We? You mean me and you?"

"No." Jaxon's raspy breathing was the only sound in the room. "Back there. The others. Stories helped pass the time. Families. Big brothers. It's what we always talked about."

Connor's limbs went numb, and he sat down hard in a plastic visitor's chair. He whispered, "I'm sorry."

"I don't know which stories are real and which are made up. They're so much… they're just stories in my head."

Connor's hands trembled in his lap. "Tell me some. I will let you know which ones are real."

Jaxon ran a tongue along his lips, looking like he was arguing with himself. He swallowed, the clack audible in the quiet of the room. His eyes remained focused on the overhead lights. "Flying kites. Racing bikes. Pillow fights. Swimming in a creek."

Connor answered, his voice little more than a whisper. "We did all those things."

"Things are so hazy. Like dreams." His breath wheezed in and out. "Like maybe I never did those things at all but only heard about them."

Connor dragged his shirtsleeve across his face, clearing his eyes so he could focus. He scooted the chair closer to the bed and reached his hand out, their fingertips brushing. "I'll help you remember. Everything."

Jaxon's hand trembled, quivering against Connor's touch. His fingers recoiled and then, after a pause, stretched and interlaced with his older brother's. "I'd like that. I want the stories to be real."

Grasping his brother's hand, Connor fought the flood of memories as they reappeared one by one. He hadn't been traumatized like Jaxon had, and yet he struggled to piece everything together. He wanted to help his brother get back to normal, but first he had to confess. "That day… My friends… I left you alone… I shouldn't have done that."

"Yeah. I wish you hadn't." His gaze lowered from the ceiling and locked onto his brother's as a faint smile crossed his face. "Long time ago, though, Con."

"Yeah, long time ago." They sat there, holding hands, hearing only the buzzing of the fluorescent lights. Connor leaned back in the chair, his brother's bony fingers resting in his own hand. He hadn't allowed himself to dream they might ever touch again, but it had happened. No matter how different things were, he felt complete for the first time in a long time. "Welcome home, Jax."

Jaxon's eyes flicked between his visitors. He opened his mouth to speak, but nothing came out. His mouth slowly closed again, and he chewed on his chapped lips. He lay back on the bed, stared at the ceiling, and whispered, the word coming out more a question than a statement, "Home?"

19

Heather felt Sheila wrap her arm around her waist. She turned to look into her friend and former boss's concerned face. "Thanks so much for being here for us."

"Honey, it's the best part of being a volunteer. I don't have to race to the next patient, 'cause I get to spend time where I want to. And taking care of you and that boy is what I want to be doing right now." A wide grin spread across her face. "And you wanna know what the second-best part of being a volunteer is?"

Heather couldn't help but smile as she shook her head.

"I get to call up to administration and tell them what needs to happen. What they going to do? Fire me? So that's what I just did. I told them we need to move this boy up to the fifth floor and get him out of this ER."

"Is he ready to move?"

"Already cleared it with Doc Queen, and he's signed the order. Medically, all this boy needs right now is that IV, some sedatives to deal with the pain, and someone to change the dressings. It's going to get busy down here, anyway, once people start stirring 'bout town, so up there'll be much quieter.

I even got him a room all the way down at the end of the hall so no one will bother him."

"Thank you." Heather hugged Sheila. "When?"

Sheila pulled the curtain back to reveal a waiting wheelchair. "Horace is ready, so ain't no time like the present."

Horace came into the room and helped Jaxon out of his bed. The boy stood on unsteady legs, leaning on Connor as Horace guided him gently into the chair. Without any personal effects to move, they were soon rolling toward the elevators as the ER nurses called out well-wishes and gave Heather hugs. Minutes later, they were on the fifth floor. Horace and Connor assisted Jaxon back out of the chair and into bed.

Horace wheeled the empty chair out of the room, and Sheila left with a promise to check in later. The room fell quiet as Connor draped his jacket over the back of a chair then flopped down into it.

Heather stood at the foot of the bed, her arms crossed as she hugged herself, her eyes dancing back and forth between the boys' faces. For the first time since learning of Jaxon's return, she wasn't surrounded by others bustling around. The quiet was unnerving.

"I'm going to find some coffee. You boys need me to bring you something back?" They shook their heads, and she slipped out the door, hearing it latch behind her in the quiet. She only took a couple of steps before her emotions overwhelmed her, and she crumpled into a chair at the end of the hall and sobbed.

She stared out the hall window at the snow-covered mountains, tears streaming down her face. She needed to be strong for Jaxon—for both her sons. They didn't need to see her cry, but how could she not bawl at the sight of him? His dull eyes had followed her around the room, obviously questioning why she had given up on him. That jagged scar running down his face seemed to accuse her of not caring about his suffering. His gaunt features and lifeless hair…

Coffee wasn't what she desired. She craved her little boy, the one gone for so long. She yearned to hear his infectious giggles as she made him pancakes on the rare mornings she wasn't racing off to a day of classes after working all night. She wished to see his eyes light up when she agreed that he and Connor could split an order of french fries. She longed to feel his little arms snaking around her neck as he hugged her.

She wanted *him* back, not the hollow shell propped up in a bed, hooked up to machines, the bony teenager who didn't seem like her son at all.

If only…

She had spent many a sleepless night, staring at the ceiling, playing the if-only game.

Her last memory of Jaxon was wrapping her arms around him at the breakfast table as she was leaving for class. He'd rewarded her affection with a big, wet, sloppy kiss on her cheek, his mouth full of cereal and milk. He'd cackled in delight, and she'd laughed along with him as she exaggeratedly wiped the mess off her face. She'd sent him one last smile as she kissed Connor on the top of the head, grabbed her car keys and bag of nursing textbooks, and raced out the door, late for school.

She never saw him again. She didn't even remember saying "I love you." She had found the time to nag them, though, reminding them to do their chores, not to watch TV all day, and not to leave the house until Harold got there.

Except Harold never showed. The boys didn't really expect him to because he had failed so many times before, but they had always backed their dad up, claiming he was there when he hadn't been. The lies had flowed freely because that was easier than them facing how much of a loser their father was. *How many times had Harold not shown up? How many times had*

Connor lied for his dad? How many times had Jaxon played in that playground by himself? How many times did I suspect they were alone but hadn't pushed because then I would've had to do something about it?

I didn't know.

But she did know—if not the specifics, the generalities. She was months away from completing her coursework for being an RN, which came with a big raise. Without Harold's steady contribution, that extra money was supposed to help her keep up with the mortgage payments so they didn't lose their house. She needed to buy clothes and food for a pair of growing boys. Maybe, she hoped, she could even save a little extra for their college years.

What was I supposed to do?

She had held Jaxon's cereal bowl in her hands that night, staring at the dried cereal stuck to the side, left from their half-hearted effort to rinse their breakfast dishes. She didn't wash it for weeks, scared to remove the last tangible sign that he had been in the house.

She had stood in the boys' room, looking at the wrinkled beds, the sheets pulled up in their best bed-making effort. Pillows still lay on the floor from a pillow fight they must have had as they waited on Harold. She knew them and knew that they must have planned to straighten up before she got home so they wouldn't get into trouble.

Connor had been reluctant to admit that his father had never shown up that day. At first, he had claimed he had been there, just like he was supposed to, but the lie quickly fell apart, and he recanted.

That change in story made the police wonder if Harold had really been there all along. They seemed to think that maybe Connor's real lie was that the man wasn't involved.

Confused and frustrated, Connor had broken down and told the whole story. His friends had shown up, and they played in the front yard. They grew bored waiting and decided to go to the park without Harold. It was close to the house and a safe place. Lots of kids in the small town went there unsupervised.

Connor had seen no harm in joining them. He'd hopped on his bike and had Jaxon follow. He made sure Jax was on the swings and having a good time. He made him promise not to leave and noted there were other kids and parents hanging around. He made him promise not to tell Mom what they had done. He had no qualms leaving to ride the dirt trails with his friends.

He wasn't worried because it was something they had done dozens of times before, he had confessed with tears in his eyes.

I didn't know. I suspected, sure, and had even heard from other moms that they had seen Con and Jax playing at the park without Harold in sight. But I didn't know-know. Maybe Harold was sitting on a bench, smoking a cigarette. Just because they didn't see him…

Heather hung her head. She had lied to herself because it was easier than admitting she'd left two little boys alone to fend for themselves. Sitting in that hospital room, staring at the husk of her boy in that bed, she grew tired of the justifications in her mind. A mother's job was to know what her children were doing. Her first priority was to keep them safe. And she had failed.

And why? Because it was also her job to put food in their bellies, clothes on their backs, and a roof over their heads. Harold never helped much with that either.

20

W ith the fresh cup of coffee in hand, David entered the hospital and headed toward the elevator bank. As he punched the elevator call button to go up to Jaxon's room, a female voice called out, "Sheriff Newman?"

David turned to see FBI Supervisory Special Agent Roxanne Porter walking toward him, a second agent in a coat and tie two steps behind her.

"You made it to Millerton fast."

She extended her hand and shook David's firmly. "I appreciate the phone call. Not often we get happy endings in this business, especially after such a long time."

A decade earlier, Roxanne had been the most junior member of the team the FBI dispatched to Millerton on the day of Jaxon's disappearance. As far as the family understood, her primary role was inside the Lathan house, serving as a liaison to Heather. She kept the frantic mother as calm as possible, helping her to understand what law enforcement was doing to find her missing son. Nothing about the case looked like a kidnapping for ransom, though Roxanne had been prepared to coach the family through that process if the need arose.

While Roxanne supported the family, her second role had been to gain their trust so she could monitor them. The majority of kidnapped children were taken by a close relative. An estranged parent, particularly one like Harold, with his history of drug and alcohol abuse, made for a prime suspect.

Trusting Roxanne, Heather had shared stories of her ex-husband's erratic behavior and struggles. Connor confessed how often he had lied about Harold's failure to show up. That information, coupled with Harold's inability to explain his whereabouts when Jaxon disappeared and the boys' clothing in his trailer and car, painted a guilty image.

As the years went by, David had stayed in touch with the FBI about the case whenever a boy's body was located. The senior agents on the original team retired, quit, or transferred to other units, elevating Roxanne to the FBI's senior agent on the case through attrition. Contact between Miller County and the FBI team had been limited over the years, sparked by possibilities that were soon disproven. If a hiker or hunter stumbled across a decomposed body, DNA tests were ordered. Often, an arrested serial child molester was then questioned about dates and locations. But without a body or a confession, little happened to move the case forward, and their contact was infrequent.

Roxanne introduced the other agent, Anthony Gonzalez, who stood out in his dark suit, white shirt, and red tie among a sea of people in jeans, sweatshirts, and scrubs—FBI agents never seemed to blend well in small towns—then turned back to business. "Do you have confirmation of the boy's identity?"

"The first confirmation was a visual by me, coupled with his recollections. His mother and brother are with him now and also believe it's him. I've requested his DNA testing be top priority for Raleigh, but I think that's a formality now."

"We can run it faster if you want. We don't want another Brian Rini." In 2019, police in Kentucky had stopped a teenager wandering the streets of Newport. He'd identified himself as Timmothy Pitzen, a boy who'd disappeared in 2011 at the age of six from Aurora, Illinois. Investigators doubted his kidnapping story when he refused to be fingerprinted. DNA testing outed the impostor as a twenty-three-year-old felon named Brian Rini, who had made similar claims twice before.

"Agreed, and I'll take all the help I can get." The friction between local police and the FBI so often depicted in movies wasn't always the reality, particularly not for a small police department without the resources of their larger-city brethren. "You need to come up and chat with the kid, anyway. I suspect he's got quite a tale."

"Have you notified Harold?"

David motioned toward the parking lot, where Harold was getting out of his Chevelle. He knew Roxanne shared the same qualms—Jaxon's reappearance forced them to question their conclusion about Harold's involvement. "Seemed genuinely surprised and shocked, but not worried the kid had reappeared. Said a couple of times he wants us to catch whoever took Jaxon. He didn't argue when I explained he wouldn't be able to see the boy without supervision."

"In other words, he's not acting like a man scared his old crime is about to be exposed." Roxanne studied the waiting father as he settled into a chair in the lobby. "I'm not taking him off my list yet, but it'll certainly make us reexamine things we thought we knew. He could still have been involved in the kidnapping. Maybe he had to settle a drug debt."

"I'm with you about the disappearance, but I don't see how he could've been involved in holding the kid alive all these years. Prison time would have made it impossible to hide the child's whereabouts without a trusted accomplice, and we've not known him to have any close friends. Since being released, he rarely goes anywhere other than work, AA, and NA. No way he hid a kid in that trailer park without the neighbors knowing. If he was involved at the beginning, I think he's as surprised as the rest of us that the kid's still alive. We'll watch the boy's response when dad gets to see him."

"We? So you want me in the room?"

David looked pointedly at Agent Gonzalez. "I don't want to crowd him, but the boy's scared and doesn't want to talk much to me. I've seen you at work, building rapport to get information. We need to find out where he was being held, and I'm hoping you might be able to get that out of him."

"Makes perfect sense. Gonzalez can coordinate transfer of evidence to our labs, and I'll assist with interviews."

The elevator doors opened, and they stepped on. With others around them, they rode to their floor in silence, waiting at each stop as people got on or off the elevator. When they reached the fifth floor, Roxanne spied Heather standing at the end of the hall and pulled David into a quiet alcove. "Has he said anything about other victims?"

"No, but that's my fear. He hasn't told us much of anything yet, but wherever he came from…" He looked out the window at the parking lot below them. The snow had been pushed into hills at the far end, and rivulets of melt ran across the pavement in the bright sunshine.

"If there are others, once his escape is discovered…"

"They could be moved or worse, killed," David finished the gruesome thought.

"Gonzalez, let's get the clothes he was wearing to our lab as well, see what we can pull off them and who and where it points to." Roxanne turned back to David and asked, "How sure are you he came from the Wattsville exit?"

"Only an educated guess. If he was hitchhiking, he could have come from anywhere, but considering where we found him and the direction he was walking, Wattsville is the only exit that makes sense if he was on foot the whole time. The next one west of that is another four miles into Tennessee. I don't see how he would have survived in last night's weather that far. It's a miracle he survived as long as he did. Plus, we would have received calls even earlier because people would have seen him walking that stretch of road."

"And to the east?"

"Seven miles to the next exit, and that one is even more remote. Since he was headed that way, it really doesn't make sense."

"So the isolation helps us by narrowing it down to a single likely exit but hurts us because it's a big search area."

"The good news is there are only a couple of roads there, but it's very rural, and houses are scattered. State patrol and the forest service have offered to get their choppers up, but they need to know what they're looking for. The park service is checking shelters, but they're mostly empty this time of year. Besides, they make no sense as a long-term kidnap holding. I'm going to send some deputies knocking on doors, but the residents up there, well, they aren't exactly big law-enforcement fans. Cooperation is very iffy." David sighed. "We need to know more about what we're looking for."

"So let's go see what Jaxon can tell us."

21

Movement in the reflections of the window broke Heather's thoughts. She noisily wiped her hand across her face and turned to see the sheriff approaching her. He motioned to the familiar-looking woman walking beside him and asked, "Do you remember Agent Porter?"

Heather couldn't help a smile crossing her face as recognition hit. Unlike the sheriff and his pursuit of her ex, Agent Porter had always felt like an ally. "Of course. Roxanne is my statistics queen."

David's faced crinkled in confusion, but Roxanne defused the moment with a laugh. "Forgive me for my rookie mistake. I was trying so hard to prove how much I had learned in the academy and tried to counter emotions with data. I've learned tons about people skills in the years since."

"There's nothing to forgive. You helped me deal with all the craziness of those days."

The day after the disappearance had been no easier than the first night. Cops had traipsed back and forth in her house, their radios squawking. They'd asked her thousands of questions. Connor had retreated to the room he shared with his missing brother, except the police entered it, too, and sorted through Jaxon's clothing and toys, looking for clues.

Worst of all, they asked over and over where Harold was, as if she would magically get an idea.

She had curled up on a couch in the den with the TV blaring, trying to drown out the noise around her. The talking head on the TV was interviewing an expert in child abductions. They raged at the incompetence of the police, how underwhelming the sheriff had appeared, how the case was spinning out of control. And then the interviewer asked if it was already too late to find the boy alive.

Heather had sat up and stared at the TV, the noise around her disappearing in a fog. The expert, in his fancy suit and flashy tie, looked right at the camera and said, "The statistics are clear. Ninety-nine percent of all kidnapped children are dead in the first twenty-four hours. The police have moved too slow on this one."

She didn't remember throwing a glass at the TV. Or the screen shattering and smoke curling up from behind the set. Or the officers standing around, slack-jawed and silenced. Or Roxanne guiding her to her bedroom and sitting her down on the bed.

"I was out of my mind." Heather wrapped her hand around Roxanne's elbow in a warm embrace. "But you—you were different than the rest of them. You helped me to breathe until I could explain what had happened, and then you told me about the studies the guy was quoting."

The FBI, like all law enforcement, knew that most missing children come home. They could wander off and get lost or end up with a friend or relative, not even realizing that people are looking for them. Kidnappings were rare, but when they did happen, the perpetrator was almost always a family member, most of whom did everything they could to keep the child safe.

A total stranger taking a child almost never happened. The sheer abnormal nature of such cases drove the extensive media coverage that formed the public perception of stranger danger.

So, yes, Roxanne had told Heather back then, a study by the Department of Justice found that eighty-nine percent, not the ninety-nine percent often quoted, of those children *who died* did so within the first twenty-four hours of kidnapping—the majority within only a few hours. In other words, for the very few who were killed, it happened quickly. The kidnapper who held onto a victim for days, weeks, or even years was far more common in movies than real life.

"I cringe when I see some TV cop saying that. I don't know why it bothers me so much when it's the same stupid shows that have a female FBI agent showing her cleavage while balancing in her high heels." Roxanne looked down at her own sensible foot attire.

"Standing beside her impossibly handsome partner," Heather added as both women glanced at the sheriff and laughed.

David grimaced. "Thanks, ladies. Way to trash the ego. But to make it worse, I'm a Southern sheriff, not an FBI agent. We're all stereotyped as Andy Griffith, Rosco P. Coltrane, or some racist slime ball. Not much glamor in that."

Their laughter dwindled to a chuckle. Roxanne's face grew serious again. "Heather, you don't know how happy I am he's back. I wish the best for your family and want to give you the space you need to heal, but we need to spend some time with him this morning. If you'll let us, of course."

Heather wrapped her arms around her chest. Roxanne was right, she had improved her people skills, but Jaxon came first. She shook her head and said, "Not now, please. He needs to rest. To recover. Can't you come back in a few weeks? Or even just let him rest a few days first? What's the point in rushing, now that he's back?"

Roxanne fixed her gaze directly on Heather's. "Whoever had Jaxon all these years is still out there. When they figure out he got away, what do you think the reaction will be? Are other kids in danger? Will he go snatch another kid to replace him? You know what that's like, so you know why we need his help. We want to catch this SOB, and we need to move quick. That's why it needs to be now."

Heather turned her back on them and stared out the window at the mountains. *Is the creep hiding out there somewhere? What if he comes to take Jaxon away again? Maybe he's in the hall right now, dressed as an orderly or pushing a broom or delivering a food tray. We have no idea what he looks like.*

She had given up cigarettes as soon as she found out she was pregnant with Connor. Over the years, she had watched her ex-husband fight his own addictions. She understood it because in times of stress, she craved with every fiber the relaxing feeling of a smoke. That particular moment was off the stress charts, so her hands shook at the thought of holding one between her fingers. She closed her eyes. Her precious Jaxon had been taken from her, and a shell of a boy had been returned. If they could prevent that from happening to another boy, they had to try.

Exhaling slowly, she nodded.

22

"Do you remember the mud pit?" Jaxon asked.

Connor knew his mother's need for coffee was an excuse to avoid the room. He felt the discomfort too. The boy sprawled under the sheets wasn't the same, haunted and changed by the years of abuse. Their conversation was halting as they struggled for things to talk about, throwing out old stories to rebuild the feelings, but everything felt forced and foreign. At everything Connor said, Jaxon just shook his head and said he couldn't remember. Connor doubted they could ever reconnect the bonds that had been broken a decade earlier.

He wanted to remember the mud pit, whatever it was, because it was the first time Jaxon had brought up something himself. Connor scrunched up his face as if that would force the memory to surface. "Mud pit?"

Jaxon's face fell, the hopefulness that had popped up dissipating quickly. "Yeah, it was one of the stories we told a lot. Makes me laugh, thinking about it."

"Well, tell me. Maybe I'll remember."

With a grunt, Jaxon sat up in the bed and crossed his legs.

He rested his hands on his knees, closed his eyes, and began. "It was a hot summer day, a perfect day to go swimming, except we couldn't go to the park without Dad. We weren't allowed to leave the yard without an adult, so we were stuck at home, in the backyard, sweat dripping down our bodies, complaining like we loved to do. With a snap of his fingers, Connor stood up and exclaimed, 'I've got an idea. Let's dig our own pool.'"

Jaxon opened his eyes and looked at Connor, a reddish tint of embarrassment crawling up his face. "Sorry. I meant you. You stood up. I'm so used to telling it as a story."

Connor shook with surprise at hearing his name in the midst of the story. It felt as though he had been listening to a campfire story told about someone else more than a conversation. Still, the memory had come crashing back to him, and he didn't want to lose the moment. "I remember it. It was hot as hell, and we wanted to go swimming. Dad was supposed to take us over to the community pool at the park, but he didn't show up. Big surprise. He never showed up when he was supposed to. I wanted to ride our bikes over there anyway, but you had this brilliant idea we could make a pool in our backyard just like rich people do."

Jaxon sputtered in protest. "I thought it was all your idea."

The older boy grinned and chuckled. "Oh, no, you went running into the storage closet and came out carrying Dad's shovel. It was like twice as big as you were, and when you stabbed it in the ground, the handle hit you on the head. But you were like, 'We're gonna build our own pool!' and kept digging."

"Funny. I thought you did all the digging."

"Oh, I did, because you weren't making much of a hole, and I took over. I guess I thought it would work, or maybe I thought it would be fun to try, because I grabbed the shovel and started tearing up the dirt. And Duke helped… You remember Duke, don't ya? That dog was awesome."

Connor laughed louder as Jaxon's eyes grew big. The memory of the day kept flooding into his brain. "Anyway, we only got a few inches dug 'cause we kept hitting rocks and had to stop and pull them out of the ground. We got tired and hot 'cause it was really hard work, so I began to think it wasn't such a great idea after all, but we did have enough for a wading pool."

"That's when you decided to roll out the hose and fill it with water."

"Me?" Connor protested. "It was definitely you who grabbed the hose."

"Whatever." Jaxon waved his hands in dismissal. "Most of the water didn't go in the hole because it turned into a massive water fight in the backyard. Water dripping off the windows and the house and everything."

Connor howled with laughter at the memory as Jaxon's smile expanded into a full grin, exposing the gaps from missing teeth. Making his brother laugh felt good, and Connor didn't want to lose the feeling, so he continued, "And the mud. It's not like we had much grass, anyway—never did—and we had this hole in the middle of the yard and the dirt we'd pulled out. Everything turned to this clingy, yucky mud that stuck to everything. The house. The dog. Each other. Duke was racing around, shaking his fur and splattering the side of the house. And that's when we started 'rassling' like they do on TV, taking big flying leaps through the air and landing in that big ol' muddy hole with a splat."

"Mud caked in ears. Dripping out of hair. Even down pants and into underwear."

"Oh, yeah, and Duke was as muddy as we were. I swear he wagged his tail, and mud flew everywhere. And then we got into trouble."

Jaxon snickered. "Mom came home."

"We heard the car door slam, and she came around the corner of the house. The look on her face. She was so mad at us…"

"But you could also tell she was trying really hard not to laugh."

"Exactly! She called us swamp monsters." Connor snapped his fingers and exclaimed, "No, it was her lizard men! You know, like that legend down in South Carolina. The lizard man of the swamp or something like that. And she called Duke lizard dog because you couldn't even see his fur anymore."

Jaxon clasped his hands and smiled broader. "Bath time for my lizard men!"

"Except she made us take off all our clothes out in the yard." Connor hooted and rocked in his chair. "She was more worried about getting mud everywhere than the neighbors seeing us naked. She warned us not to touch anything until we were in the bathtub. And she made Duke stay outside. He was howling his head off 'cause she wouldn't let him come in."

"Except… you snuck out and let him in."

Connor wiped a hand across his eyes, tears of laughter rather than sadness over lost time. "Oh, yeah, I had forgotten that too. And that time it was me, for sure. He was so excited to be back with us he ran through the house, leaving muddy paw prints everywhere. Then he jumped up on my bed, twisting around in celebration, getting mud all over my bed."

"And on the walls!"

"Oh, yeah. Mom was so mad, and I got in so much trouble all over again. I tried to tell her you let Duke in, but she didn't believe me."

"A mud-pit swimming pool. That was so cool."

"That whole day was so cool. Getting in trouble and all." Connor balled his hand up in a fist and stuck it out toward his little brother, but Jaxon flinched and shrank back into his pillow. His face went white, and he pulled the sheet up to his chin and quivered. His reaction horrified Connor, and the laughter inside him faded, replaced by a revulsion toward whoever had changed his brother so much. He looked at his outstretched fist and exclaimed, "Oh God, no, Jax. I wouldn't hit you, dude. Never."

Jaxon raised a single finger from his hands holding the sheet and pointed at Connor's fist. "But…"

"A fist bump. That's all it is."

The boy raised an eyebrow. "Fist bump?"

"You don't remember. We used to do it all the time." He had to remember how much his little brother had forgotten. He lowered his arm and loosened his fist. "It's a way of celebrating. Kinda like a handshake but cooler."

"But how…"

"Look, Jax, it's easy. Just ball your hand up like this." Connor tightened his fingers. "Now, reach out and tap your knuckles to mine."

Jaxon relaxed his grip on the sheet and slowly sat back up in bed. He looked down at his hand and curled his fingers. With a sheepish glance for approval from his brother, he reached out slowly until their knuckles touched. "Fist bump," he whispered.

"Fist bump." Connor rested his fingers against the bony fingers across from him. He could feel the nervous shake coming through the light touch. "We used to do it every night before going to bed and anytime we got into trouble together. It was just our thing."

Jaxon hung his head. "I'm sorry. There's lots I don't remember."

"Don't be sorry, bro. I'd forgotten the mud pit." Connor wrapped his hand around his little brother's fist. "We'll remember it all together. I promise."

23

Heather opened the door and ushered the sheriff and FBI agent into the hospital room. The two boys fell quiet, their conversation halted mid-sentence as they focused on their visitors. Jaxon scooted to the side of the bed closest to his brother's chair until they were almost shoulder to shoulder. Connor draped his arm around Jaxon's neck.

Connor's defensive move unsettled Heather—not so much his desire to protect the boy as the casualness of the gesture. He was being a big brother, offering comfort to his weaker sibling while defending him from the intruders. She wondered whether he would have yielded so quickly as she had and allowed Jaxon to be peppered with their questions. In retrospect, her protest felt timid and insincere. Her own protective maternal instincts should have flared up and battled the intrusion.

She took a deep breath and reminded herself that the questions were about the other children. She had to allow this to help them. She could protect both her boys and help others too.

"Jaxon, uh, honey," she said as the two boys tightened their grip on each other, "Sheriff Newman and Agent Porter need to ask you a few questions. Is that okay?"

Before he had a chance to answer, the FBI agent pulled a chair to the foot of the bed and sat down, making herself small and unthreatening. She took on a quiet, calm tone. "Call me Roxanne."

David attempted to emulate her by folding his lanky frame into a chair beside her. His posture wasn't nearly as convincing. Still, the boy relaxed with a glance to Connor for reassurance.

Heather took a hesitant step toward the bed, but there was no room left. She scanned the room for somewhere to sit, but no empty chairs remained. She leaned against the wall and crossed her arms, doing her best not to feel out of place.

Roxanne said, "We want to find the place you've been all these years and the people you were with. Can you help us with that?"

Jaxon's eyes opened wide, and the little color he had drained out of his face. He gripped Connor's arm hard and shook his head. "I don't wanna go back. Not ever. I can't go there. Please don't make me."

Roxanne leaned and reached to comfort the boy but stopped herself. She settled back into the chair and let her hands drop into her lap. Connor squeezed his brother with a reassuring hug. She shot the boy a smile meant to relax him. "You don't have to go anywhere near it. You can stay right here with your brother and mom."

Feeling Roxanne's glance at her, Heather unfolded her arms and let them fall to her side. She avoided the agent's gaze.

Roxanne spoke softly and reassuringly. "We need you to describe it so we can find it. Nothing else. Just describe. Can you do that for us?"

Jaxon squeezed his eyes shut and balled his fists. "I don't want to talk about it. Not about him. Not that place. Ever."

"I can understand that. I would probably want to forget it

all, too, but what about the others, the other kids who lived with you? Don't you want us to get them away from there too?"

Jaxon pulled the sheet tight against his chin. "It's too late. There haven't been any other kids in a long time. Just me." A loud gulp as he swallowed followed by the softest whisper. "And him."

Heather took a tentative step forward. *If there aren't still kids there, can't they delay the interrogation? But what if he said that just to avoid questions at all?*

Roxanne glanced up at her, seemingly thinking the same thing. "How long has it been just you and… him?" She waited for an answer then prompted, "Days? Weeks?"

Jaxon shrugged, a slight movement under the sheet. "I don't know. A bunch of weeks at least. The leaves were still on the trees outside, but it was already getting cooler." He turned away from her and pleaded to Connor, "Please. Make them go away. I don't want to talk about him."

The older boy glared at Roxanne and held his brother tighter. She kept her eyes focused on Jaxon's face, willing the frightened boy to look at her. "Then let's talk about the house itself and not him, okay? Can you tell me what it looked like?"

The two boys exchanged a look, Jaxon's eyes begging. Connor leaned forward until their foreheads touched. They whispered an exchange undecipherable to the others in the room.

Heather blinked back the tears filling her eyes. With the two boys in profile, Jaxon's scar was hidden. For a moment she saw what could have been if he had never disappeared, the two brothers tightly bonded throughout their childhoods.

They fell silent, and Jaxon sighed and slumped on his pillow. He closed his eyes and said, "I don't know much. I mean, mostly, I stayed in the basement."

"Mostly?"

He swallowed and continued, his trembling voice soft, "Sometimes, not real often, he made me do chores outside. Things he didn't like to do."

"Like what?"

"Dig holes. Chop wood. Pile up debris that got knocked down in a storm. Stuff like that."

"Okay, let's start with that. Can you describe what it looked like around the outside of the house?"

"Trees as far as I could see. The house was in this small clearing, but we were surrounded by woods."

"Could you see any other houses?"

"No."

"Hear cars on a road?"

"No."

"Ever hear people talking or music playing or any sounds of neighbors?"

"No."

"Could you hear anything at all?"

"Birds. Coyotes singing. Sometimes a jet way up in the sky. I always wondered what it was like, having the freedom to fly anywhere you wanted, to go somewhere different."

"I'm sure." Roxanne asked softly, "What would he do outside?"

"Go to the outhouse. Work on his van."

"Outhouse? So no bathroom inside?"

"I don't think so. None I ever saw."

"Did you go to the outhouse?"

"Only to empty the buckets we used in the basement. That was one of my chores."

Heather put a hand up over her face in horror and connected eyes with Roxanne. The FBI agent nodded some sympathy toward her before turning her attention back to Jaxon. "Could you see the van?"

"Not always. Depended on where he parked it."

"How often did he leave in the van?"

Jaxon shivered. "Not much. He said most everything he needed came from the mountains."

"Good. Good. So he hunted for food? What did he catch?"

"Rabbits. Squirrels. Deer. Bear. Got an elk once, but that was a few years ago. He was real freaked out about that."

"Why?"

"It had a radio collar on it."

Roxanne and David exchanged looks before she continued. "That's great. Did you see it? Remember if it had a number on it?"

The boy shook his head. "Nope. He got rid of it before he got the elk back to the smokehouse."

"Smokehouse? So he cured his own meat? Is that what the wood chopping was for?"

"Yeah. And for the still and to heat the house."

"Still? So he made his own liquor?"

"Yeah."

"And to heat the house? So no propane tanks?"

"Nope."

"Electricity?"

"Nope."

"How about running water?"

"He got water from a hand pump in the yard."

Roxanne chewed on her lip. "So, let's go back to the van. What color was it?"

"More than one color." He held up his hands and stacked them to indicate two layers. "Dark brown on the bottom half and a real light tan on the top half."

"Ford? Chevy? Something else?"

He shrugged.

She chewed on her pen. "Windows all the way down either side of the van and on the back doors?"

"No. Just up front."

"Was it the same vehicle the whole time you were there? Or did he get a new one at some point?"

"Same one. Always had rust and dents and stuff like that."

"You're doing great. That helps tons already. What can you tell me about the house itself? Stone? Wood?"

"Wood except stone around the bottom."

"Wood slats like this?" She drew a series of parallel lines on her pad and turned it to him.

He sat up and opened his eyes to look at her drawing. "Sort of, except they weren't straight like that. The edges were curled and really rough and uneven. And not painted or anything."

"Hand-hewn boards like this?" She sketched another series of lines, but this time showing rough-cut boards.

Jaxon nodded.

"Windows?"

"Just two windows in the front, on either side of the door. And little windows along the ground."

"Little windows? How big?"

He moved his hands indicating foot-and-a-half wide by half-foot tall.

"They were to the basement?"

He nodded.

"Okay, you're doing really well. Can you tell me about inside the house? How many rooms?"

"Just two. The front room and the kitchen."

"No bedroom?"

"No. He slept in the front room. It had a bed and a chair and the fireplace."

"What did the kitchen have in it?"

"An old wood stove, a table, and a chair."

"Just one chair?"

"Yes."

"You didn't eat with him?"

Jaxon looked incredulous and shook his head.

"Any windows or doors?"

"No windows." He gulped. "The only door was to the basement. It had a padlock on it."

She scribbled some notes before looking up. "Can we move into the basement? Can you describe it?"

Beads of sweat formed on the boy's upper lip. His breathing accelerated. Connor leaned forward to him and whispered, his words just loud enough for Heather to decipher, "You all right?"

The boy quivered and took a series of rapid breaths. "I'm okay."

"Go ahead and tell her. I got you."

"Okay." He turned to her, exhaled, and said, "Door off the kitchen. Wood steps down. Dirt floor. Stone walls."

"And the little windows?"

"Way up high."

"Too high up so you couldn't see out them?"

"Sometimes. If others were in the basement with me and we didn't think he was coming, one of us could stand on the other's shoulders and look out."

Roxanne and David whispered to each other at the foot of the bed. Connor wrapped his hand protectively around the back of Jaxon's head. The younger boy rested against his older brother's shoulder.

Heather stood in the middle along the wall, watching the exchange and feeling isolated. She resented Connor being more protective than she was but was thankful he was there for his little brother. Uncomfortable with her own lack of a role in the room, her arms had worked their way back up and folded across her chest as she leaned against the wall. She felt the need to insert herself and spoke up, "Look, Jaxon can't really tell you much. Can we leave him alone?"

Roxanne straightened in her chair and smiled. "Jaxon's told us tons. The house is something that was once common here—

an old mountain shack built with hand-hewn wood with a stone cellar on a large piece of private land. The national park has some of these maintained, but the rangers would have noticed smoke from chimneys and smokehouses, so this has to be off park property. We know it's remote because no neighbors or livestock can be heard. And we know it doesn't have plumbing and electricity, which narrows it down considerably. Most of the old places like this have been abandoned and have rotted away, but this one is still livable. If we can narrow down the location, we can ask neighbors in the area. Just because people don't visit the house doesn't mean people don't know about it. So, please, just a few more questions, and we'll leave you alone."

Without waiting for a response, Roxanne turned her attention back to Jaxon. "Can you tell us about the night you escaped? How you got out? What you saw as you were leaving the house? If you can do that, you will tell us enough to find it."

Heather turned her attention back to the head of the bed to see if Jaxon could keep going. But the boy wasn't looking at her—he was looking at his older brother. Connor smiled at him and nodded.

Jaxon shivered, turned, and looked out the window, the jagged scar dark against his pale face. He clutched the blankets and pulled them tightly under his chin.

24

I lost count of the days since he had last opened the door. I hadn't heard his footsteps or the creaking of his bed or the scrape of a chair or the slamming of a door. No logs dropped in the fireplace. No pots and pans clanged on the stove. All I heard was silence.

I couldn't reach the windows to look out for him, not without someone else to boost me up there. And no one else was in the basement with me. No one had been there for months, not since that last boy had trudged up those steps and not come back. He had been furious about that because summer was over, and he didn't like to hunt in the winter. He said it was always easier in the summer.

I didn't like it either, because I was totally alone. No one to talk to. No one to sleep beside.

But why was it so quiet?

Maybe he had gone off hunting for a new kid. I hadn't heard the van crank up and leave. I wouldn't have missed the sound of an engine starting. No way I would've slept through that.

But still, I didn't hear him. The silence was wrong. It scared me. I would sit down there, looking up the steps, half hoping the door would open and he would still be there.

The other half of me prayed the door never opened again.

The problem was, I was hungry. I mean really hungry. When he tossed food down, I always knew to make it last a few days. I never knew when he would throw more down. But he had never been this long, so I had run out. Not a scrap.

The last time he had opened that door had been a couple of weeks earlier, and I wasn't sure he was going to throw food down. He leaned against the frame, wheezing and hissing. No new kid was thrown down, but he didn't call me up the steps, either. He just glared at me.

I knew he hated me. Always had. I thought maybe he had finally decided to come down and kill me. After all, he didn't need me without a kid for me to tend to. But he didn't come down. He just stared. And wheezed. Minutes, hours passed while he leaned against the doorframe, looking at me as I tried to hide in the shadows.

Finally, he reached behind his back and grabbed a bucket of food. He tossed it down to me, but it hit the steps and tumbled, clattering across the floor. The slop spilled out, and the rats came from the shadows. I wanted to chase them away —it was my food, and I was starving—but I didn't dare move until the light from upstairs was blocked and I heard the door slam shut and the lock slide into place.

I chased the rats away and gathered my food in the bucket. It wasn't much. They had gotten some of it. But I could make it last a few days.

But more than a few days passed. He didn't come back, and I didn't know where he was. I started debating how long I would last. What if he wasn't coming back? What if I could get away? I could have crept up those steps and forced open that door only to find him sitting there, waiting and watching for me, grinning that twisted, gap-toothed smile and twirling the ax handle he liked to use for the most heinous beatings.

I licked water from the walls and searched desperately for crumbs. Not for the first time, I caught a rat slowed by the wintry cold, slammed its head against the stone wall to kill it, and sank my teeth into it. Rats were better tasting than some things, and it was too cold for insects.

That last day, the day I escaped, the light outside was gray and cold. I could barely see in the corners as I searched for something—anything—to eat. I was sitting there, thinking I was going to starve to death, and I made a decision. Just like that, snap, and I knew what I had to do. I didn't want to die in that basement—a shocking thought, considering how little I had to live for.

I didn't expect to get far and figured he would catch me and kill me for trying to escape. I knew I wouldn't make it. I just didn't want to die without trying.

I put a first tentative foot on the bottom tread of the wooden stairs and listened to it creak. I held my breath and waited for the storm of his footsteps, for the door to be yanked open, for him to glare down at me in fury at my boldness. I remained frozen as minutes slipped by, listening, but only the groaning of the wind answered me before I gathered enough courage to move to the next step. Still more ticks of the clock until the next. And the next and the next. The shadows of the brief winter day shifted across the room as I moved cautiously from step to step, always prepared to scamper back down.

Hours passed before I stood at the top, trembling as I pressed my ear against the door. Tree branches clacked against each other as the wind groaned. Ravens squawked as they fought over food in the woods. A rat scurried in the walls.

But not a human sound reached my ears. No footsteps. No voices. No breathing.

With sweat dribbling down my back despite the cold, I

reached out with a quaking hand and turned the knob. The latch slipped away from the strike plate with a loud, echoing clack. I squeezed my eyes shut, dreading the storm of approaching boots.

But I heard only silence.

Maybe another hour passed—I don't know, I've never owned a watch—until I built enough nerve to push on the door. It didn't move. An unseen but often heard padlock held a hasp closed on the other side. I looked in the shadows of the basement as if some previously hidden tool would come to sight, but I knew every square inch, and it held nothing useful.

Nervously wetting my lips, I grabbed the handrail with each hand and kicked with all my strength, which wasn't a lot. The door held solidly in its frame. I slammed my shoulder against it. Despite the intense pain the impact caused me, the door didn't release.

But I also realized something. He wasn't in the house. No way he wouldn't have heard me banging on that door. I didn't know when he would return, or who might be with him, but I had a chance at freedom for the first time in my life.

Sheer desperation to escape filled me. I pushed, shoved, and clawed before a crack appeared in the wood panel of the door. I wriggled my fingers into the splintered wood, desperately prying the hole bigger and bigger until I could squeeze my arm through and grasp the padlock. I yanked and pulled but it didn't give. I screamed in frustration and twisted hard. With a sudden snap, the door yielded. I stumbled into the kitchen and fell face-first onto the floor.

For the time ever, I was out of the basement without him.

Then again, maybe he was watching.

I bolted to my feet and looked through the dark house. His shape rose from a shadowy corner where he had been waiting, laughing at my feeble escape attempt. His meaty hand slipped the wide leather belt from around his waist, and he raised it high over his head in a clenched fist. As I heard it whistling through the air toward me, I cowered and wrapped my arms around my body, bracing for the sting of the flaying swipe.

The pain never came. I peeled my eyes open and looked where he had stood, but only the shadows of tree branches danced on the wall. He had never been there.

I rose to my feet and staggered through the kitchen and into the den. Shadows morphed into recognizable shapes. Logs lay stacked against the wall, but the fireplace was dark and cold. A small table held dirty dishes and glasses. A Mason jar sat half-filled with clear moonshine. A stench hung in the air.

I worked my way through the shadows to the far end of the room and reached for the exterior door, convinced it would be tightly locked, but the knob turned easily in my hand. I slipped out onto the sloping wooden front porch, its supports rotting and termite infested. A board under my foot squeaked.

I breathed in deeply and felt the cold air. A few snowflakes fell, and I realized I was cold. I didn't have a coat or shoes because he never gave them to us. We used burlap bags as blankets at night and wrapped them around our feet during the day for warmth. Maybe he had something else, but I couldn't go back in the house to search. He might be in there drunk or asleep.

I cast one last glance back at the house and fled into the surrounding woods. Branches smacked across my face. My feet slammed into rocks. But the pain meant little compared to the elation of being outdoors. I whooped and hollered, celebrating my victory, and I ran as far as I could.

I didn't stop until the reality hit me. I was free.

25

Connor held his breath as if he was alone in the house late at night watching a horror movie on TV. But unlike some Stephen King story, he knew the ending—the boy had survived, because he sat beside him with his head leaning on his shoulder. Still, he couldn't help worrying that the monster might win instead.

Before hearing the details of the escape, Connor had only allowed himself to think briefly about the nightmare his brother must have endured before he chased the thought away. A fleeting imagined scene wasn't the same as hearing the words blow by blow, the shaky little voice hammering the reality home.

He ran his hand along Jaxon's torn fingers, the ones that had beaten the frame of the door and ripped the lock off. Admiration for his little brother's resolve filled him. He doubted that he would have had the strength and nerve Jaxon had shown.

He made a silent vow. No matter what, he would protect Jaxon every minute for the rest of their lives, never to let him out of his sight. Never again would he fail his little brother.

Roxanne paused in her note-taking and asked, "Can you tell me the man's name?"

Jaxon sucked in a breath and shook his head. "No."

"That's okay. We don't need to do that yet." Roxanne chewed on the end of her pen. "Let's talk about what you saw as you left the house. It'll help us locate it."

"Not much. The road was dark, and it was snowing."

"So there was a road all the way up to the house?"

"Sort of, but not really a road. It was pretty overgrown, but the brush wasn't as thick as it was in the woods. It was just wide enough to get the van through the trees."

"So not paved. Was it gravel or just dirt?"

"I stepped on rocks. I couldn't really see them, though, because of the brush."

Jaxon coughed, a deep, phlegmy sound. Everyone paused, and Connor remembered the doctor's warnings about his brother's weakened immune system and his long exposure to cold. Connor grabbed the plastic cup on the bed tray and filled it with crushed ice and cold water from the pitcher. He held the cup in a trembling hand as his brother sipped. With a napkin, he wiped a rivulet of water from Jaxon's chin. The boy cleared his throat and nodded that he was ready to continue.

Roxanne asked, "How long of a walk until you saw anything else?"

"I was running 'cause I didn't want to get caught. Maybe ten or fifteen minutes, and then the woods ended."

"Excellent. Really helpful. What did you see when you came out of the forest?"

"A big field with an old house and a mobile home behind it."

"Like a farm?"

"Maybe it was once. I don't know. It was just like a big field."

"Did you knock on the door?"

"No. It was too close to where I came from. I was scared he might still wake up, find me missing, and come after me." He quivered. "Besides, you could tell no one lived there. Two of the walls and the roof had collapsed. The windows in the remaining walls were broken, and burn marks ran up the sides. I peeked, trying to find somewhere to hide, but snow was piling up inside, so I didn't try to go in very far."

Connor noticed David tense and sit up, but the sheriff motioned Roxanne to continue.

"The exterior walls… Brick, stone, or wood?"

"Wood, except this one with, like, real boards, all straight and smooth like that first picture you drew."

"Clapboard." She smiled and scribbled notes. "What color was it?"

"It might have been white, but it was hard to tell in the snow and dark. Anyway, the paint was chipped away and faded."

"What about the mobile home?"

"It was dark. Didn't look like anyone was in it. I didn't want to stick around, though, so I kept going on the road."

"You're doing awesome, Jaxon. Was this on the same road through the woods?"

"Yeah. It was hard to find the path, but it took me all the way out to the pavement."

"Great. At the pavement, did you see a mailbox? Sign? Anything?"

Jaxon looked up at the ceiling as he searched his memory. "Yeah, an old mailbox covered in vines. I didn't know what it was at first because, well, I haven't seen one since… Anyway, it said US Mail on the door. I don't remember a number or name or anything like that. It was rusty and didn't look like it was used any longer."

"You see any other houses?"

"Two way off the road in their own fields down long gravel

driveways. One of them had big floodlights on a barn, I think, but the houses were dark. I was scared to go to them in case they were friends of his. I figured I should get as far away as possible, so I walked down the paved road, toward some light down the way."

"How far?"

"I don't know. Probably took me an hour or two to get to the big road."

Roxanne scribbled in her book. "Okay, so this was all on a two-lane road. Considering you were walking in snow, that may have been four or five miles. Did you see any more mailboxes along the way?"

"Yeah, sure."

"Remember what any of them said? Or numbers?"

A shake of the head.

"You see any other buildings before you got to the highway?"

The boy shrugged. "Mostly just a few more houses and barns until I got to a big building."

"Like a warehouse?"

"No, like maybe a factory or something. I'm not sure, but it had lights, and you could hear humming and water splashing. I don't mean a little water—like a whole lot of water. There were a few cars in the parking lot, but it was the middle of the night, and I didn't see anyone. I tried to get in, but it had a big fence and a gate."

David looked up and asked, "Water splashing? Was it near a river?"

Jaxon recoiled against the deep voice, shrinking against his brother. Connor wondered at his reaction but hugged him with his one arm to indicate he would keep him safe. Jaxon licked his lips and answered quietly, "Yeah, the river ran beside it."

David turned to Roxanne. "If it's the Wattsville exit, that

could be the hydroelectric plant up there." He turned back to Jaxon, "Any signs you remember?"

"'No trespassing' and 'danger,' but I don't remember what all they said."

Roxanne put a hand on David's knee and took over the questions once more. "It's okay, Jaxon. You're doing terrific. What did you do next?"

"I saw a big road on the other side of the river from the building. I followed the road I was on across a bridge and then to that big road."

"What did you see?"

"There were two big blue signs with red stripes on top shaped like a shield. They said 'Interstate 40.' One pointed under the bridge and to the left and said 'west.' The other pointed right and said 'east.'"

"And you went east?"

He nodded.

"Why east?"

He shrugged. "Because it was closer. I mean, I had to go one way or the other and just picked one. But I'm glad I did."

Startled, Connor turned his attention away from the FBI agent and back to his little brother. "Because you wanted to come home?"

"No. I mean, yeah, I wanted to come home, but I didn't know where home was."

"So why are you glad you went east?"

"Because sunrises are to the east. I've never seen one."

Connor felt his breath catch in his throat. He pulled his brother close and whispered, "I'll take you to see one tomorrow."

26

D avid and Roxanne slipped out of the hospital room and huddled near the window. Roxanne asked quietly, "Recognize the place?"

"Sounds like Wattsville for sure, so that narrows things down a great deal. But a falling-down old farmhouse with an abandoned mobile home? There are more of those than you might think."

"And the old cabin?"

"Before the Great Smoky Mountains National Park was created, that was logging land. Hundreds of cabins were scattered across the mountains with hand-hewn boards for walls. But most of those have long since decayed and collapsed except for a few restored for tourism on park property, and no one could live in those undetected." David stared out the windows at the mountain ridges between them and Wattsville. "And the cellar is very confusing."

"I thought lots of houses had stone cellars?"

"Not here. Not the way he described it." David turned to her. "Most places had what are known as root cellars or some variant—

apple cellars, potato cellars. They're typically outbuildings carved into the side of the mountain that maybe have a small wooden building built above 'em. But that's not what he described. He talks about a cellar under the main house, dug so deep that the windows are at ceiling height from inside but ground level from outside."

Roxanne pursed her lips. "So it's deep, which took a long time to dig."

"And with windows. Glass was expensive in old Appalachia, and it would only have been used for the main floor if at all. More likely, it was added later, which is an odd thing to do to an old house. Either way, someone went to a lot of time and expense. And that's not a lumberjack."

"So a lumber company foreman or even owner?"

David shrugged. "Possible, but I was thinking someone hiding a common crop… moonshine. Scotch-Irish families up here have been making it forever, even though it was illegal to distribute after the civil war because the government wanted the tax-stamp money, and the value skyrocketed further during prohibition. An old farming family could grow corn out in the open fields and look totally legitimate but haul part of the crop back into the woods to manufacture liquor and use the cellar for storage and hiding."

"Which is why you tensed up in there. You recognized something."

David looked back out the windows. "Maybe. One of the leads we followed out that way when we were checking up on sex offenders. And he happens to be the descendant of a long-time moonshining family."

"We should pull his file again."

"There is no file, at least not on him. Both his father and brother racked up numerous charges—drugs, alcohol, assaults. But this guy has never been arrested for anything."

Roxanne cocked her head. "But if he was never charged,

what made you think of him when you were checking on sex offenders? He wouldn't be in the registry."

"Because I went to school with him. He got expelled from high school, and the rumor was it was for touching a little kid. I didn't really know the details, had only heard the rumors, but it's not something you forget. I went out and visited him myself."

"And?"

"He was mad I remembered the story. He confessed it really did happen and told me about it, but he swore it was something stupid he did as a teenager. Said he had always regretted it and never did anything like it again."

"Did you believe him?"

"Wasn't sure, but he didn't act like a guy trying to hide something. He told me more than I knew about the thing that happened when we were teens. And he didn't have any problem with us searching his place for any sign of Jaxon. Didn't ask for us to get a warrant or anything. Kept saying he didn't have anything to hide."

"And you found nothing?"

"Nothing at all. Not a sign Jaxon or any kid had ever been inside his trailer. No porn, not even a computer."

"His trailer?"

"Yep. A mobile home on his family's old farm, behind their old farmhouse, which had been destroyed by fire a few years earlier." David looked up. "A fire started by a meth lab, by the way. It exploded and killed his older brother. I stood outside that house as they pulled the body out, so I know what the house looked like, how it fell in."

Roxanne stiffened. "Now I understand your reaction. But no old log cabin with a stone cellar?"

"None that I know of, but I wasn't really looking for one, either. Until today, I've never heard of or cared about an old home up that way, but his family has owned that land for a couple hundred years, so there would have been old homes there at some point." David pulled his cell phone from his pocket. "But I'm going to get the tax department to pull the plats and see if they have record of a house while we're watching Jaxon get reintroduced to Harold."

"You still think Harold was involved?"

David paused with his finger above the screen of his phone then shook his head. "No, probably not, but we're about to find out. The kid's reaction to him will tell us a lot."

27

W hen the door opened, Connor quit his quiet chattering with Jaxon and focused on the visitors. The sheriff and FBI agent entered first and stepped to either side of the doorway, their bodies as tense as a pair of mountain lions prepared to pounce.

Harold slipped through the door behind them, disheveled —unshaven, hair mussed, ragged clothes—and obviously unsettled by the large audience. He glanced nervously at Heather, who had shrunk against the wall beside the window, positioned between her sons and her ex-husband with her arms crossed.

Harold opened his mouth, but only a whistle of air escaped. He swallowed hard, coughed, and croaked, "Jaxon?"

Connor felt Jaxon tense and turned to see his brother's eyes widen, carefully assessing the newcomer but not showing any extreme signs of fear. "Who…?"

Connor wrapped his calloused hands around the fingers gripping his arms and smiled to reassure his sibling, "It's okay, Jax. It's Dad."

Jaxon's gaze came back to rest on Harold. A puzzled look clouded his face. He kept his grip on Connor's arm and asked, "Dad?"

Harold took two steps toward the bed, but Jaxon shrank away and leaned against his brother. Seeing the reaction, Harold stumbled backward and shot an angry look toward David, who had tensed up. He wrung his hands and dropped his head. "Yeah, son, it's me."

Roxanne motioned to the empty seat at the foot of the bed. "Why don't you sit here and give him some space? This all has to be very overwhelming for him."

He looked to Heather, who nodded in reply, before he reluctantly sat and clasped his trembling hands together.

Connor felt the tension in the room. He knew the sheriff wouldn't easily lose the long-held suspicion of his father, but Harold wasn't helping things with his nervous behavior. In a bid to help his dad, he turned to the boy in the bed. "Did you know that Dad had a best friend called Jackson? That's where the name Jaxon comes from, even though it's spelled different."

"Really?" The boy's face crinkled, and an eyebrow rose.

Harold studied his shaking hands and managed to steady them. He looked up and licked his lips. "My best friend in my army unit, except he spelled it the old way. J-A-C-K-S-O-N."

"And I'm named after him?"

"Yeah, sort of. A lot of our buddies had unusual names or at least unusual spellings. He and I were boring. Jack and Harry."

"Why's boring so bad?"

Harold looked nervously around the room. "It's not. But when you're young, you get focused on things like that. Just the way it is, I guess."

Jaxon smiled a little. "Did he like you used his name?"

Harold ran his hand through his thinning hair and

grimaced. He looked like he really regretted the conversation. "He never knew. He was killed by an IED over in Afghanistan before you were born."

Jaxon took the news of death without even a flinch, unlike the others in the room. "Who's an IED?"

"It's a what. An IED is a bomb. Just an army term." Harold gazed out the window, his eyes glistening in the sun. "Jack was my anchor over there. We kept each other sane. When we got hit, the Humvee flipped over on its side. I crawled out, took shelter, and scanned for the threat. But no one shot at us. Nothing. Just quiet. I checked myself and didn't have a scratch on me, but when I started checking the other guys, there was Jack, bleeding and gasping for breath. We called for an evac, but it didn't get there fast enough. I held his hand and promised to call his wife, tell her he loved her. And then he died."

The room was so silent they could hear birds through the closed window. Jaxon asked, "Did you call her?"

He whispered, "Yeah. Hardest call I ever made. And then I went and got falling-down drunk."

David and Roxanne exchanged a glance. It was the most sympathy Connor had ever seen them show his father. The man wasn't acting guilty or even like a parent. He seemed simply lost.

"I wanted to honor my friend, but I also wanted to make it unique. It couldn't just be Jack. So, Jaxon. With an x." Harold cleared his throat and turned to the boy. "Jackson would be proud you have his name."

Jaxon dropped his eyes and fiddled with the blanket, opening and closing his mouth but not speaking.

Harold said, "It's good to have you home, Jax."

Jaxon relaxed his grip on his brother's arm and sank into the pillows. His eyes shifted around the room, over the monitor showing his vital signs, the IV bottle feeding him nutrients, and the array of medical equipment on the wall above his head. His voice sounded small as he squeaked, "Home?"

Harold smiled at the little joke. "You got me, Jax. It's not home yet, is it? But soon enough, you'll be going home and sleeping in your own bed in your own room. Your mom and brother will be right there for you. Doesn't that sound nice?"

Jaxon didn't answer but asked instead, "Won't you be there too?"

Harold glanced at Heather. "For visits, when your mom's okay with it. If you'd like that."

"You don't live there?"

"Sorry, buddy, no. We were getting divorced when you… left." He shot a look at the sheriff.

Jaxon's head rested against Connor's chest, and his eyes drifted shut. "Oh. I didn't know that."

They exchanged surprised glances at each other. The separation certainly hadn't been a secret because the boys understood the custody limitations, but maybe it was just another forgotten detail.

Jaxon's breathing became deeper and steady as he drifted off to sleep. Soon, soft snores came from the boy. Harold stood to leave, but Connor stopped him. "Dad, it's not you. The doc's giving him some sedatives, and he's real tired. Maybe you can try again later."

Harold smiled weakly. "I understand. The kid needs time to rest and recover. He doesn't need a bunch of strangers hovering around his bed. Not me, for sure." Harold opened the door to leave but paused and looked pointedly at the sheriff. "And certainly not you. Why don't you stop hanging around the hospital and go find the son of a bitch who hurt my son?"

Harold's shoes squeaked as he walked down the hall. David turned back to the room as if to defend himself, but Heather brushed past him and into the hall. He was met with a harsh glare from Connor as he cradled his brother.

With a sigh, David nodded to Roxanne, and they left the room.

28

"Harold, wait."

Heather walked quickly down the hallway to catch up with her ex-husband. He slowed and ran a hand across the day-old growth of whiskers on his face. "It's okay, Heather. I'm just another stranger to him."

"You're not a stranger. You're his dad."

He reached out and gently placed his hands on her shoulders. "No, I'm not his dad. I never was. I might have fathered him, but I've never been his dad. Even less so for him than Connor."

Becoming pregnant had certainly not been part of their high-school plans. Neither was being married. So she was only angry, not surprised, when he announced he had enlisted in the army. He had told her not to worry, claiming that he would send money to care for Connor. And he did—for a while. And he even came home for a few visits during breaks in his first year of training. But once he left for his first year-long deployment to Afghanistan, the phone calls became sporadic, then ceased altogether.

He surprised her by showing up on her doorstep when he

returned stateside. He was quieter, more serious, and even talked about a future in Millerton after getting out of the army. They married and moved to Fort Bragg to build a life together. Shortly after that, they received double news—he was being deployed for a second tour, and she was pregnant again.

Afghanistan went poorly for him the second time. The loss of his best friend, Jackson, changed him profoundly. She'd been proud to name her son after a man she barely knew but had heard so much about. But when Harold came home after the second tour, he struggled to use the name and even suggested they change it. They fought often about it. He would storm out of the house and spend the evening drinking with buddies. In many ways, those nights alone were easier for her, because when he was home, he often awoke from nightmares, screaming and sweating.

When she'd finally had enough, she demanded a divorce. To her surprise, he agreed. He moved out of the house and agreed to give her full custody of both boys with only limited visitation rights for himself—only at the house and with her specific permission. He claimed he wanted to be involved in the boys' lives, but his empty promises usually ended in disappointment. Jaxon was too young to understand, but she knew that Connor felt the sting.

After Jaxon's disappearance, Harold served several years in prison for drug charges, under a cloud of suspicion about his son. When he returned, he was bitter and struggling, but he seemed determined to be there for Connor. Despite a few slips, he had mostly maintained his sobriety.

"The past is past, Harold. But you've worked hard the last few years to build a relationship with Connor. You can do the same with Jaxon."

His eyes were downcast. "At least with Connor, I had something to rebuild. But with Jaxon… I never really knew the kid.

Honestly, if I had passed him in the hallway today without you telling me who he is, I wouldn't have recognized him."

She didn't mention she had barely recognized him herself and shifted the conversation. "Not sure I've said it, but... I'm proud of your patience with Connor. Giving him time to come around to you."

"Time is about all I have to offer."

"Good. Because time's what he needs. He's seen how you've changed."

He turned away. "One hundred sixty-three days. Not even a half year yet sober."

"And longer than last time. You've told me to celebrate the steps. You may have fallen off the wagon twice this year, but that's better than last year or the year before. I remember whole years you didn't have two days without a drink."

"Heather, you don't get it. I want a drink when I get up in the morning and even more when I go to bed at night. I crave it in a way I can't explain. I can't think about anything other than getting through one day, today, without a drink. Then I can say I made it one hundred sixty-four days."

"And you'll make it."

He walked a few steps but stopped and turned around. His hands were shaking, and his face was red—he seemed angry, and she suspected it was directed at himself. He gritted his teeth. "The whole time I was in that room, looking at that boy in the bed, all I could think about was running out and getting drunk. I can taste the beer right now. What kind of father could I ever be to him?"

"You aren't gonna, are you? You aren't going to get drunk?"

"I want to. Bad. But... no." He looked down the hall to Jaxon's closed room door. "You know why?"

"Because you're stronger."

"No. Because I can't even remember the day Jaxon disappeared. I don't remember promising to watch the boys. I don't remember where I was or what I was doing. I don't remember anything at all except waking up a few days later with some Asheville cop's gun in my face as he yelled at me to put my hands up."

"Harold…" She wanted to stop him from going down that path again.

"When they figured out who I was and tried to tell me what had happened, you know what I was worried about?"

"Harold…"

"I didn't care I was sitting there, buck naked. I didn't know where I was or who I was with. Worst of all, I didn't even care my son was missing or they thought I might've had something to do with that. Hell, I wasn't sure I didn't have anything to do with it because I couldn't remember. But the one thing I understood? I could see a whiskey bottle sitting on the bathroom sink and a glass pipe on the floor. I wondered if I could have some of either—or both—before they slapped the cuffs on me."

They stood in silence in the hallway, the nurses at the station watching them warily. Heather took his hand. "That was a long time ago."

Harold ripped his hand away. "Not for me. For me, it was yesterday. Don't tell me to forget it, because I don't want to forget it. It's the only damn thing that keeps me sober. That"—his hand shook as he pointed down the hall—"and those two boys."

He turned his back on her and walked to the elevator bank. He pressed the call button and looked at her as the doors opened with a ding. "I'll be here whenever they're ready for me. I'll never make up for what I've done, but it's all I've got to offer."

29

After they saw the couple talking upstairs, David and Roxanne wanted to ensure that Harold left before they did. They raced down five flights of steps and waited inconspicuously in the corner of the hospital lobby as Harold walked across the parking lot, toward his car.

Confident the man was leaving, they moved into the vestibule. David said, "I can't take him off the suspect list with the way Jaxon reacted. He's scared of that man."

"He's scared of all men."

David's eyebrow rose as he thought through Jaxon's reactions. "Not Connor. He clings to that boy."

"Exactly. 'Boy.' Connor may legally be an adult, but he's still a teenager. And in Jaxon's memories, Connor's a boy not that different in age from others who would have been held victims in that hellhole. He's someone to trust and someone who would protect him."

David leaned against the cold glass. "But his reaction to Harold was visceral. You saw how wide his eyes got. He doesn't react as poorly to other men."

Roxanne turned to face him. "Oh, yeah? What did he do when he saw your deputy last night?"

"Ran, but that was when he had just gained freedom."

"And when he arrived at the hospital. Did he open up to Dr. Queen or Nurse Sheila?"

"Hell, Roxanne, I don't warm up to Dr. Queen either. Sheila is much easier to talk to."

"How did he react when he first saw you?"

David watched the water running over the asphalt from the melting snow. "Fine, I surrender. He didn't care much for me either."

"Look, I'm not taking Harold off the suspect list—I'm not taking anyone off until we learn more—but I don't see anything that makes him stand out either. I did back then, but not now." She turned to face him. "Jaxon didn't react well to him because he's a man, and after the last ten years, he has a big fear of any adult man. Harold was someone who came in and out of his life, so he has no particular affinity for him, unlike Connor, so he's a stranger to him today—just like you or the doctor or any other man. I didn't see any signs he recognized him at all."

David leaned his forehead against the glass and closed his eyes. The chill helped slow the scramble of thoughts bouncing around his brain. "Which means I focused on the wrong guy."

A blast of cold air hit them as the outside doors swooshed open. A woman walked in, chatting on her phone with barely a glance in their direction. The interior doors closed behind her, cutting off her chatter.

Once they were alone again, Roxanne said, "We focused on him because no one else crossed our radar. We had thousands of insignificant little leads, none of them worth much. Nothing pointed in any direction except the boy disappearing without a struggle, which meant we assumed he went with someone he knew. It made sense to focus on a family member, and Harold was the only one, but none of us were ever sure. You know that."

"I also know I was the lead investigator, so it was my job to get it right." David stood up straight, feeling determined. "And now we have a new lead. A house somewhere off the Wattsville exit. Unfortunately, the tax office isn't showing an old house with a cellar on the McGregor land. All it shows is the house and the trailer, just like I remember."

"Doesn't mean one's not there."

"No, of course not." David stared into the parking lot. "But it sure does make getting a search warrant a lot harder."

"So maybe we just go visit. He talked to you last time."

"Yeah, maybe. But last time, we were knocking on every door, looking for a lost child. This time would be basically an accusation. And if he refuses to let us search and he does have kids there…"

Roxanne completed the thought. "Then he's alerted we're that close, and he gets rid of them. So maybe we ask some neighbors if there is an old house? Go knock on doors and see if anyone recognizes the description Jaxon gave us?"

"Maybe, but finding people up that way willing to talk to the law is about as hard as finding the right abandoned house. Even harder for the FBI. Run, Rudolph, run." His reference to Eric Rudolph, the infamous domestic terrorist who detonated a bomb at the 1996 Olympic games in Atlanta, wasn't missed by Roxanne. The FBI led a relentless manhunt in the North Carolina mountains until he was eventually caught scrounging through a dumpster behind a grocery store by a small-town rookie police officer. Throughout the search, rumors floated that locals had helped the fugitive with food and places to sleep. While that was never proven, many enjoyed watching the frustration of the FBI agents as they struggled to catch their target. One of the most popular T-shirts in tourist stores in the region read *Run, Rudolph, Run.*

Roxanne asked, "Do you have a better plan?"

He studied the mountains to their west. "Maybe. An old high-school buddy lives up there. He grew up in Wattsville and moved back to the old family land after retiring from the military, but he knows the area and the people out that way much better than I do."

"Then let's go see him."

"Not quite that easy. We might have hung out together in high school some, but we've only seen each other a few times since. And he's not a big fan of the badge. I'll call and find out if he'll see us." David tossed a glance over his shoulder at Agent Gonzalez waiting in the lobby behind them, his red tie stark against the white shirt. "If I can convince him to let us come by, you two need to look much less like federal agents."

"Give us five minutes to change."

30

Nurses' voices filtered through the closed door, and their shoes squeaked on the tile floor as they went about their rounds. PA announcements too muffled to understand sounded more like squawks than words. A raven flapped past outside, the noise of its wings audible through the window. Somewhere in the distance, a horn honked, and an engine revved.

The sounds indicated a world continuing to revolve outside the room, but inside their warm cocoon, the Lathan family rested in the quiet comfort of reunion. Jaxon lay back on the pillows of the inclined bed, slowly inhaling and exhaling in a restless sleep. His fingers twitched with his dreams as his hand rested on Connor's arm. The older boy sprawled in a chair, his head tilted back at an awkward angle, allowing soft snores to emerge from his open mouth. The equipment surrounding the bed hummed and beeped, a soft mechanical background rhythm behind the boys' breathing.

Heather stood at the head of the bed and admired her boys. Her fingers ran through the thick mat of hair on Jaxon's head while her mind imagined stroking the soft, silky mane of a little boy years ago, sitting in her lap as he sounded out words from a picture book. She wanted to step out in the hallway and call Donna to come work on his hair, but she didn't want to risk waking them.

The hair stylist would do wonders for the boy, not just make him look better. She had a knack for listening and making someone feel like she had all of the time in the world for them. Heather had shared her dwindling hopes for finding the boy while settled in Donna's chair as scissors snipped. They'd compared notes between Connor's mischief and Donna's three children's antics. After each layoff at a town factory, when more jobs went overseas, they mapped out plans to revive Millerton and, more immediately, ways to help those suddenly without jobs. They planned fundraisers and covered-dish suppers.

A simple call to Donna, and she would come scrambling. Heather smiled to herself, recognizing that Donna would show up if for no other reason than to be the first outside the family to witness the return of the missing boy. Demand for appointments in her chair would increase as she passed on what she had seen and heard. And she would plan how to help. Heather wouldn't be able to pay for anything in town for weeks as the town rallied around her. It's what Millerton did.

She tucked Jaxon's hair behind his ear with a gentle swoop of her finger and then slid her light touch across his forehead. She traced the bridge of his nose, relearning the shape of his face. The boy's eyes shot open with a start, and he jumped, but a smile spread across his face as recognition grew in his eyes. They stared at each other as she let the tips of her fingers bounce over his chapped lip and along the peach fuzz on his chin. Her caress traveled up the side of his face before tracing the scar along the side of his face. "Will you tell me how this happened?" she asked.

He turned his head away, and the smile faded. "You don't want to know."

"I know all of Connor's scars. And I want to know the stories behind yours. That's what families do—share scars."

Awakened by the soft conversation, Connor leaned forward over the bed and pointed at a small scar on his lower right arm. "Skateboard into the side of a parked car down at the Dollar General. An old white Cadillac. I bled all over the hood. Old Man Tompkins was so pissed about that."

Heather shook her head at the profanity, but Connor continued in his carefree way. With a giant grin across his face, the boy's finger traced a faded inch-long pink line peeking above his eyebrow. "Wiped out my bike into a fence post trying to impress Cecilia Wyatt with my mad skills. She laughed her ass off, but she also said 'yes' when I asked her to go to a movie as blood dripped down my face."

Connor stood tall and lifted his shirt to his shoulders, exposing a toned abdomen. He pointed at the center of his chest. "This scar is where she broke my heart when she dumped me and started dating Carlos Estrella. Guess she liked baseball stars better than BMXers."

Jaxon sat up and squinted as he studied his brother's hairless chest. "I don't see a scar."

Connor slowly lowered his shirt. "It's a joke, Jax."

Jaxon flopped his head on the pillow and stared at the ceiling. "Oh."

Heather smiled at the disappointed look on her eldest son's face. He had slipped naturally back into the role of big brother, trying to get the younger boy to laugh at his silly jokes. She hoped time would allow Jaxon to ease back into their banter, but he wasn't ready yet.

The younger boy turned his head and looked out the window. The wind whipped around the corner of the building. He exhaled deeply and whispered, "Never let them see you."

Heather leaned over Jaxon, tears filling her eyes, and softly kissed the scar. "You never need to hide your scars from us."

"Not the scars." Jaxon's gray-blue eyes drifted down to look into her face. "That was his first rule. Never let them see you."

"Who's them?"

"Anyone. If someone came to the house, we were supposed to stay quiet and not draw attention to the basement. Never let them see you."

"A lot of people visited?"

He paused in thought. "No. We could go months between. Hunters sometimes stumbled out of the woods. Or somebody heard they could buy moonshine, though it wasn't true, 'cause he didn't sell to people he didn't know, and people he knew wouldn't dare show up at his house."

He adjusted himself in bed. "A preacher showed up several times."

Heather and Connor exchanged a puzzled glance. She asked, "A preacher?"

"We giggled because the preacher kept asking him if he had been saved. Hell, we needed saving, not him, but the preacher never had a clue we were there. The last time the preacher came, he pointed a shotgun at him and told him to never come back or he would get to see God up close and personal." His eyes focused on the ceiling tiles above his head. "I hope he has met God really up close now."

She replied, "I don't think God will waste any time with him before sending him straight to hell."

"Nope."

She reached to trace his scar, but he pulled back. She tucked her hand to her side and asked, "None of the visitors ever saw you?"

"Never." Jaxon ran his tongue along his chapped lips. "Until the hiker. He's the only one who ever did."

"Hiker?"

"We were sitting in the basement like always when we heard him come out of the woods and ask for directions. He said he was hiking the Appalachian Trail but took a side trail and got lost. His voice sounded real happy, like a guy just out to have fun. He called out, and then…"

Connor and Heather exchanged glances, waiting for Jaxon to continue. "Then *he* answered. He didn't sound mad or angry but almost nice. He told him real calmly how to get back out to the road. Took his own sweet time telling him too. Guess he didn't have that shotgun close. Anyway, the hiker would have left, but…"

Heather reached out to stroke Jaxon's hair and was surprised to see her fingers quaking. *Do I really want to know what happened?* Connor's scars came from childhood antics, silly stunts to impress his friends or some girl. But Jaxon's scars were delivered by someone else. Dread filled her as she quietly asked, "What happened?"

Jaxon picked at the bandage on his left hand. "You gotta understand, it'd been really bad for a couple of weeks. He had gone hunting and left us alone. We rationed the food, but we never knew how long he would be gone. You want to make it last, but it's hard when you don't know when more is coming. By the time he got back, we hadn't eaten for a couple of days and were starving."

"He brought back a deer or something?"

A wry smile crept across the boy's face as if he was the only one in on the joke. His eyes clouded. "Not that kind of hunting. For a new… boy."

"Oh." Heather swallowed hard. "Did he find one?"

"Yeah." Jaxon turned his head away and looked out the window. His voice became mechanical and emotionless. "He had one, but the kid was real sick. He shoved him down the steps and told us we better get him healthy or else."

"What did you do?"

"The only thing we ever could do was give kids food and water, and for normal sick stuff, that worked. Well, usually it worked. But we were out of food and real low on water. And this kid told us he was a diabetic and needed insulin every day."

Jaxon inhaled deeply. "A dictionary teaches you tons, but it doesn't do everything. *Diabetes—any of various abnormal conditions characterized by the secretion and excretion of excessive amounts of urine.* We didn't even understand what to look for. *Insulin* was a little more helpful because it said *glucose—a crystalline sugar*."

He pulled the blankets up to his chin and closed his eyes. "But we couldn't ask for sugar. You didn't ask *him* for anything. You took what he gave you. And you figured out how to deal with everything else. We tried. Tried everything we could think of." He took a slobbery breath. "But... he didn't make it."

Connor leaned over until the boys' foreheads touched and whispered, "That ain't your fault, Jax."

"I know. Sometimes, it just happens." His eyes fluttered open. "But see, we knew what would happen next. We knew how mad he would be. He had just gotten the kid, and now he was going to have to go hunting again, or one of us would have to..."

Jaxon swallowed, and he turned his eyes away from them. "It was just Kevin and me then. We were older than what he..."

He squeezed his eyes shut. "We'd failed. And he was madder than I'd ever seen."

31

I dug the grave. I always did. He said it was one of my jobs.

I liked most days I got to be outside, but not that day. He sat on a tree stump with that shotgun across his lap. He pointed it at me and asked if I thought I was faster than buckshot. It was like he was daring me to try.

It wasn't the shotgun that kept me from running. It was Kevin. He was still locked in the basement. If I didn't come back, he would be all alone.

I got winded and leaned on the shovel to catch my breath. A dirt clod zinged me in the back of the head, and I fell to my knees. "Stop being lazy!" he yelled and threw more clumps at me 'til I staggered up and started digging again.

"Damn useless boys is what you two are. You got one simple job—keep the young 'uns I bring ya alive and quiet 'til I'm ready for 'em. If you can't even get that right, why do I waste my time feeding ya and keeping a roof over your stupid heads?"

Another dirt clod pegged me between the shoulder blades. I kept digging as fast as I could as he ranted. "Now I've got to go back out huntin', and it's your damn fault. It's getting hard out there with damn cameras everywhere. Even on those damn cell phones people carry. They take videos with 'em, and the police can look at 'em later and see ya even when people don't remember you were there. Didn't use to be that way, but that's what I have to deal with and all cause you two ijits can't keep a boy alive."

When the hole was deep enough, I rolled the body of that little kid into it. He landed all twisted, but he was facing up. It was like he was looking at me as I started shoveling dirt in as fast as I could. I was pushing dirt so hard and so fast, and I got dizzy—lack of food, I guess, and I fell in the hole. My face was right against that kid's face.

He kicked a bunch of dirt on my head and yelled, "Maybe you should just go right ahead and dig two more holes so I can put you and your damn useless friend in 'em and be done with both of ya. Dumbass useless brats."

I scrambled out of the hole and went back to work. When all the dirt was piled back in that hole, he jammed the shotgun in my back and marched me over to the shed to hang the shovel back up. Then he walked me back through that house to the cellar door. I waited while he unlocked the padlock, and then I started down the steps. He shoved me really hard in the back, and I rolled head over heels to the bottom. Kevin helped me sit up and whispered about how crazy he was getting.

That was Kevin and me from the very first day he got there, years and years earlier. He was a tough little kid from the beginning. He didn't sit around bawling like the others. He sure didn't just curl up and die like some of them. We played checkers with pebbles and a board drawn in the dirt. We read the few books we had down there, stuff kids had with them when they got taken. He invented a game with that dictionary we found, asking each other the meaning of the next word. We shared our food rations with each other and told each other our real names, though he was smart enough to embrace

Kevin as his name. We shared stories about our lives before we got there.

I always knew he liked Kevin better than me. Every time that damned door opened, it was Kevin's name he called, not mine, and I often wondered why. I didn't care, but I was thankful, at least until that door would shut and the darkness enveloped me. Then I would sit in the shadows with my ears peeled for every creak, or groan, or scream. I prayed for the sounds to stop, but when they did, I dreaded the silence even more. I stared up the steps at the locked door, waiting, dreading as much for it to open as for it to not.

And then the door would open, and my friend would stumble down the steps. I would wrap my arms around him, hold him, let him sob against me.

And then one day, the door opened, and Kevin hung his head and started to stand up. But he didn't call Kevin's name. He shoved this new sniveling little kid down the steps and told us to welcome our new brother. That hadn't happened in a long time, but Kevin was happy because that meant his name wasn't always called. And when that kid left, another new kid came. And another after that one.

For some reason we never figured out, he let both of us live. We tried to take care of the kids he brought, we really did, but most only lasted a few months. Long stretches would pass where it was just Kevin and me, but he mostly left us alone down there. He said we were too old. We could hear him coughing and wheezing, getting drunk and stumbling around. Those were the best times, when it was just us, but it never lasted, because he would go hunting again. Then he would tell us we needed to do a better job with the new one.

And the latest one had only lasted a few days. We'd failed.

We were sitting there, whispering, when we heard a hiker coming through the woods. We looked at each other all wide-eyed. We knew if the guy had emerged from the woods a half hour earlier, he would have seen me digging that grave.

Kevin whispered, "Will he see it?"

I shook my head, "Shouldn't. I spread leaves over it."

I scrambled up onto Kevin's shoulders and peeked through the window. Between the two of us, we had become tall enough to get a look at the outside world that way, and we took turns climbing up like that.

"What's he look like?" Kevin asked.

"Scraggly beard but not like a mountain man. Purple T-shirt, fancy hiking shorts, boots, and a real bright bandanna tied around his hair."

"College boy," Kevin said mockingly. The man hated all sorts of people and bucketed them into groups. Guvment people. College boys. Rich pricks. Tourists. And he could say it in a way you just knew how disgusting they were.

"Yeah, exactly. He's got a fancy-looking backpack and all sorts of gear. Looks rich."

"What're they saying?"

"Getting directions. Said he got lost off the Appalachian Trail."

"Wow." Kevin was quiet for a second. "It must be close."

"I guess."

"That means maybe others aren't too far."

I looked down at Kevin and realized he was getting himself all worked up. I should've noticed. If I had, I could've stopped him from yelling, but I didn't, and the next thing I knew, he was shouting, "Down here! Help! Help! We need help!"

I jumped off Kevin's shoulders and grabbed him. "What are you doing?" I hissed.

"It's our only chance," he replied. "We can get away. Go home."

The hiker must've heard him, 'cause he leaned down and

looked through the window right at us. His eyes grew wide, and he asked, "What're you two doing down there? You okay?"

I tried to grab Kevin and stop him, but he answered anyway, "We're kidnapped. He's holding us. You gotta help us get out of here. Please! Please!"

"Kidnapped? Really? Who—"

I'm not sure if I saw the ax or heard it first, the glint of the blade coming down or the sickening wet noise as it sunk into his brain. The guy's eyes rolled up in his head, and he fell against the glass, shattering it. Blood dripped down the wall inside. He coughed and sprayed blood. And then... he stopped. Blood ran down his face and dripped off his chin, puddling on the floor in front of us.

We saw the boot come down on the back of the guy's shoulders. He pulled the ax out with a horrible sucking sound even worse than when it went in. He wiped the ax off in the weeds and sank it back into a log on the woodpile being built for the coming winter.

I wish he had kept the ax. It would have made things go faster. We heard the sound of his boots clomping across the floor over our heads. He ripped open the door and stomped down the steps. Maybe we should have rushed him, tried to get past—maybe we would have made it. But we cowered.

I stood with my hands out in front of me, begging him not to kill Kevin and pleading for his life.

He backhanded me. The ring he always wore caught my ear. I felt it rip down the side of my face, to my lips. The skin flapped down around my jaw. I watched a tooth fly through the air and bounce off the wall. The world swam, and I fell backward onto the ground. Before I could move, he kicked me hard in the stomach. I curled up as he kicked over and over.

Kevin shouted at him to stop, and he grabbed his arm and pulled him off-balance, but just for a second. And then I heard the crunch as the man's fist shattered Kevin's nose. Kevin screamed, a muffled wet sound, but then I heard him get hit two, three more times. Kevin fell to the floor, blood dripping from his nose and mouth, his eyes rolling back up into his head. The man kicked him in the ribs, and Kevin coughed, splattering us both with his blood.

I tried to beg, but my jaw wouldn't work. Blood was running down the back of my throat. I pushed up to speak, and he smiled. The sick bastard smiled at me and raised his foot, a mud-splattered boot with a steel toe and heavy tread. He slammed it hard on top of Kevin's head, flattening it. My friend's eyes bulged as blood was forced out his nostrils. Those big boots slammed into him over and over.

And then it was done. He leaned over me, grabbed my hair, and pulled my head up. I cringed, sure I was about to feel the last fist of my life. He leaned into my face, the stench of his breath overpowering me. His spittle flew as he whispered, "This is all your fault, boy. Your job is to make sure they follow the rule—*never let them see you*. Including this one here. I'd let him live all these years for you, and this is how you repay me. You ungrateful little shit."

He dropped my head back onto the dirt. One of Kevin's teeth was in front of my nose. I remember being amazed at how long the root was.

He stomped back up the steps and opened the door. Before he closed it, he said, "Look at the mess you made." And then he shut the door and snapped the lock closed.

It was almost dark outside, and I could barely see Kevin, so I dragged myself across the floor and asked him if he was okay. When he didn't answer, I wrapped my hand around his. His fingers were icy cold, but his eyes were fluttering. He breath was ragged, whistling in and out. I think he tried to speak, but I couldn't understand him. Or maybe I imagined the whole thing. We lay like that, face-to-face, even after his eyes dimmed and his breathing stopped.

32

Connor turned a chair at the end of the patient hall around so he could face out the window and stare at the snowcapped mountains. His mind buzzed in horror at the story he had heard. His body was balled up with his feet pulled up in the seat to his butt, his arms hugging his legs against his chest, and his chin resting on his knees. A forgotten Mountain Dew bought from the vending machines, his excuse for leaving the room, sat sweating on the table beside him.

Lost in his thoughts, he didn't hear Heather slip out of the patient room until she wrapped her arms around him from behind and kissed the top of his head.

He leaned his head back against her and looked up into her eyes, not surprised to see them filled with tears. He wanted to cry, scream, shout, go beat the shit out of the man who had done those horrible things to his brother. With effort, he focused instead to remain steady for his mother. "How did he do it? Survive... that?"

Heather kissed his forehead and sighed. She opened her mouth, struggled for the words, then closed it again and shrugged. "I don't know."

Connor closed his eyes, thinking of the little brother he remembered, tottering around with picture books until he could start sounding out words. He would demand that Connor read to him, but Connor grew tired of the same stories over and over and would invent tales instead. They had argued one night after Connor had Winnie the Pooh being carted off by space aliens and the X-Men battling the aliens. Jax argued that wasn't how the story went.

By the time Jaxon was in the first grade, he was reading at a fourth-grade level, books assigned by Connor's teachers that Connor hadn't cared about reading and had left lying around the house. The older boy was the daredevil, pushing the limits with his bicycle or the skateboard he got from Jared down the street, climbing trees, or wading into creeks. He loved video games and action movies but never cared much for reading. His interests hadn't changed much in the intervening years.

His breathing tightened, and the tears he didn't want to shed threatened. "I failed him."

Heather squeezed him tightly. "Con, no. You never failed him."

"Yeah, I did. I had to go off with my friends and left him all alone in that playground. If I had stayed with him, that pervert would never have come up to us. And if he had, I would've known better than to fall for the lost-dog thing." He crossed his arms and hugged himself. "What kind of brother abandons his little brother?"

"A nine-year-old boy who was being asked to do far more than he should ever have been asked." Heather squeezed his shoulders and forced him to look at her. "That's what you were, a little kid asked to grow up too quick. You want to blame someone? Blame me. What kind of mother leaves two little kids at home all by themselves?"

Connor unfolded himself from the chair and stood to face

her. He wrapped his mother into his arms, holding her tight against his chest. "Mom, no. What were you supposed to do? Sit in the house and watch TV all day while you collected some stupid welfare check?" He sighed, feeling his breath blow through her hair. "If we had stayed together, he would have been safe."

Heather returned Connor's hug. "Don't play the if game, Con."

Connor relished the comfort of his mother's hug all the time. Over the years she'd held him that way, comforting him from a skinned knee from a fall off his bike, a black eye from a fistfight with his best friend—they made up the next day—and even the heartbreak of dating off and on in high school. With guilt, he realized his little brother hadn't experienced the same comfort in years and had needed it much, much more. "I look at him lying in that bed and think of all of the pain he has suffered… I can't help but wonder if I could have prevented it. It's not an if game. I wish he hadn't had to put up with that crazy maniac all these years."

Her voice was muffled against his shoulder in reply. "Fair enough, Con, but you never gave up. I did. I see him in there and realize, deep down, I had assumed he was dead and would never return. What kind of mother does that?"

Connor's stomach clenched as he hugged her tighter. "You put your energy into me because I was the one who was here. Nothing wrong with that. And I think you did a damn good job of it too."

They hugged tighter before breaking apart, Heather sniffling back her tears. "You did turn out pretty good."

"All because of you." He stared at the closed door, both dreading and wanting to go back in the room. "He's going to be even more messed up than Dad—this is PTSD squared. How's he ever going to get back to normal?"

Heather wiped her eyes and straightened her blouse. "Well, that's our job. We're going to have to be there for him every step."

Connor looked wistfully out the window. "I'm game. I owe him that. I don't think I'll ever let him out of my sight again."

33

D avid piloted his SUV west on the interstate through the Pigeon River Gorge, the pair of federal agents following in their own black SUV. He glanced across the highway to the point where Deputy Patterson had picked up the boy the night before and shuddered. He'd been out there, all alone, so desperate to escape the horrors. Other than the highway, though, no other sign existed of other humans. Not a single building. No power lines or lights. Absolutely nothing other than mountains and trees.

To think that kid probably was in Miller County all along, and David hadn't figured it out. He gripped the steering wheel tightly, vowing to rescue any other kids before the sun set. But he had to find the house somewhere in that vast wilderness.

The tall mountains towered over either side of the highway, blocking the direct sunlight from the road except for a few brief hours every day. The snow berms lining the highway, the efforts from the previous night's snow plows, were melting and sending sheets of water across the road. The road crews were busy spreading salt brine to keep it from refreezing overnight.

David slowed as he entered Tennessee and passed the turn-around point his deputy had used the night before. He took the first exit, its green sign reading "Wattsville," and followed the two-lane road as it doubled back into North Carolina. The snowplows had cleared the path as far as the power plant, but only ruts through the snow greeted him after that, a fitting symbol of the isolation of the community. He engaged his four-wheel drive and cautiously moved down the road.

Wattsville was built in the 1920s by the utility company erecting the dam across the Pigeon River. With no roads leading to the area and limited access to the river, the houses, school, and community center supported the isolated families. The formation of the surrounding Great Smoky Mountains National Park and the Pisgah and Cherokee National Forests in the coming decade cemented the isolation.

As more modern power plants were built and the workforce slimmed, the school and community center were closed, and houses were abandoned. The opening of the interstate in the late sixties made things worse by highlighting how much closer Tennessee was despite the fact that the few remaining citizens of Wattsville paid Miller County and North Carolina taxes.

David understood how little allegiance the residents felt to his county. He had to think hard to come up with when he had last been in the area himself, realizing it had been on a fishing trip three years earlier. He resolved to come more often. The residents were voters, after all, even if most of them didn't bother. They still deserved to see their sheriff.

He spied a gravel driveway on his left. Plowed clean, it snaked its way through the forest. David bumped his vehicle off the road and followed the half mile of twists and turns until he emerged into a clearing. A timber-frame house with a green metal roof stood in the center. Smoke curled from the chimney and was swept away by the stiff morning breeze.

They came to a stop in front of the house, parking side by side. David signaled to the FBI agents to stay inside the car.

The reason for his caution appeared in seconds—a pair of Plott Hounds, one black and one brown brindle, raced from the back of the house and circled the arriving cars, snarling and snapping in warning to the visitors. Bred in the mountains for hundreds of years as bear hunters, the large dogs were sleek, muscular, and fierce. Loyal to their owners, they were excellent protectors against both human and animal invaders.

The front door of the cabin opened. Colonel Buck Sawyer stepped onto the wide front porch, crossed his arms, and glared at his visitors. He had close-cropped gray hair and wore a red flannel shirt, tan Carhartt jeans, and scuffed work boots. His demeanor matched the attitude of his dogs, unwelcoming of the intrusion.

David waved a tentative hello from the safety of his car. The colonel scowled but nodded in recognition. He pursed his lips and whistled, the shrill sound echoing off the nearby barn. The dogs fell silent, turned, and raced across the gravel and up the steps in leaps. They circled the colonel's legs with tails wagging and sat on either side of him, sentinels watching the guests warily and waiting for commands.

David stepped from his vehicle and motioned for the agents to join him. Once on the porch, he extended his hand to shake while the dogs sniffed at his legs. "Good to see you, Buck. It's been a long time."

"Years," the colonel replied and refused the handshake. He glowered at the other visitors standing behind David. "Still can't believe you asked to bring Fibbies onto my land."

The shedding of their suits for more casual clothes did little to help the federal agents blend. Dressed in blue jeans, hiking boots, and windbreakers, they looked more like city slickers out for a day hike than the mountain people who lived in the area. Roxanne remained unflustered and introduced herself. "Surprised an old army colonel has so little regard for a federal agent."

"My upbringing in these mountains gave me a natural dislike to anything out of Washington. My time in the army confirmed it. Nothing good comes from that swamp."

She waved her arm toward the mountains rising on the horizon. "Brings tourists to the area for the Great Smokies, right?"

"Tourists? They bring litter, traffic, and crime, but everyone caters to them, right?" The colonel harrumphed. "But they don't let those of us who live here hunt in the park. They don't even let us take our dogs to walk on the trails. Not to mention they evicted my ancestors—and lots of other people's ancestors—to create your little playground."

David stood silently. He had heard the rant before from many of the longtime locals. Buck needed to get it out of his system before anything productive could happen.

"Hell, Washington at least acknowledged they treated the Cherokee poorly with the Trail of Tears, so they let 'em have a casino on their reservation to earn some money from them tourists. But we hillbillies didn't get squat when they took our land. Just a bunch of empty promises like the Road to Nowhere. You know what I'm talking about, agent?"

Roxanne shook her head and stayed silent. David worked to keep the smile off his face, knowing she understood the game as well as he did. Buck needed to work himself down.

"Family cemeteries are up there, centuries old. And they promised people they would be able to visit them anytime they wanted. Even promised to build a road to make it happen. Eighty years ago, that road was promised, and it's still not built. They lied to the mountain people to get them to move. And they continue to lie to them every year when some slick politician promises this time will be different if only you'll give him your vote."

Figuring Buck was about done, David took the time to

interject. "Blame me. I asked the FBI to Miller County to help me find the worst kind of man there is."

Buck glowered at the agents for a minute longer before slowly turning to the sheriff. "What type of man?"

"One who hurts kids."

David knew his tactic had worked as Buck's eyes flicked across the faces of his visitors. Without another word, he pushed open the front door and waved them inside.

34

Connor stuck his head through the door and scanned the hospital room. "Mom's not in here, is she?"

Jaxon sat up in the bed, smiling at Connor's return. "She went to the cafeteria to get some lunch."

"Awesome. I have a surprise." He slipped inside and let the door latch shut behind him before setting a grease-stained white paper bag on the bed tray. He ripped open the bag and unwrapped a cardboard tray full of thick, hot french fries. "Fresh from Abe's Market."

The smell filled the room, making Connor salivate. Jaxon picked one up, bit into it, and closed his eyes, clearly savoring the taste. "Wow, these are awesome. I've never tasted something so good. What are they?"

Connor picked up a fry and inhaled the scent himself. "French fries. You don't remember these?"

"*A strip of potato typically cooked by being fried in deep fat,*" Jaxon recited as he stuffed another one into his mouth and chewed thoughtfully with his eyes closed.

"You really don't remember sneaking over there from the park to get these?" When Jaxon shook his head again, Connor waved his hand in dismissal. "Doesn't matter. Guess you were too little."

Connor puzzled over why his little brother lacked memories of so many of the things they had shared. The experience of surviving in that horrid place had taken more than years. He decided to see what he could replant. "Mom would let us ride our bikes around the park while she read a book or something, but we weren't allowed to leave. Right across the street from the entrance, though, was Abe's Market—just a little convenience store, but it's got a deli in it, and man, is the food awesome."

Jaxon chewed, his attention rapt on Connor as the older boy continued. "Mom stopped at Abe's all the time for groceries, and we would go watch Abe's wife make sandwiches and stuff. We loved to eat there, but Mom couldn't afford that. But when we got cravings for these fries, we would scavenge the park for change. If we searched the trails and dug in the sand, we usually came up with enough money. Then we would sit on the curb out front of Abe's and eat them all before going back in the park. That way, she'd never know what we'd done."

Jaxon chewed, his mouth crammed full of fries. He swallowed and mumbled, "Was that the same park? You know, that day…"

"Oh, God, I'm such an idiot. I shouldn't have… I mean… Stupid of me to mention the park." Connor crumpled into the chair and watched his brother chew.

"It's okay, Connor. The park's a fun place. Lots of good memories. The swings. Riding bikes to it. Stuff like that. It's the only one in town, right?"

"Yeah, it's the only park here in Millerton." Connor leaned back in the chair and sighed, wondering how such crystal-clear memories were lost on Jaxon. "When you get out of here, I'll take you down there. I mean, if you want. I'd get it if you never wanted to see the place where it happened."

"I do want to go… if you'll take me."

"Of course." He chewed a fry. "Abe's son runs the deli now, but he makes the food just like his mom used to. I'll buy you one of those hot-roast-beef sandwiches you always wanted. I can afford it now 'cause I'm working."

"You work? What do you do?"

"Assembly-line stuff in one of the factories here. One of the maintenance guys is teaching me how to weld on my breaks. Says I'm a natural. I've been thinking about going to community college to learn more about it. I know it's weird for me of all people to actually want to go to school, but this is different."

"Sounds like a cool place. Maybe you can get me a job there too."

"No way." Connor laughed at the disappointed look he received. "Mom's probably already figuring out how to get you enrolled in school. She would've kicked my butt if I hadn't graduated."

Jaxon paused, a french fry dangling from his hand. "But… I've never been to school."

Connor cocked his head. "You went to first grade."

"I meant, you know, not in ages. Not that I remember."

"I hadn't really thought of that." Connor clasped his hands, interlaced his fingers, and rested his chin on them. "Guess we'll have to figure out how to get you caught up, but I'm sure Mom will. Must be some way."

"I don't know. Seems like it would be easier to just get a job instead."

"It's hard enough getting a job around here and no way you do it without at least a GED. To do any of the specialty stuff like welding, you really need a technical degree."

"Oh." Jaxon upturned the bag, but nothing fell onto the tray. He shook it then wet his fingers to pick up the crumbs on the tray. He crumpled the bag and settled back onto his pillow.

He opened his mouth and belched, the sound echoing off the walls.

Connor burst out laughing. "Dude, Mom hears you do that, and she'll kill you." Jaxon paled and shrank back. Connor leaned forward and grabbed his brother's hand. "No, I didn't mean it… not literally. I meant she lectures me that stuff like that is rude."

"Really?" Jaxon's eyebrow rose. "You can't burp?"

"Nope, and don't even think about farting, either." He settled back into his chair. "Don't worry. I'm sure she'll go easy on you. It's weird, realizing how little you remember."

"I want to, though. I want to remember all the things you remember."

Connor sat up and snapped his fingers. "You remember Duke, don't ya? Helping us with the mud pit?"

A smile crept across the boy's face, and he nodded. "Yeah. A yellow lab. Big and furry."

"He passed away, but I got a new one from the pound. You'll really like Trigger, 'cause he's a lot like Duke. Even kind of looks like him, at least to other people, but I know he's different. I can't wait for you to come home and meet him as soon as you get out of here."

"Wow." Jaxon licked his lips. "Home. I don't know——"

Connor thought Jaxon would be eager to get out of the hospital and go home, so he was surprised to hear him hesitate. But before he could ask, the door opened, and Heather entered the room. She sniffed the air and glared at Connor. "Do I smell french fries?"

The boys looked at each other and laughed. Connor raised his hands and grinned innocently. "Delivered special by the cafeteria."

"Don't give me that cafeteria BS. I work here, remember, and the fries never smell that good. You went to Abe's, didn't you?" She placed her hands on her hips, a stance Connor knew well as the ain't-buying-that stance. "You know junk food isn't good for your brother right now. He needs nutrition."

With a finger pointed at Jaxon, Connor replied, "I don't care what the docs say. Anything that puts weight on him is good." Seeing the retort building in his mother's eyes, he stood and wiped his hands. "Love to chat more about this, but I'm going to be late for work. And you know how you taught me to always be on time. Always do what your mom says, Jax. That's my motto."

Heather crossed her arms and stared at him, but she didn't stop his retreat.

"Don't worry, little bro, I'll stop by first thing tomorrow morning. Maybe I'll bring sausage biscuits from Abe's."

The last sound he heard before the door latched shut behind him was Heather saying, "Don't you dare."

35

D avid waited impatiently as the visitors settled into leather wingback chairs under the arching timber-frame ceiling of Buck Sawyer's cabin. A fire crackled in a massive stone fireplace on the far wall of the large main room. The dogs trotted across the wooden floor and curled up on a pair of wool rugs on either side of the mantel, their alert eyes monitoring all movement. Buck went into the adjoining kitchen and prepared four cups of steaming-hot coffee. After delivering the drinks, he tossed a log onto the fire and settled into his chair. "Talk."

David recapped the story of finding Jaxon on the highway and his tale of escape. When he finished, he paused for a second and locked eyes with Buck. "Now, a falling-down farmhouse with a trailer behind it describes a bunch of different places around here. I can even think of a few sex offenders in the county who live in a place like that. But I can only think of one person who lives in a place like that in Wattsville and who has a history of messing with a little boy."

Buck grimaced. "Matt McGregor."

"Yep, his old man, Rick, beat the ever-living crap out of him in front of the high school for touching that kid. Matt got expelled, and his younger brother, Mark, dropped out. I didn't see much of either one of them for years."

"Until Mark blew up the house."

"Exactly." David turned to Roxanne. "The McGregor clan dates back a long ways in these mountains. Certainly before the Civil War and probably even before the Cherokee were evicted with the Trail of Tears. They struggled as lumberjacks and farmers, but they hit their stride with moonshine. McGregor shine was known as some of the best around, and they made a bunch of it. Except they lost the touch."

Buck stood and stirred the fire. "When their grandpappy died, the recipe must've gone with him, 'cause Rick's shine was crap, and his kids didn't do much with it, either. Matt made some small batches from time to time that weren't bad, but Mark didn't think there was enough money to be made, not with all the tourist stores selling their version of moonshine. Though how the hell anything legal can possibly be called moonshine escapes me."

David continued the story, "Mark was the smarter of the brothers, though that isn't saying much because Matt could barely read and write. Mark figured out how to make meth, and Rick used his old moonshine distribution network to sell it. Great plan right up until Mark screwed up the lab and blew up the house. Killed himself in the process. I was out here the next morning as they pulled his body out of the house."

Roxanne asked, "Matt wasn't hurt?"

David shook his head. "Matt was living in a trailer behind the house. Turns out Rick had banned him from the house after the high-school incident. Said he was no longer allowed to live under the same roof."

"And Rick?"

"Wasn't home. Maybe he was delivering product. Maybe he was with one of his girlfriends or a hooker—the two boys had different mothers. Anyway, he came driving in the next morning… in a two-tone brown-on-tan van. The same damn van they've had for years."

"Where's Rick now? He still alive?"

Buck shook his head. "No clue. I haven't seen or heard anything from either one of them since I moved back here. Rumors bounce around, and people claim to have seen Matt from time to time, but that's really it. People avoid him."

Roxanne spread her arms. "Because of the incident with the boy back in high school."

Buck leaned back in his chair. "Some, but Matt's always been strange. A nasty mean streak. No one's ever liked being around him."

Roxanne counted off the connections on her fingers. "So you have a falling-down farmhouse blown up by a meth lab, a trailer behind the house, and a two-tone van. All things Jaxon's described. What about the house with a cellar? That's the thing we need to find."

David turned back to Buck. "I'm hoping you can fill in the blank, because I don't know anything about an old house with a stone cellar. Nothing shows on the property records. I could call in a chopper to fly over and tell me if something is there, but I'm hoping you'll save me the time. We need to get up there."

Buck stood, leaned on the mantel, and stared into the fire. "His great-grandpappy's house is back up in those woods. I was up there a few times as a little kid, and it sure sounds like the same place."

"Stone cellar?"

"Yep. They stored moonshine in there 'cause it was nice and cool. Used to buddy around some with Mark when I was eleven or twelve, and his daddy would make us haul that stuff up and down those steps. I did it because Rick would beat the tar out of me as fast as he would one of his own."

"The house still there?"

"Don't know. Haven't been there since middle school." He turned to face them. "Look, hanging around Mark was okay, but I didn't like his daddy. And I sure didn't like being near Matt, 'cause he was so weird."

Roxanne leaned forward. "This was before the incident in high school?"

"Yeah."

"So what made him so weird before that?"

Buck paused and looked into the air. After a few seconds, he said, "The boy was just cruel."

"Like how?"

He sighed, and his shoulders slumped. "People up here hunt, but it's for food. No one takes pleasure in killing animals just to kill them. But Matt was different. He would torture the hell out of little animals just to hear 'em scream. I couldn't stand it. So I stopped hanging around."

Roxanne and David exchanged knowing glances. What Buck described was classic early-serial-killer behavior. David asked, "Can you draw me a map to the house? I've got a SWAT team on standby, but I need to understand how far up in there it is."

"Sure." Buck collapsed into his chair and stared at the ceiling. "But you need to know something else about Matt. High school wasn't the last time he touched a kid."

David slammed his coffee cup down and leaned forward. "He did it again?"

"Yeah. This was after Mark was killed. I was home on leave when my dad had cancer, so I guess this would be about seventeen years ago. Daddy told me rumors were flying around that Rick was fuming 'cause he had caught Matt again. People were mad and threatening to string him up, but Rick told them not to worry, that he was gonna cure the boy good. Fix him once and for all."

"Cure him? How?"

Buck could only shrug. "I'm sorry, David, but I don't know. I was dealing with my daddy dying, not the McGregors."

David squeezed his hands until his knuckles turned white. "No one thought to report it to the police?"

"That's not the way things work up here. We handle things ourselves."

Roxanne piped in. "Doesn't sound like it got handled at all. No one thought he might do it again? Particularly since he had already done it before?"

Buck's face grew red. "We screwed up, yeah, but don't act like we're the only ones, and don't go blaming the people up here. The high school didn't report it way back when the first one happened. And it's not like the Catholic Church didn't keep moving pedophile priests around. Or the Boy Scouts didn't maintain a secret list of banned volunteers but didn't bother to share it with other youth organizations. Hell, schools all over the country transferred teachers rather than dealing with it. We all keep burying the crap and hope it stays buried. So, yeah, we made the same damn mistake."

David raised his hands to calm them. "Yeah, and I questioned him ten years ago and let him go. So let's just fix this today and stop him."

36

C onnor whistled as he walked out the exit door of the hospital parking lot, his house keys jangling in his hand. His brother was home, and his mother was happy—what could make the day any better? The warm sunshine hit his shoulders in answer, a beautiful day following the stormy night. He stepped out to the curb, looking for his ride, but a glance at his watch confirmed he was a few minutes early. He tilted his head back and savored the sun.

"Need a ride, Con?"

He opened his eyes and saw his father leaning against a pillar, his cigarette smoke curling around the no-smoking sign. He couldn't help but smile at the sight, but he declined the offer. "Got an Uber coming."

Harold looked around the parking lot. "Uber? In Millerton? Thought that was a city thing."

"It's a job, Dad. Anyone with a car can do it."

"Why you need an Uber, anyway? Your truck running okay?"

"It's fine. I just rode in with the sheriff."

"Oh."

They watched a crew raising a satellite dish on a TV truck near the emergency-room entrance. The cameraman was running a cable and setting up his equipment. A reporter was brushing her hair.

Harold swept his hand toward them. "Vultures. Be careful of them. They made me look so bad back then."

"I think they just followed the finger the sheriff was pointing."

"Yep." He glared at the crew. "Still, be careful."

"I don't think they recognize me. I was a little kid back then."

"They'll figure it out." Harold looked up at the wall of windows of the hospital. "How is he really? Jaxon?"

"Tough kid. The stories he tells..." Connor shuddered. "He's doing better than I would be, considering what he's been through. Struggling with everything. And he's so different than I remember."

"I expect he is different. A lot different. I don't know a lot of things, but I do know how hard it is to overcome things when you've seen horror. And he's seen a lot worse than I ever did."

"Yeah, I guess you do know." Connor squinted against the sun and avoided his father's eyes, wondering how the man always managed to turn a conversation back on himself.

Harold took a deep drag on his cigarette and blew the smoke high in the air. He returned the glare from an elderly couple coming up the walk from the parking lot, as if daring them to say something. After they passed, he said, "You're a good brother, and that's what he needs right now. Love, support, time, and being there for him. Give him that, and he has a chance."

Connor looked toward the entryway by the main road but didn't see his ride coming in yet. He turned back to his father. "That wasn't enough for you."

Harold dropped the cigarette to the ground and crushed it under his foot. "That's on me, son, not you. I was weak, already dabbling with drugs and drinking too much before I even came home. So, no, I was a lost cause. Y'all did what you could, but nothing could have saved me then."

"And now?"

"I'm working on it. For your brother up there. For your mom. For you. All I can do is one step at a time."

They stood together as a breeze flapped their jackets. A paper cup bounced across the parking lot. Connor asked, "You staying sober?"

Harold looked down at his feet. "One hundred sixty-three days. But I won't kid you, Con, it's hard. Every day is hard."

Connor had seen Harold sober up many times, but it never stuck. His father had always been glib about it, pretending he didn't have a real problem, saying "no sweat." To hear him say every time they saw each other now that it was still difficult gave him hope in a weird way, because it told him how hard his dad was really trying. "Almost six months. I'm proud of you."

"I can't think about months, Con. I'm too weak for that. I don't look further ahead than today. That's it. It's all I can focus on. Making it to one hundred sixty-four days."

Connor nodded. "Then I'm proud of you for today."

Harold looked away, but not before Connor noticed the moistening of his eyes. His father's voice came out choked. "I'll take that. It means more than you'll ever know."

They stood in silence for another minute before Connor said, "Guess the sheriff really knows now that you had nothing to do with Jax's disappearance."

Harold tapped another cigarette out of the pack in his hands. "I used to hate him for accusing me, for thinking I could ever do that to my own boy. But looking back, I get it. I might have been just sick enough to have caused actual harm to him."

"But you didn't have anything to do with Jaxon's disappearance."

"I had everything to do with it. I was supposed to be there that morning, watching you boys. Taking you to the park myself. All I had to do was show up, and I couldn't even manage that. I was more in love with booze and drugs than my own sons."

"Yeah, well, I was supposed to stay at the house. And I wasn't supposed to leave Jax alone while I went off with my friends."

Harold stared hard. "It's my burden, son, not yours. Don't you dare take it on."

Connor leaned his head back and watched a cloud float through the sky. "Maybe we all failed him. Maybe that's the only way to look at it."

"Maybe." Harold flicked the lighter open and let the flame touch the end of his cigarette. He inhaled deeply and blew a series of smoke rings. "Or maybe it's just freakin' bad luck it happened at all. Kinda like driving over an IED in the middle of a road."

Connor watched the smoke float through the air, blurring with the cloud in the distance. He didn't want to argue, so he changed the topic. "You ever going to quit those?"

"One bad habit at a time, son."

They stood in silence for a few minutes, a father and a son still trying to find their way around each other. Connor said, "You said you used to hate the sheriff for accusing you. Not anymore?"

"Still working on that, won't lie. I deserved to get arrested for the dumb shit I was doing, but I didn't deserve him letting everyone think I would hurt Jaxon." Harold stared off at the mountains in the direction of Wattsville. "Mostly, though, I'm mad about all that time he wasted focused on me, when he could have been out there searching for Jaxon. Not sure I can ever forgive the sheriff for that."

A car with an Uber sign pulled up to the curb. Connor waved at the driver and stepped toward it. He looked up at the fifth-floor windows as he opened the car door. "You said we need to give him love, support, and time. Do you think that will really save him after all he's been through?"

Harold studied the glowing end of his cigarette before answering. "I'm done BSing people, so I gotta say I honestly don't know. But without that, he doesn't stand a chance at all."

"Then it's what we'll do for him. You and me both. Make up for failing him ten years ago."

As the Uber worked its way out of the parking lot, Connor watched his father through the back window. *Maybe,* he thought, *I'm getting my brother and my father back at the same time.*

37

"Empty," Lieutenant Teddy Gilman announced to the sheriff as he exited the mobile home. His team followed him in their heavy tactical gear then climbed back into their waiting armored vehicle.

David stepped into the trailer and glanced around. The air held a vague moldy smell. The stained mattress was stripped bare, the couch tattered, the sink empty of dishes. Rat droppings littered the floor. A dried snakeskin lay in a cobweb-covered corner. Matt McGregor hadn't lived there in years.

Back outside, he took a deep breath of fresh air and strode toward his car. He waved his hand toward the narrow road disappearing into the woods. The armored truck roared up the path in the lead, followed by a K-9 SUV and three patrol vehicles. David fell in behind them with the FBI agents taking up the rear.

The tactical debate had been brief. Their background intelligence was sketchy, based on Jaxon's story and Buck's crude map. A highway-patrol helicopter had flown over the house to confirm its existence and location but spotted no movement below them and no smoke from the chimney.

Unfortunately, they also saw no place to land, so access would be limited to a ground assault. Waiting on additional resources from another county or the FBI's Incident Response Team might have been the safest option, but they dismissed the idea. If kids were in that house and needed rescuing, the risk was worth taking.

Their only choice was going in fast and loud, so Matt would hear them coming. He would already have heard the helicopter and probably had discovered the missing boy, so their time was short. If he took off running, the K-9 could chase him down. And if he didn't run, speed and surprise were the only advantages they had. Matt unfortunately knew every hiding place in that remote section of mountains, and they didn't know any.

Tree branches scraped along the side of the SUV as David fought to keep the vehicle in the ruts created by the vehicles in front of him. His radio crackled with Gilman's voice. "I see it. House at a hundred yards. No movement. Everyone, lock and load."

They entered the clearing, the back doors of the armored vehicle flinging open before the vehicle came to a stop. The heavily armed men hit the ground running and spread quickly around the house. The K-9 SUV slid to a stop, and the driver jumped out with a Belgian Malinois straining against its leash and barking in excitement. The patrol vehicles blocked in the two-tone van. Their occupants, with shotguns in hand, fanned out around the perimeter.

David barked into his microphone, "What you see, Gilly?"

Gilman's voice squawked back, "No movement, no sound in the house. Front door ajar. We have side windows covered. No rear door. We need to get a look inside, so going to break the windows."

"Go."

At the sheriff's command, movement was swift. SWAT

members on either side of the house stood and broke windows. With flashlights mounted on the barrels of their weapons, they scanned the interior.

"Five. I've got a body on the floor. Repeat: body on the floor."

Gilman's calm voice replied. "You have a bead on him, Five?"

"Ten-four."

"Movement?"

"Negative."

"Adult? Child?"

David held his breath as he waited for the reply. "Adult."

"Five, keep your bead. Three, can you see the whole room?"

"Ten-four. All clear. Looks like a kitchen in back, but I can't see for sure."

"Sheriff, we're ready to breach."

David moved up behind a tree near the porch. "Watch your crossfire, gentlemen. Entry team, go."

With the men on the side windows covering the interior, two men mounted the front steps and pushed open the door. One went low and to the right and the other higher and to the left, their rifles sweeping the room as their voices boomed through the house. After a pause, David's radio cracked with the first report. "Body on the floor DOA. Other rooms cleared."

David entered the house right behind Gilman and shined his light in the face of the body on the floor. The cold air had slowed decomposition, but the face of the man crumpled on the floor was still too bloated to positively identify. Besides, David barely knew Matt McGregor and hadn't seen him in years. He could only guess it was him.

"In here, Sheriff."

David stood and followed the voices into a cramped

kitchen. On one wall was a wooden door. The screws holding the hasp were ripped from the wall, a remarkable feat for the boy to have accomplished in his weakened state. The cellar side of the door and frame hinted at the ferocity of his efforts to escape, with long scrapes and cracks in the wood from his attempts to scratch his way out, bloodstains marring the surface. The upper panel was shattered from the basement side, matching the boy's description of putting his fist through the door. A clear, small, bloody handprint gripped the doorframe, probably left as Jaxon threw his thin body against the door to break it open.

Two SWAT-team members eased down the steps, the flashlights on their rifles probing the shadows. David paused at the top step, his own flashlight picking up a glint on the tread. He looked down and saw it was a bloodied fingernail. He looked at the claw marks on the back of the door and shuddered. The poor kid had ripped it out in his frenzy to escape.

He carefully stepped over it and descended into the darkness, gasping against the stench rising from the basement. The only light filtered through the narrow, shattered windows near the ceiling. The wind whipped in, chilling the room enough that they could see puffs of their breath. Following the powerful beam of his flashlight as it scanned the room, David took in the contents. A small pile of books was stacked neatly in one corner, including a dog-eared *Merriam-Webster's Dictionary*. A crumpled blanket was near an indention in the floor. A metal pail filled with excrement was tucked in one corner.

Most remarkable was what wasn't there. No furniture, not even a thin mattress for comfort. No changes of clothing. No toys. No food. Not even a second bucket for fresh water. The books appeared to be the only luxury, and everything else was sheer depravity.

The weight of the horror of the room made David tremble. He couldn't imagine staying down there for an hour, even with the comfort of his thick coat and outdoor gear. He muttered, "How did that boy survive this place for ten years?"

Gilman could only shake his head in reply.

Revulsion enveloped David, and he had to get out, get to fresh air. He couldn't feel his feet moving, though he heard his boots clomping up the steps as distant echoes in his mind. His eyes locked on the shattered open door above him. The kid had clawed his way out of the subterranean hell and then walked miles out to the interstate, all while David had finished paperwork in his office, eaten a warm meal, relaxed in an over-stuffed recliner, and watched some Netflix. And when the first sightings had been broadcast over the radio, he had remained under the warm covers, not wanting to go out in the cold, snowy weather.

He stopped and stared at the body on the floor of the main room. Tests would prove it, but he knew it was Matt McGregor, a man he knew existed, yet never suspecting the depth of his depravities. Most frustratingly, it was a man who would never feel the cold steel of handcuffs being snapped around his wrists, all because the sheriff had barely even suspected him.

Jaxon had been cowering in that basement a decade ago while he had stood not a half mile away, having a conversation with his kidnapper. He hadn't even thought to look around for other places to hide a boy.

He stumbled across the porch and into the yard. He leaned against a large poplar tree and vomited, a first for him at a crime scene—it never happened even during his rookie year. But this was different. He wasn't sick from what he saw. He was disgusted by what he imagined. Jaxon sat in the darkness, waiting on someone to come, on someone to rescue him. Kids came and went, lived and died, and David's biggest worry had been how his divorce might affect opinion polls.

He straightened and wiped his hand across his mouth. With a deep breath of fresh, cold mountain air, he turned back to where Roxanne and Agent Gonzalez stood, both carefully avoiding looking at him. He wanted more than anything to get into his car and leave but instead took a halting step toward them when his radio rattled to life.

A young deputy's voice came over the air. The man had been assigned to the perimeter of the clearing. "Sheriff? We found graves. God help me, there's at least a dozen of 'em, maybe more."

38

It was still dark outside when the elevator doors slid open and Connor walked out onto the fifth-floor hallway. The night nurse at the station glanced up and scowled at the dog beside him. She opened her mouth as if to protest but paused and closed it again. With a shake of her head, she looked down at the records she was documenting and continued scribbling notes.

Connor exhaled and reminded himself to look confident, as though the dog was supposed to be there. Claws clacked on the linoleum floor, Trigger's tail slowly swaying to and fro as he sniffed the air. Convincing the dog to accept the service-dog vest had been a challenge. He had scratched and clawed at it and panted all the way over to the hospital. But his head was high as he sniffed the unfamiliar smells. He looked nearly as confident as a service dog.

Almost at the end of the hall and successful in his smuggling routine, Connor was shocked when Jaxon's room door opened and Nurse Sheila exited. She blocked their path and examined the dog. "And who might this handsome creature be?"

Connor swallowed hard. "His name's Trigger."

"Mmm-hmm. And I see Mr. Trigger is wearing a service-dog vest."

He glanced over his shoulder, half expecting security to round the corner. "Yes, ma'am."

"We have lots of therapy dogs come visit patients. Volunteers take them around and just make people smile. You should consider it. After all, it takes a lot less training to be a therapy dog than a service dog. And it would keep a young man like you out of all sorts of trouble."

Connor gulped. "Good idea."

"In the meantime, seems the doctor wants Mr. Jaxon in there to get out of his room some. Walk around a little. Stretch his legs. Maybe even get some fresh air. I'm thinking a big brother would be better than some ol' volunteer nurse helping him do that."

"Even better idea."

"Perfect. And you can take Trigger on those walks." She looked down at the dog and smiled. "Just like a real service dog would."

"Yes, ma'am."

She walked past them, humming "Who Let the Dogs Out."

Connor watched her go down the hall and reached down to rub Trigger's head. "I guess we got away with it, huh?" He chuckled. "Sort of."

He turned and knocked softly on the room door before opening it enough to stick his head inside. "Morning, Jax. You ready for a visitor?"

Jaxon was sitting up in the bed. The nutrient-rich IV fluid and three-meal-a-day routine had already added color to his pale complexion. His hair had been washed and trimmed by Heather's stylist the night before. With the added bonus of a full night of sleep in a bed with pillows, and he looked like a new person. "Yeah. You bet."

"Good, because I have someone special with me." He pushed open the door, and the dog bounded into the room and threw his front paws up on the side of the bed. His tail wagged with enthusiasm, a blur of yellowish fur. He chuffed softly and grinned with his tongue lolling across his jaw.

Connor had expected Jaxon to lean forward and wrap his arms around the dog's neck, but instead, he scrambled back in the bed against the rails on the far side. He drew his legs up tightly against his chest and wrapped his arms around them. His eyes opened wide, and a squeak slipped out of him.

Shocked at the reaction, Connor sternly commanded, "Trigger, down. Sit." The dog dropped his front paws to the floor, and his furry butt quickly joined them, the tail sweeping the floor slowly. He tilted his head over his shoulder and looked quizzically at Connor, a soft whine escaping his open mouth.

Worried, Connor asked, "Jax, you okay? I'm sorry. I'm so sorry. I should've told you what I was planning."

Without taking his eyes off of the dog, Jaxon asked, "What's that?"

Connor looked from the dog to the frightened boy and back. "This is Trigger. He's the dog I got after Duke died."

"Trigger?" Jaxon's arms relaxed their grip on his legs, and he allowed himself a glance up at Connor.

"I thought since he looks so much like Duke... I'm sorry, I didn't think. Mom says I never think things through."

"He's... just"—Jaxon looked around the room, appearing to be at a loss for words—"bigger than I thought."

"Bigger? Duke was almost as tall as you were when you... you know, disappeared."

Jaxon let his legs slide flat on the bed. "Sorry, it's just... I can't really remember touching a dog. Stories, yeah, but not for real."

"Let me take him back down to my truck, and then I'll come back up and chat with you."

Connor picked up Trigger's leash and turned for the door. "Wait."

He turned back to face his little brother, worried he had screwed things up by moving too quickly. But Jaxon was sitting up, eyeing the dog carefully. "He's friendly? I mean, he won't bite me or anything, right?"

"No way. Trig's a gentle giant." He reached down and rubbed the dog's ears, rewarded with an adoring canine look of affection.

Jaxon inched his hand forward. "Can I"—he swallowed and continued—"touch him?"

Connor eased the dog forward to the edge of the bed and told him to sit. He held an ear gently between two fingers. "Here. Feel."

The boy's hand trembled as he reached out and let his fingers brush the tip of the ear. Trigger waited patiently as his hand ran down the ear and across the head. "I think he likes me."

"Of course he does. Trigger likes everyone. Well, except for the sheriff, but…" Connor shrugged.

With his hand stroking the dog's head, Jaxon looked up and smiled. "He goes everywhere with you?"

"No, I wish. Most places don't allow dogs."

Jaxon cocked his head. "Does the hospital?"

A chuckle slipped out of Connor. "No dogs allowed."

"But how…?"

"A friend of mine loaned me the service-dog vest. He bought it off eBay or something because his beagle isn't a service dog, either. I've never used it before, but he told me places can't ask, so I thought I would try. Worst thing that could happen is they make me take him home, and then he would sleep all day on my bed."

Jaxon looked up incredulously. "He comes inside? Sleeps on your bed?"

"I forget how little you remember." Connor settled into the chair beside the bed and let Trigger's leash slip to the floor. "For me, I'd come home from school and find Duke curled up in your bed. Or on hot summer nights, Duke would decide I was too hot to sleep beside, and he'd pad across the floor and stretch out on your empty bed. When Duke died, I almost couldn't stand how lonely our room felt. Your empty bed… no dog sprawling in mine… it was too much. I begged Mom to let me get another dog because I couldn't sleep alone. It was too… vacant." He rubbed Trigger's shoulders slowly. "You don't know how many tears have soaked into his fur. I don't think I could have slept without him."

Jaxon leaned forward in the bed so his nose touched the dog's. The two sniffed each other. "I get it. The worst nights were being alone. After Kevin died, being all alone in that place was hard. I wish I'd had somebody to keep me company."

The boys sat in the silence of the room, the hum of medical equipment a background to the sound of dog panting. Their hands stroked the fur as they were each lost in their memories.

"Do you think," Jaxon asked quietly, "he might get into the bed with me?"

"Sure, if you ask him."

"How do I do that?"

"Pat the bed with your hand and say 'up.'"

Jaxon slid back against the far rail, creating a wide space. His hand gently tapped the covers beside him, the attached IV line bouncing in the air. "Up."

The dog turned his head and looked at Connor. "You heard him. Up."

Trigger sprang into the bed, tail wagging furiously as he licked Jaxon's face. The boy giggled in delight and let his hands explore the dog's thick neck and chest. After a few moments,

Jaxon slid back onto the pillow. Trigger stretched out and rested his head on the boy's chest.

Connor grinned, his brother's happiness warming him even as he struggled with the knowledge of the years of darkness between them. Trigger was one more bridge helping him heal. "I got one more surprise for you."

Jaxon looked up in anticipation. "What?"

"Ready to see a sunrise?"

39

E xhaustion weighed on Heather as she exited the elevator and turned toward the hospital room. She nodded at the nurse at the station as she passed. The woman opened her mouth as if to say something but hesitated and smiled instead.

Heather's overnight shift had been a challenge, especially since she had never slept the day before. During her breaks, she slipped up to Jaxon's floor and looked in on him. They chatted haltingly, getting reacquainted until she had to go back to her own floor.

Her coworkers suggested she take time off. She had plenty of vacation banked—it wasn't as if she had needed to take it before—and even a little money saved up. She was in a very different place than she had been when she was struggling to make ends meet in nursing school. She thought she might just take some time when Jaxon came home, but for the time being, it was as convenient to work, since they were in the same building.

The other nurses understood and cheered her on, but they also pestered her with questions about what the police had learned so far. The Asheville TV station seemed to know as much as she did about the investigation, which in both cases was virtually nothing. Neither the sheriff nor the FBI had given her much information in their updates.

She worked her full shift, clocked out, and rode the elevator to the fifth floor. As she approached the end of the hall, the laughter of the boys floated through the closed door and reached her ears, a magical sound that swept away her tired feelings. Jaxon was home, and from the sound of it, the brothers were making up for lost time. And so would she. Screw the bills. They would figure it out. Maybe she would let her friends do that online fundraising thing they had talked about on break. It couldn't hurt.

She pushed open the door and stood transfixed at the scene. Connor was sprawled sideways in the chair, his legs draped over one of the arms and his feet dangling. Trigger was lying in the bed, wagging his tail as he licked Jaxon's laughing face.

"What is that dog doing in here?" she demanded.

Connor turned to her and displayed the aw-shucks-just-having-fun grin that always came with his mischief. "Looks to me like he is licking Jaxon's breakfast off his face."

"You know what I meant. How did you get him up here without anyone stopping you?" She spied the service-dog vest through Jaxon's fingers as he caressed the dog, answering a part of her question. "Where did that vest come from? You know he isn't a service dog. That isn't right, Connor."

"I don't know. He sure seems to be doing a good service making Jax happy, so I think he's a service dog."

She had to smile at the truth in that. The boy sitting in the hospital bed was as different from the one the day before as either were from the boy who had disappeared so many years ago. The puckered scar crossed his face, but the skin around it glowed. He appeared to have already put on some much-needed weight, filling out his gaunt cheeks a bit. Shining from the previous evening's shampooing, his hair was no longer knotted and tangled.

Most importantly, his smile warmed the room, even with the missing teeth. The worry creases in his face were smoothing out to reveal the smooth skin of an adolescent.

"Well, you'll get to explain all of that to the hospital when they catch you. And remember, I work here."

"Nurse Sheila has already seen him. She said they want Jax up and walking the hallways today, and Trigger could go with him for support."

"She does know he isn't trained for any of that, right?"

Connor blushed. "I don't think we fooled her at all. She didn't care and even said they have therapy dogs visit, and they do the patients a lot of good. Said I might oughta consider volunteering."

"Sounds like Nurse Sheila. She always had my number when I trained under her." Heather chuckled. "You know, Con, a lot of my patients look forward to their visits. You should do it."

She stepped forward and ruffled the grinning dog's head. "I've got to agree—he looks like he belongs."

Jaxon looked up, his eyes shining brightly. "So he can stay?"

She shrugged. "Until the hospital complains, yeah. But he has to go home when Connor leaves. Deal?"

"Deal," the boys said together and laughed. Connor reached out his hand balled into a fist, and Jaxon responded with a fist bump.

"Connor took me to see a sunrise!" Jaxon exclaimed.

"What? Where?"

"Don't worry, Mom," Connor explained. "Nurse Sheila got us a wheelchair, and we rolled down to the waiting room on the east wing. We didn't leave the floor, and she was with us the whole time."

Her eldest son had always been impulsive. She had told

him many times that she thought his motto was "act first—think later." Rather than being scolded by the words, he laughed them off. But he was finally maturing.

She looked at the dog and grinned to herself. Okay, he was somewhat maturing. Still, she had to trust him, especially with Jaxon. "So what'd you think of it?"

Jaxon's eyes widened. "It was amazing. Like purple then pink and rays of light sparkling. It was… was… magical."

"Wow. Sounds wonderful. Maybe I can see one with you."

"Con said he would come take me again tomorrow. Come see it with us."

Connor sprawled back in the chair, his hands clasped behind his head and his legs dangling. A bright grin was spread across his face. She was warmed by their camaraderie. Her family was back together.

"I think I will."

40

They make me laugh, but that makes me sad too. I know I will disappoint them some day because they want me to be sweet, innocent, six-year-old Jaxon who disappeared from that park so many years ago—the little kid who loves french fries, curls up with Connor and reads, sleeps with a dog in his bed, and rides his bicycle.

But I'm not him. I can't ever be him. I know the stories, but I don't know how to *be* Jaxon. The only person I know how to be is Teddy, a kid who grew up in a cold, dark dungeon doing whatever it took to survive until the next day.

I watch the two of them bantering. She pretends to be angry at Connor for bringing Trigger into the room, but she isn't really mad. She doesn't slap him across the face or pull his hair or push him down and kick him.

And Connor brushes it off like her scolding doesn't matter when I can tell he wants to please her. They can be that way because they have each other. And always have had each other.

I don't belong with them. I don't fit.

I have—had—Kevin, the only brother I've ever known. All those years, we huddled together for warmth, swapping stories and making up adventures. Playing games with sticks and pebbles. Reading the dictionary in the light from the little windows. That's real.

Sitting in a bed, getting three meals a day, laughing at corny jokes, and scratching a dog's ears can't be real.

They want me to remember my life before. So do the doctors and nurses and the psychiatrist who comes by and talks.

But I can't remember before. My memories—my real memories—start in that dungeon. Whoever and whatever I was before that nightmare began is tucked away so deep that I don't think I can ever unearth him. I've got him carefully compartmentalized and buried like one of those graves I dug.

Before is nothing but stories we told each other to distract ourselves from the hunger, the pain, and the despair. We told and retold them so many times they became nothing more than tales. My *before* is no more a reality to me than Kevin's *before*—or Joey's or Chad's or Mike's or Jimmy's or Dave's or that of any other kid who shared our existence. The stories told of each other's parents and friends and siblings became as powerful and life-sustaining as our own, so our own personal *before* became meaningless. *Before* is more dream than memory.

I wish my *before* was as real to me as it is to these people. I really do. Not just for them, but for me. I've never been as happy as I've been these last few days. And I don't want it to end.

I wonder if maybe I was happy *before*, but I don't know. They tell me I was, but I don't know how they would really know. I don't remember playing with friends, fighting with my older brother, throwing sticks for dogs, or riding bikes. I don't even think I know how to pedal a bike because I can't remember riding down a hill with the wind whistling through my hair.

I want what they are offering. A brother. A mother. A

father, even if he isn't perfect. A dog to sleep in my bed. A bed with covers and clean sheets and pillows.

I want to get up every morning and watch the sun rise.

Mostly, I want to forget that place I lived in and the things that happened there. I don't ever want to think about it again.

But the sheriff and FBI agent won't let me forget yet. They stop by my room and ask me to verify it's him. They show me a photograph of his rotting face, and in a glance, I know it is.

I can't catch my breath. The air in the room is gone. My vision grays. The room swims. My hands shake. Sweat rolls down my face. All I want to do is run. Connor's arm around my neck anchors me. I can only stammer, "It's him."

The sheriff's face is filled with concern as he takes the photo back from me. "His name was Matthew McGregor."

"Matt." I whisper his name for the first time since I escaped. I hadn't wanted to say it out loud for fear it would somehow summon him. I don't want him to find me and drag me back.

"Don't worry, Jaxon. He's dead. He'll never hurt you again."

Yeah, he will. He'll haunt my dreams forever. "Did you shoot him?"

"Uh, no. He was already dead."

That makes no sense. How does a monster just die? "How?"

"We don't know yet. Heart attack, maybe. Could have been a stroke. An autopsy will tell us. But it doesn't matter how. He's dead."

Yeah, it matters how he died. He doesn't deserve to die that easily. He deserves to suffer as much as Kevin and all the others.

The sheriff looks around, blinking. He's struggling with what to say. "Your description was perfect. You led us right to him. The burned-out house. The trailer. The road. The van. The house. Even the basement was exactly how you told us."

Of course it was. Why would I lie about that? What else don't they believe?

"We also found the graves." He nodded toward Roxanne. "The FBI is sending a specialized team. It's called an Evidence Response Team. They're going to help us exhume the bodies."

Exhume. I always liked that word in our dictionary games. *To disinter. Dig up. To bring back from neglect or obscurity.*

Like me. I've been exhumed, not that differently than Kevin will be. They will exhume his body too. "Why not leave them there?"

Connor pulled me close. "So they can go home to their families. They deserve that, not to be left out there in the woods."

"But how will you know who their families are?"

Agent Porter came to the side of the bed. "DNA testing."

DNA. Nucleic acids that are usually the molecular basis of heredity. That's one of those words where the definition doesn't really help you understand what it means. "How does DNA tell you who the family is?"

She sat on the edge of the bed. "Everyone's DNA is unique, but it's also based on their parents' DNA. So we can take DNA from them—their hair, for example—and match it to a database of missing children. That match tells us who they are and who their family is."

"You have everyone's DNA?"

"Most missing kids, yes. Really old cases are tougher because the protocols were different then, but now we collect DNA on every missing child."

"So all those kids, the ones who came through there… You'll be able to match them and find their families?"

"Yes, we should. As long as they were reported missing."

"But what good does that do? You're just telling their parents they're dead. Don't they already think that?"

"Think about your friend Kevin." She ran her hand through Trigger's fur. "He disappeared like you did, and his family is left wondering what happened. Don't you want Kevin's family to know what happened to him? Maybe you could even meet them someday and tell them what a great friend he was to you and what a comfort he was. Wouldn't that be great?"

I look around at them standing in my room and realize they don't understand. I don't think it will comfort Kevin's family to find out their son is dead. I don't think his family will like it at all. I survived, and he didn't. I think they will hate that. And I think they will hate me.

41

D avid watched the elevator-floor indicator count down as
they descended. "That poor kid."

Roxanne said, "He's luckier than the rest of them. At least
he got away."

The sheriff nodded and looked down at the floor. "The
look on his face when he saw Matt's photo… sheer terror. I'll
dream about that for a long time."

"He'll probably have nightmares about that man for the
rest of his life. We can only hope he'll find a way to put him
out of his mind, and that's going to take a lot of support and
counseling."

"And a very supportive family, which he's lucky to have.
Connor is so devoted to him, protective like a big brother
should be. Heather is strong and independent, used to working
hard to get what she needs. Even the dog, not that there is any
chance in the world he's a service dog"—David grinned—"is
going to be there for him every step of the way."

The elevator reached the ground floor, and the doors slid
open to reveal Harold Lathan waiting to go up. The collar of
his fleece-lined denim coat was turned up, his John Deere hat

pulled down low over his head. David spied the reporters milling outside the entrance of the hospital and guessed the reason for the incognito look. "Harold, if you'll let me know when you're coming in, I can get a deputy to help you pass them."

Harold glared directly into the sheriff's eyes before stepping back to let them pass. "I can manage without your help."

David ignored the angry tone. "I was coming to find you. If you have a few moments, I can give you an update about the case and what we know."

Anger raged under the surface of Harold's face. "A reporter from the Asheville paper called me. Asked if I had any comment about you finding the house my son was held in, right here in Miller County. Is that true?"

"Damn it." David and Roxanne exchanged glances. He was frustrated the reporters were already digging up the story before they had a chance to control it. "Sorry, I didn't want you to hear it that way."

"I'll take that as a yes."

David paused before answering. "Yes, it's true."

"Was it a McGregor?"

The sheriff cocked his head and studied Harold's face. "Did you know Matt?"

Harold stepped back. "Damn it, you still think I had something to do with it?"

"I didn't say that."

"But I saw how you looked at me." Harold shoved his hands in his pockets. "No, I didn't know them. They were older. Gone from high school before I got there. I knew they were a source of liquor and drugs—everyone knew that—but I was pretty squeaky-clean in high school, believe it or not. Some beers at parties was about it."

"You never bought meth from Mark?"

"No. I didn't get messed up with drugs until after my

second tour. Mark blowing himself up was legend by then." Harold looked at David with disgust. "The reporter also said you found a dozen or more graves."

"We don't have a count yet."

"So more than the hiker and his friend Kevin Jax told us about? 'Cause I figure you can count that high. I'm guessing you found a bunch of kids that maniac killed."

David swallowed and glanced around to see who was listening. He guided Harold to a corner of the waiting room and lowered his voice. "Yes. More than two. We honestly don't have a count yet."

"I guess I'll find out from the newspaper when you do know."

Harold turned to walk away, but David reached out and grabbed his arm. "Look, I'm sorry. I stopped by to update Heather and the boys and haven't had a chance to catch you. I'm trying to keep all of you informed, but I didn't know the media already had some of the details. You should never have found out that way, and I'm sorry. I'll be glad to answer any questions you have and help your family in any way."

Harold spun back, his face red and his eyes narrowed. He spoke in a fierce whisper, spittle flying from his lips. "Help? Sheriff, we needed your help ten years ago. You were so busy blaming me, trying to bury me under as many charges as you could dream up, you couldn't even look around your own damn county while some pervert did God knows what to my boy. Guess once you get a *count*, we'll find out how many little boys lost their lives because you were too busy blaming the wrong man. Maybe you should go explain to those families why you let their kids die."

Harold stomped to the elevator bank and slapped the call button hard enough to make people in the lobby jump and stare. When the doors opened, he stepped inside, spun around, and glared at the sheriff.

When the doors closed and hid the view, David felt his body go limp. He leaned back against the wall and looked up at the ceiling. "That went well."

"Victims' families are often angry. You know that."

He shook his head and looked out the window, anything to avoid Roxanne's eyes. "I'm used to their misplaced anger, but this is different."

"How so?"

"Because it's not misplaced."

"That's not fair. He was *a* suspect, not *the* suspect, but he was a very good suspect. Estranged father. Known mental health issues with his PTSD. Drug and alcohol problem. You know how often that profile turns out to be the right suspect, and no one saw anything that gave us any other leads. What else were we to do?"

David leaned his forehead against the glass windows that overlooked the parking lot and sighed. They could have done *something*. He had stood in Matt McGregor's trailer and talked to the man. Listened to his denials of involvement and his promise of straightening out his life. David had taken McGregor's willingness to have his trailer searched as a sign of innocence.

He squeezed his eyes shut and tried to block out the pain of regret, but he knew the truth. "I failed that kid."

42

Heather looked up as the room door opened. Harold stuck his head through and scanned the room. Her two sons sat on the bed in an embrace. Jaxon, unnerved seeing Matt McGregor's photo, had broken down as soon as the sheriff and FBI agent left the room. Connor had him wrapped in a bear hug, doing his best to console his younger brother.

Harold said, "Maybe I should come back later?"

"We're just trying to give him some family time, so you might as well come in."

He looked down the hall as if hoping to find an excuse before slinking into the room and settling into a chair. He crossed his legs and shifted his weight, trying to get comfortable. He reached out to pat Jaxon's leg, hesitated, then withdrew his hand. He dropped his eyes and uncrossed his legs again as he waited. Heather would have felt sorry for him if she didn't have bigger issues.

Jaxon's sobs slowed, and he grew quieter. With a big sniff, he broke from the embrace and leaned back on his pillow. He wiped his eyes with his good hand. His voice came out choked and strained. "I'm sorry. I don't know why I'm crying so much."

Heather leaned over him and smoothed his hair. "It's okay. You've earned the right to cry."

He shook his head. "No. I'm not supposed to cry. It's weak."

Harold's voice boomed in the room. "Bullshit."

Shocked, Heather turned to look at him. "What?"

"You heard me. That's the kind of macho bullshit I always thought—the kind of bullshit that got me into the mess I was in."

He stood and walked to the side of the bed. He rested his hand on the boy's bony shoulder and looked him in the eye. "Listen to me, Jax. Whatever that guy taught you about weak..." He closed his eyes and took a deep breath. "The strongest thing you can do is deal with how you feel. It's taken me too damn long to figure that out, so understand that with your family, you can cry anytime you need to. We'll never think that's weak. You got it?"

Jaxon blinked his eyes. "Family?"

"Yeah, family. In front of your brother or mother... or me. It don't matter. Family'll never think less of you for crying. We're gonna help you get through this."

Heather straightened and looked at Harold's determined face. She hadn't heard a speech like that from him in a long time, maybe never. But he was right, and it helped her make a decision that had already been tickling the back of her mind. Jaxon needed to get out of the hospital.

He didn't need the constant interruptions of doctors and nurses taking his blood pressure, listening to his heart, or asking him how he was every few minutes. They were doing their jobs and doing them well, but she could change his dressings and make sure he took his medications. And he certainly didn't need cops arriving unannounced, asking questions and upsetting him. He needed to be safe with his family so they could protect him and help him heal.

She leaned over and kissed his forehead. "We're going to get you discharged and go home."

Jaxon sat stock-still and stared at her. Harold's face filled with surprise. Connor's head snapped around, and he raised an eyebrow as he asked, "Home? Today?"

"Today. Tomorrow. As fast as we can. All three of us." She cocked her head at Trigger wagging his tail from his perch on the bed. "Fine. All four of us." She caught Harold's eye. "And we expect you to come by every day too."

She had expected the boy to be excited, but instead, Jaxon's face was clouded with doubt. "Will they let me go?"

"I don't see why not. They've already said your injuries aren't that serious, that what you need are good meals, lots of rest, and time to heal. The IV is coming out today, anyway. We can make sure you get your antibiotics. They aren't doing anything else for you except monitoring. The sooner you're sleeping in your own bed, the faster you can get better."

"Will the doctors come there?"

She chuckled at the vision of doctors doing house calls. "We'll come in for any appointments. Dr. Sorenson, the psychiatrist, will want to keep seeing you and help you work through things, but we live close, so that won't be hard."

With the softest mumble, he said, "I'm not sure it's a good idea."

Connor leaned against the bed, lowering his head so he could look Jaxon in the face. "I think it's a great idea. Mom and I work different shifts, so we're trying to get things done at the house and then come down here to spend time with you. This way, we can all be home together. One of us is always at the house."

"I don't want to be in the way."

Connor scratched the dog's ears. "In the way? Are you

kidding? You'll keep Trigger company while I'm at work. He gets lonely and would be in your bed the whole time. And he won't have to pretend to be a service dog anymore."

Jaxon ran his hand across the dog's fur as Trigger's tail thumped against the mattress. He turned his eyes up toward them. "I don't know if"—he sniffled—"if I belong there."

Connor wrapped his fingers around Jaxon's, cocooning his brother's smaller hands in his own. "Well, I know you belong. You belong in my room." He paused and corrected himself. "In *our* room. I want to come home from work and find you there, keeping *our* dog company. I want to wake up every morning and see you there."

Heather fought the tightening in her chest. She needed to be strong and try not to cry again. But she was so proud. Connor was playing the role he should have always been able to play—protective big brother.

And Jax. Her Jax. He was so different, but he was home. Finally. "We want you there."

Jaxon's eyes flicked from face to face, and his mouth opened, but words didn't come out. As tired as he had to have been of crying, the tears flowed again. He buried his face in the dog's neck, muffling his cries. Heather's vision of him blurred as her own tears flowed, but she pulled him close, her heart filling as Connor said, "Welcome home, little bro."

43

D avid climbed the narrow steps and opened the door to the second-floor situation room located over an old hardware store on Main Street near the sheriff's department. In the three days since the FBI's Evidence Response Team had been at the McGregor farm, the flood of evidence had quickly overwhelmed his small conference room at the station, and he'd needed to find extra capacity.

The landlord was thrilled at the good fortune to lease the space after it had sat vacant for so many years, a victim of the Walmart by the interstate sucking retail away from the small town. He even offered a vacant ground-floor storefront next door for press briefings, once they moved the dust-covered display shelves of a five-and-dime closed years earlier.

The large room was dingy but adequate for their needs. Portable whiteboards had been hauled in and set up around the perimeter. Crime-scene photos were taped to their surfaces with scribbled notes identifying them. Arrows were drawn to connect one scene to another. A scattering of folding tables served as desks for sheriff's department detectives and FBI agents, who sat side by side as they typed on open laptops or chatted on cell phones.

Over the years, David had worked in a few such war rooms, though they were usually filled with the urgency of a manhunt or preparation efforts for a raid. He could feel the room humming with a sense of purpose, but he missed the raw energy of pursuit. No mystery existed in the identity of the perpetrator. DNA results had confirmed it. The fiend was already dead. There would be no dramatic takedown or the associated adrenaline rush, no satisfying conclusion of putting the bad guy in jail or watching him die in a hail of bullets.

The people in the room, though, didn't seem to share his feeling of missed opportunity. Agent Gonzalez headed up the FBI's efforts to identify the bodies found in the graves. Their labs would turn results around much quicker than the state labs. Once a victim was identified, the sheriff's department coordinated with the appropriate local law enforcement to notify relatives and to review the original investigations into the disappearances.

David and Roxanne worked together as circus ringmasters, keeping the investigation coordinated and information shared.

He settled into a metal folding chair at the end of a table covered in folders of notes then signaled for Agent Gonzalez to start.

"The Evidence Response Team has completed its search for additional graves and are satisfied that all bodies have been recovered. They were located in a tight grouping in a clearing and laid out in an orderly fashion, the oldest situated at the farthest point from the house and in a line to newest nearest to the house. Our final count is eighteen."

Gonzalez paused for a moment and let silence fill the room before continuing. "Fourteen of those were young male children between the approximate ages of five and eight. Of the remaining four, the two who appear to be in the oldest graves are an older male and a female in her late teens or early twenties. Two more graves are also clustered, estimated to have been dug about three years ago—a male in his early twenties and a male in his early teens."

David prodded with questions to keep the meeting flowing. "Let's start with the children. How many are identified at this point?"

"Six of the fourteen have been identified." Gonzalez stood and pointed at a map of the Southeastern United States, littered with pushpin markers. "Their abduction points and the victims have striking similarities, showing a pattern. All disappeared from midsized blue-collar towns within a few-hundred-mile radius of Wattsville—Tennessee, Georgia, Carolinas, Kentucky, and Virginia. The victims were all white and from working-class families, mostly single-parent, and were five to seven years old at the time of disappearance. Their abductions all occurred during the summer months when school was out and from places commonly frequented by children—parks, playgrounds, fields."

"The local police departments suspect abductions?"

"They all suspected it as a possibility, but none of them had any strong indications. The children all became isolated from their friends for one reason or another, and hours usually passed before anyone became suspicious. By that time, no one could recall any specific suspicious behavior that caught their attention, though all were also in locations where people didn't know everyone, so seeing a stranger didn't ring alarm bells."

Roxanne turned to David. "I've fed the information to our behavioral analysts for their insight. The thought is McGregor preferred these midsize towns because he would have stood out in a more sophisticated urban environment or in a wealthy neighborhood, and everyone knew each other in tiny towns, so they would remember a stranger. He probably looked just like another unemployed worker or dad working a late shift and killing time in a park as he patiently waited to spot a child alone. Then he could use a ruse like the lost dog to isolate the kid without drawing attention."

David scanned the map. "And no one ever spotted a pattern?"

"Sadly, no. Counting Jaxon, we now have seven identified victims kidnapped from six different states, all at least a year apart. They all appeared to be isolated."

"So many kids, though…"

Roxanne grimaced. "And you know the statistics as well as I do. NCIC logs over four hundred thousand missing-children reports every year in the US. Most are recovered alive within hours. Those who aren't are usually associated with family abductions. Since these victims' families were headed by single parents, the estranged partner was often a suspect. Other relatives came into focus as well."

Agent Gonzalez hesitated and looked up from his notes. "And sometimes we see patterns where they don't exist. We have police departments contacting us with old cases, but we rule them out. They aren't any of our victims."

David picked up a paper clip and started twisting it out of frustration. "So how are we doing on the eight still-unidentified children?"

"We're using the geographic and age pattern to scan for other possible matches. Already have a few DNA submissions coming from local police who didn't suspect an abduction but assumed a child had wandered into the woods or drowned in a lake or river. Thus, they never submitted DNA to our database. And others will turn out to have been in the DNA database all along, but it takes time to churn through all the possibilities. The technicians are working it as fast as they can."

"I get it. Good work so far." David folded his hands together. "How about the adults?"

"As we suspected, the older male in the first grave is Rick

McGregor, Matt's father. The autopsy confirmed he died a violent death, a beating with a blunt object—perhaps an ax handle, baseball bat, or even a tree branch. The left ulna is shattered"—Gonzalez held his arm up in front of his face and rubbed the forearm—"which the ME suspects is probably a defensive wound to his lower arms from trying to ward off the blows."

"Estimated date of death?"

"Still working on narrowing that down, but estimating fifteen to twenty years."

David consulted his notes. "We can narrow that down some. We know from Buck he was seen in Wattsville a little over seventeen years ago. Sometime after that, I stopped him personally, driving that van in a routine traffic stop."

Roxanne added, "The question for the analysts is whether Rick's death was the trigger, but we don't think so. We believe he did act as an inhibitor because of his disapproval, but we think something else happened. There appears to be too long a lag, probably several years, from Rick's death to the first kidnap."

"Why do you suspect a gap?"

Gonzalez picked his report back up. "Because victim number two, the female, appears to have died two or more years after Rick but before the first child victim."

David drummed his fingers. "But we still don't know who she is?"

"No."

"A relative?"

"No, DNA rules that out. She's not a genetic match to any of the McGregors and has not matched to any missing person we know of."

David leaned back in his chair and stared at the board. "Okay, so he kills his father in a fit of rage. And then a couple of years later, he kills an adult female. And then a couple of years after that, he kills his first boy. So was she an experiment? Maybe an easy target like a prostitute for him to try out what he wants to do?"

Roxanne smiled. "Very good, Sheriff. The BAU might have an opening for you."

David shook his head grimly. "No, thanks. I want to go back to normal crime." He turned back to Gonzalez. "Looks like we identified the one adult killed three years ago."

"DNA records submitted by the family of Chance Victor Street were a confirmed match to our young male. He disappeared three years ago at the age of twenty-three. An avid outdoorsman from Northern Georgia, he enjoyed solo hiking during the day and often separated from others during his through-hike on the Appalachian Trail. In fact, in the previous two years, he never came close to finishing the trek because he wandered off so many side trails to see other sights. He liked to go at his own pace and not be constrained with exact plans, so no one was surprised when he didn't show up at his planned shelters. Concern grew several days after he was last sighted, as fellow hikers compared notes and realized no one had seen him. By the time authorities were brought in, the possible search area was very broad, including towns off the trail where he might have met and hung out with new friends, a pattern in his history."

"So we never even knew he was missing in Miller County."

"Nope. The Great Smoky rangers had been included in the missing-person notices since the trail runs through the park, but no one had any real idea where the man even went missing." Gonzalez flipped a page and read, "Final autopsy results are being completed, but the skull of the deceased reflects blunt-force trauma consistent with an ax as the likely cause of death. We found the entire contents of his backpack in his grave with him, so everything points to this being the hiker Jaxon witnessed being murdered."

"Which means the teenage boy found in the next grave must be Kevin? Killed the same day, according to Jaxon," David added.

Gonzalez shuffled folders. "Early teens, deceased approximately three years, with multiple fractures consistent with long-term abuse similar to our survivor. Multiple broken bones and a crushed skull consistent with our survivor's story of a significant beating that was the probable cause of death. Still unidentified, though his DNA is uploaded and being scanned against the missing-children database."

"But no hits?"

"Not yet. With the pattern of the other young victims, though, we have focused our search parameters. Unfortunately, the lab's pushing hard with all the other IDs as well. He's in the same queue as the rest of the young victims."

David tapped his pen on the table. "Well, we know he was taken after Jaxon because he told us about Kevin's arrival. And we know they are about the same age. So let's start with the date Jaxon disappeared and go forward two or three years. That should narrow the search down a good bit. And I think it will help Jaxon so much if we can tell him we found Kevin's parents. Can we make him a top priority?"

Roxanne nodded. "I agree. Besides, identifying him might help us solve one of the other great inconsistencies the profilers are confused about—Kevin and Jaxon."

"How so?"

"We have fourteen victims that make a clear pattern. All young males abducted, abused, and died before they reached puberty. The hiker we know stumbled onto the scene and was killed. The father enraged Matt for some reason, but it is a clear case of patricide. The woman remains a mystery. But those two boys are the other big mystery."

David leaned back and exhaled. "What made Kevin and Jaxon special enough to be allowed to live into their teens?"

44

Tammy—not Dr. Sorenson because she just wants us to chat—asks me how I feel. It's her favorite question.

Matthew was a lunatic.

How does that make you feel?

I watched little kids die.

How does that make you feel?

He beat Kevin to death right in front of me and then made me dig his grave.

How does that make you feel?

Honestly, Tammy, I feel scared and happy and mad and sad and all of that at the exact same time. And I'm really freaked about leaving the hospital and its warm beds, fluffy pillows, three meals a day, nurses checking on me, and security guards on the doors.

The doctors are freaked too. I heard one of them telling Heather I should stay longer so they can make sure the antibiotics are working, my stomach is handling food okay, and my wounds are healing. She reminded him she was a nurse and could do those things and still get me back to the hospital for follow-ups. He finally agreed to the discharge as long as she kept bringing me back to talk to Tammy.

Psychiatrist—a medical doctor who diagnoses and treats mental, emotional, and behavioral disorders.

Which means they think I'm crazy.

I figured Tammy would object to me leaving, too, but she didn't. "I think going home will be good for you. Your own bed. Your own space. How does that make you feel?"

Argh.

"I don't belong there."

"Why do you say that? Where do you belong?"

"I don't know. But I don't deserve to be there."

She's wearing one of her bright knit sweaters. This one is purple and green with giant blue snowflakes. I guess they're supposed to make you feel happy, but I find them distracting. She leans forward with her notebook clutched in her lap. "Don't you want things to get back to normal?"

"Normal? Why do I get normal when they don't?"

"Ah. Sounds like you're feeling some survivor's guilt today."

We've talked lots about this. Damn straight, I'm suffering from survivor's guilt. I'm alive, and they're all dead. All those little kids. I can't even remember all their faces. Or their names. I've tried. They were scared and hungry and tired. He did awful things to them, and now they're dead. And I can barely remember some of them, just like I can't remember my past.

The hiker too. A nice guy tried to help us, and all it got him was dead.

Mostly, I feel guilty that I survived and Kevin didn't. What if Matthew had beaten me to death instead? He was right—it was my responsibility to make sure everyone followed the rules. *Never let them see you.* If Matthew had taken it out on me, then Kevin would still be alive, recovering in a hospital room with his family around him and going home.

Kevin knew the rules. He called out, but it was my fault. I should have stopped him. Maybe if I had, we both would have escaped and survived.

"Kevin deserves to be going home. Not me."

"You deserve this, Jaxon. You've earned it."

I know she's wrong. I haven't earned it at all. But they take me home anyway. We slip out one of the back entrances and past the dumpsters to Connor's waiting pickup truck. We drive around the building, and they point to the main entrance and laugh. A pair of sheriff's department cars are parked there with the doors open, as if they were going to pick someone up. Reporters and cameramen crowd around them, taking pictures and shouting questions.

Decoy—Something used to draw attention away from another.

We drive through some neighborhoods of small one-story houses with front porches and sidewalks, all looking more or less the same to me, until we pull into one of the driveways. A bundle of brightly colored balloons is tied to the mailbox. A sign proclaiming "Welcome Home, Jaxon!" is staked in the front yard.

Inside the house, Heather says we should relax in our room while she heats a casserole for a big celebration lunch. "Don't worry. We have enough food to last 'til kingdom come. I think everyone in town brought something over."

Connor pushes open the door to his room—he keeps saying "our," but I can't do that yet—and we go in.

He scoops a wadded-up T-shirt off the floor and tosses it into a basket then sits on the bed pushed up against a wall by the window. Tennis shoes and boots are on the floor. The desk between the two beds has a laptop and a pile of comic books. His bed has a red-and-black patterned quilt. The pillow sticks out from underneath it. He waves his arm around. "So what do you think?"

Posters are tacked to the light-blue walls. The first one that catches my eye is a bright-red car flying down an open high-way. "Wow."

"That's a Lamborghini."

"You going to get one?"

He laughed. "Sure. With my next raise."

"Is that a friend of yours?" I point to a guy with a white-and-blue jersey, holding a football.

"Cam Newton? We don't exactly hang out, but he's cool."

"And…" I point at the next poster, a guy in shorts, shooting a basketball.

"Stephen Curry. Also not a friend."

"And him? Does he play sports?" A guy in blue jeans leans against a pickup truck.

"Blake Shelton. Plays awesome music."

"Is she your girlfriend?" A beautiful woman with long blond hair thrown seductively over her shoulder.

"Carrie Underwood? In my dreams."

I study the posters. "Where do you get all of the pictures?"

"Mostly at a consignment store downtown. We can get you some."

I nod slowly. "I don't know people like this."

"They don't have to be people. Maybe we can get you a sunrise coming over the mountains. I've seen some like that down there."

I walk over to the closet and run my hands down the clothes. The closet is full of his jeans and shirts and hoodies and coats. "Whose clothes are these?"

"Mine."

"All these are yours?" I've never had more than a pair of pants and a shirt, and they had to last until he remembered to get something else, which wasn't often.

"You can try them on if you want. I've got old stuff in there too small for me. Maybe they will fit."

I look over at him sprawled in the bed. He's not big like

Horace back at the hospital, but he's still tall and muscular. I'm just short and skinny. I don't see how any of his stuff can fit me.

"We can find you clothes down at the consignment store too. Or the Walmart out by the interstate. Don't worry. Plenty of room in the closet."

I walk over to my side of the room and touch the bed with my hand. It has a picture of a guy holding what looks like a sword. I point at it and look at Connor with a question on my face.

"*Star Wars*. You used to really like it."

I walk over to a small bookcase with little kids' picture books and action figurines. I pick up one who looks just like the guy on my bedspread.

"Mom didn't want to change everything." He leaned back against the wall. "I guess I didn't, either. We even kept all your pants and shirts in those drawers."

I sit down on the bed and look around.

"Don't worry, Jax. We can change it all. Get you stuff. Make it home again."

Connor's side of the room grew and evolved over the years. My side, however, is as lost as that little kid was ten years ago. It tells me again how little I belong here.

Connor's nice. I like him, really, but he's not a brother to me like Kevin is.

Was.

We shared the darkness together. Brothers of the dark.

But here I am. Missing my brother and gaining one at the same time.

It's not right.

I don't belong here.

45

"Thanks for letting me do this." Harold cut the twine holding the trunk of his Chevelle closed to reveal his surprise.

Heather wrung her hands and forced a smile for her ex-husband. He was trying, really trying, to be a father. Winning Connor over hadn't been easy after years of broken promises and lengthy disappearances, but he had made progress. Helping Connor buy that beat-up old pickup truck certainly hadn't hurt. The man wasn't creative enough to try a different tactic, so she wasn't surprised when Harold had called and told her he had a present for Jaxon. Since they had only been home from the hospital for three days, she thought it was too soon but had reluctantly agreed.

"Where did you get it?"

Harold rested the bright-red bicycle on its kickstand and stepped back to admire it. "The consignment store downtown. I had to oil the chain and sprockets and adjust the brakes, but it runs fine now. Then I sanded the rust off the frame and painted it the same color as the one he had as a kid. Thought maybe it would remind him of it."

She shuddered and looked away. "It might."

He looked up at her, his head cocked to the side. His face paled. "Oh God, I didn't think. I'm so sorry. I'll take it away."

She reached out and touched his arm. "No, don't. He'll love it. It just…"

"I'm such an idiot. The police found his bicycle in the park beside the swing set that day."

She did her best to smile. "Yes, but it's silly. This bike is totally different. That one was a little kid's bike."

"But the red. I wanted it to remind him, and didn't think it would remind you too. I'll take it back and paint it purple or something."

She placed her hand on his forearm. "Harold, it's okay. It caught me off guard, but you're right. It probably will remind him of happier times, and that's perfect. We need to do everything we can to take him back to normal. Besides, I can't remember the last time I've taken time off work, and I'm glad I've spent some time with them, but two teenage boys underfoot the whole time is a little noisy. Getting out of the house will do them both some good."

She waved off his protest and turned up the short walkway to the front door. Video-game noises squawked through the screen door, the constant sound of two teenage boys at play, but now it was both her sons and not Connor and one of his buddies. She hollered to be heard over the racket. "Boys. Your dad has something for you."

Within seconds, the screen door squeaked open and banged shut as the boys exited the house, the soles of their tennis shoes slapping the ground. "Cool," exclaimed Connor as he raced up and grabbed the handlebars. Jaxon froze halfway down the walk, the color draining out of his face as he stood and stared at the bicycle.

Harold and Heather exchanged a worried glance. She strained to keep her voice steady through her concern that his first connection was the same as hers—to the day he last rode his bike. "It's a present from your dad. Do you like it?"

He swallowed hard, and his voice came out shaky. "Uh, yeah. Thanks."

Connor bounced on the balls of his feet, looking back and forth between his parents and his brother. His face brightened. "Let me get mine, and we can ride around together."

"I don't…" Jaxon shifted his gaze to his brother. "I don't know how to ride it."

Connor stopped bouncing and raised an eyebrow. "But we used to ride everywhere. You never forget how to ride a bike, right?"

Heather walked over to Jaxon and stroked his hair. "It's been a long time, right, honey? You forgot how is all."

"Y-y-y-yeah, that's it."

"Well, we can't put training wheels on it, 'cause that would look silly." A nervous laugh slipped out of Connor, earning him a dirty look from his mother. He dropped the smile from his face. "Don't worry about it. I'll teach you, Jax. Jump on."

Heather absorbed the younger boy's nervous look and nodded encouragement to him. He hesitantly stepped forward and slung his leg over the middle bar. As Connor held tightly to the seat and handlebars, Jaxon balanced and pleaded, "Don't let me fall."

"Don't worry, little dude, I've got ya. Just pedal slowly."

Jaxon remained frozen, his toes planted on the pavement. A puzzled look crossed Connor's face, but he shrugged it off. He released the handlebars, guided Jaxon's left foot onto the pedal, and waited for the boy to do the same on the other pedal. Without the benefit of movement, the bike remained balanced only because of Connor's grip. Replacing his hand on the handlebars and gripping the back of the seat, Connor walked forward slowly to give Jaxon the sensation of move-ment. He carefully removed his hand from the handlebar and walked holding only the seat, allowing Jaxon to get the feel of the movement of the front tire as the younger boy's knuckles turned white under his firm grip.

He patiently explained the hand brakes and dismissed the gears with a wave. "We'll get to those later, but first I want you to pedal." With a cautious rotation of his feet, Jaxon was soon propelling forward. Connor jogged alongside, shouting encouragement. The front wheel wobbled a few times, but he was soon moving fast enough to turn Connor's jog into a determined run.

Connor released his hold on the seat and kept pace alongside. He continued to coach and encourage, but Jaxon had full control. Connor slowed and fell behind as he watched his brother ride around in the street.

Jaxon looked over his shoulder and realized Connor was several steps behind. He panicked and didn't look where he was going. The bike crashed into the curb, sending both boy and bicycle tumbling through the air. He hit the grass in the yard and somersaulted, a tangle of legs and arms flying in the air.

Heather gasped and ran toward him. Harold and Connor reached him first, so she had to elbow her way past them to see the extent of his injuries. To her surprise, he was sitting up and laughing.

"Did you hurt yourself?" she asked.

He held up his left arm, the ripped shirtsleeve exposing a raw scrape and a trickle of blood on his forearm. He shrugged and said with a grin, "It's nothing."

The horror of his past rippled through Heather again. He wasn't simply acting tough, as some boys would. Compared to the things he had experienced, a scrape really was nothing.

He righted the bike and climbed back aboard. With a little help from Connor, he restarted his pedaling and was soon riding up and down the block. Smiling, Jaxon regained his confidence and extended his distance in front of his brother, too far to stop a fall but never out from under the watchful gaze.

Harold stood beside his ex-wife as she alternately gasped and held her breath. "Connor's good with him, isn't he?"

As she started to answer, Jaxon wobbled again and struggled to correct his balance. Connor reached out to steady the bike, but the younger brother regained control himself. The boys' laughter floated across the yards.

With a hand against her throat, she coaxed herself to relax. She couldn't take her eyes off them as she answered Harold. "I went into the den the other night, and Connor was teaching him how to work the TV remote control. Jaxon is fascinated with movies, like he's never seen one, but didn't seem to know how to turn the TV on or off, change the channels, or even adjust the volume. It's the craziest thing, all the basic stuff he has forgotten, but Con hangs in there and shows him."

"He's going to make a great dad someday." Harold paused for a moment. "Much better than I ever was."

She risked taking her eyes off the boys for a minute and turned to Harold. "You taught Connor how to ride a bike, remember?"

He looked down at the ground, but the faintest smile showed on his lips. "I remember you upset when Con came in crying, a big scrape on his knee and a tear in his jeans."

She shrugged. "Well, moms worry about those things, but he got over it quick. And you got him right back on that bike."

"Yeah." Connor had stopped running beside his brother and instead stood in the road and watched him ride. Harold grinned as the bond between the boys grew. "But I wasn't around to teach Jaxon, was I?"

"No, but Connor did. And he's doing it again. Those are skills he learned from you."

"But I missed teaching him myself." He sighed, a long, low sound of mourning. "I missed so much."

Heather wrapped her arm around his waist, an expression of affection she hadn't shared with him in years, and squeezed. "We can't change the past, Harold. Let's vow not to miss tomorrow, okay?"

46

S weat ran down Connor's back despite the cold air. He leaned over, hands balanced on his knees, and sucked in a lungful of air. Both pride and exhaustion coursed through his body as he watched Jaxon ride in big looping circles in the road, amazed by how fast the boy had learned how to ride his bike.

Relearned, he reminded himself. *Even better, remembered.*

The shock of hearing Jaxon say he didn't know how to ride a bike had dulled. He simply meant he had forgotten, as he had forgotten so many things, locked away in that dungeon all of those years. Everything would come back to him. Connor would have his little brother back again.

"Give me a sec to get my bike. We'll go find some trails."

Jaxon braked and wobbled a little before getting his feet planted firmly on the pavement. He nodded toward Heather, who stood shoulder to shoulder with Harold in the front yard, watching them like hawks. "She'll be okay if we go off like that?"

Connor flashed his brilliant devil-may-care smile in the

sun. "When I promise her I won't let you out of my sight, yeah. And don't worry—I won't." He ran around the back of the house and pulled open the squeaky door to an old storage building. Pushing aside a lawnmower and some yard tools, he extracted his BMX bicycle and rolled it into the yard. Rust speckled the faded green paint. The handlebar grips were wrapped in tape to hide their wear. He brushed the spiderwebs off and oiled the chain, mentally noting how many months had passed since he last rode—back in the heat of summer, he thought, with a couple of buddies after high-school graduation. The pickup truck Harold had helped him buy had become his preferred method of transportation, but it would be fun to trail ride again.

He mounted the bike and rode to the front of the house, skidding to a stop on the grass in front his parents. They were being friendlier and warmer than he had seen in years, probably ever. Over the last couple of years, as Harold had so obviously been trying to rebuild a bridge with Connor, they had declared a tenuous truce and were polite to each other. He knew that was for his own benefit, not theirs. Without a common child, they would long ago have gone their separate ways.

Now that they have both sons back, maybe…

But he couldn't let his thoughts get ahead of him. "Cool present, Dad. I think he got the hang of it again quick, so I'm going to take him out on some trails if that's cool."

Heather chewed on her lip as she watched her younger son circling in the road, only a few wobbles noticeable. "You think he's ready?"

Harold smiled at Connor and said, "With his big-brother guardian, he'll be fine."

She reluctantly nodded her agreement. "Just be back for dinner."

Before she could change her mind, Connor waved and pedaled down the drive, motioning for his brother to follow. Jaxon quickly fell alongside, and they chatted as they cruised at a comfortable speed. They zigged and zagged through the neighborhoods, turning right and then left, aimless and having fun. They slowed at each intersection as Connor urged Jaxon to look both ways for cars, even if he had the right-of-way. Safety first, he admonished, feeling adult in his words.

After half an hour of riding aimlessly, they pulled up to the end of Broad Street, across from Abe's Market. The road to the left twisted up into the mountains and into the next county. The road directly across entered the town's industrial park, a collection of aging manufacturing plants that provided the backbone of jobs to Millerton. Many had closed over the years, their parking lots sprouting tall weeds and closed off with rusting chains. Connor worked in a factory inside the complex, hoping to never hear that his own employer was going bust. Since it was a Saturday, the plants were mostly closed and quiet, the blinking traffic light dancing on the overhead wires in the breeze with no traffic to control.

To the right was the entrance to the town park. During a summer Saturday, ballgames would be played on the open fields, walkers hiked the network of paths, and kids played on the swings. But the colder days of winter found the park mostly empty.

Connor looked at the options. The mountain road was too steep. The security guards at the industrial park would chase them out. And the park.... well, the park was a bad idea. He said, "Let's turn around."

"Oh. Is it late?"

"No, I just thought…"

Jaxon pointed at the park. "What about in there? Can we ride there?"

Connor looked at his brother. "Are you sure you're okay with that?"

Jaxon shrugged. They rode their bikes past the entrance signs and down the main road, swerving around the humps built in the pavement to slow cars. The ballfields on their left were empty, muddy from the snow that had melted off days before. Behind the fields, a nature trail wandered through the woods, but no one ventured into the cold shade. Farther down on their right, they pulled into a nearly empty parking lot in front of a children's playground. Three kids climbed playsets built over beds made from chunks of recycled tires that provided a soft landing from falls as a mom sat on a bench in the sunshine reading a romance novel. Another child was being pushed in a swing by her mother.

Balancing on one foot, Connor looked around and swallowed hard. "Doesn't it freak you out to be back here?"

Swiveling his head to scan the area, Jaxon looked perplexed. "Why would it?"

Connor didn't know what reaction he had expected, but he hadn't been prepared for a total lack of response. He couldn't believe Jaxon didn't even recognize the place. Maybe he had blocked it all from his memory.

"This… it's the last place I saw you. My friends wanted to race on the bike trails, and we knew you couldn't keep up, so I told you to stay here on the swings. When I came back, you were gone."

Jaxon looked around, his eyes glistening in the sunlight. His voice broke. "Oh. That was here?"

"Your bike leaned up against that tree over there." Connor pointed toward an ancient, spreading oak, its thick branches devoid of leaves in the midst of winter. "You couldn't see up in there in the summer 'cause of the leaves, and I thought you were hiding in it to scare me. We climbed it all the time."

Jaxon's eyes got big as he scanned the towering tree. "Climbed up into that?"

"Yeah, sure. We pretended we were paratroopers and jumped off that low-hanging branch and rolled in the grass when we hit." He pointed to a thick branch near the base of the tree and shook his head sadly. "But you weren't there, either."

"What did you do then?"

They straddled their bicycles and listened to the kids play as memories of paralyzing fear coursed through Connor. "We searched the bathrooms over there then rode around the trails, looking for you, thinking maybe you went wandering down one of them. We debated whether you went home, but it didn't make sense you would leave your bike."

Connor couldn't stop the memories. At first that day, he had been frustrated, convinced Jaxon was hiding to play a joke. As time passed and their search spread out, the frustration turned into worry that he had run into a friend and taken off with him—he wasn't so much worried about Jaxon's safety as for his own level of trouble. After all, they weren't supposed to have left the house, and he, being the older brother, was responsible for taking off to the park and for leaving his brother alone.

But his mind kept picking at the bike. Even if Jax had gone to a friend's house, he would have taken his bike. He loved that thing. No way he would have risked it getting stolen, unless he forgot. Kids forgot stuff all the time, but that would've been a big thing to forget.

As the morning had turned to afternoon and then into evening, the worry grew into a fear and finally a panic. His friends had grown quiet, their own doubts mounting, and he finally knew he had to tell his mother what had happened. He was going to be in so much trouble, but they had to find Jax and figure out what had happened.

His last thought as he rode home to tell her was that he was going to kill his brother if he found him hiding and laughing. But by the time night had fallen and the police were combing the park, he was praying that they would find him hiding and laughing.

Connor asked, "Where did he come from? That man? The woods? The bathroom?"

Jaxon looked around, scanning the perimeter of the playground. "The parking lot, I guess. I don't really know."

"His van was parked there?"

He shrugged. "I guess so."

"You don't remember?"

Jaxon shook his head and looked down at the ground. He whispered, "I don't know."

Connor nodded and stared at the empty parking lot, which had been filled with vehicles that summer day. He couldn't tell if he remembered a brown-on-brown van with a man sitting in the shadows, cigarette smoke curling out the window, or if the power of suggestion now that he knew the story made him think he did.

His voice was quiet as he wrestled with the memories. "They asked me over and over what I saw. Was there a strange car I didn't recognize? Maybe someone hanging around I didn't know? And worse, was I sure Dad hadn't shown up? Did I see him at all that day?" He squinted into the sunshine. "Now that I finally know what happened, I wonder—did I see that man and not know it? If his van was parked here, I would have ridden right by it. I wouldn't have thought he looked weird or out of place at all. He would have seen us leave and known we left you alone."

A hand wrapped around Connor's elbow. "Even if you'd seen him, you couldn't have known what was going to happen."

"But if I hadn't wasted all afternoon scared to tell anyone I couldn't find you…"

"They still wouldn't have found..." Jaxon looked at the playground. "It was too late."

"The sheriff talked to him. Remembered what he had done and drove out there just to ask him. But he didn't know about the van. If I had remembered the van, described it to the police…"

"Stop it." Jaxon's voice was strong, firmer than Connor had heard since he had come home. He was surprised to see tears welling up in his younger brother's eyes. "I wasn't the only one, remember? Lots of kids came through that place. And they disappeared the same way. Not a trace. So don't beat yourself up, okay? Please."

Connor reached over and squeezed his brother's shoulder. Just a few days ago, it was so thin that it had felt skeletal, but muscle mass was already rebuilding. "Sorry. I shouldn't have brought you here."

"I don't think I could ever go back inside that house. It's… evil." Jaxon squeezed the handlebars and twisted the grips. "But here? An awful thing happened here, and I wish it hadn't, but it was once. And for me, it's more a story than a memory."

He sighed and looked around at kids playing, the tree swaying, and a plastic sandwich wrapper blowing across the grass. His voice was distant and soft. "I don't remember it, the day I disappeared. Or my life before. I'm sorry, I know everyone expects me to remember stuff, but I don't."

Connor nodded as if he understood, though he had to admit to himself that he didn't. He remembered everything about that day. He didn't get how he could remember every second, and Jaxon didn't even recognize the place.

He shook off the confusion. He had made a pledge to his brother to help him remember, so he needed to be patient and strong. "It's okay, Jax, not to remember everything. But when you do, I'm here for you. No matter what you remember."

Jaxon wiped his sleeve across his face with a loud sniff, leaving a grease streak on his cheek. "Cool."

"Still want to trail ride?"

Jaxon nodded. The brothers took off down a muddy path through the woods, laughing as they rode.

47

S tepping into the situation room, David felt the buzz of excitement. Each day, the FBI forensics team was able to identify more victims, allowing families to understand, after all these years, what had happened to their loved ones. And the sheriff's department continued to flesh out the background of the McGregors to understand the timeline and ensure all angles had been investigated. Each afternoon, everyone shared information at a roundtable meeting.

That morning, they had identified the lone female victim. Lieutenant Gilman had been digging through her background. But David started the meeting with their primary focus. "I understand we identified two more boys."

Agent Gonzalez handed across two folders. "Two minor children consistent with our pattern, boys who disappeared when they were six and eight years old, respectively. One was from Abingdon, Virginia and the other from Dalton, Georgia. Both disappeared during summer months without any valuable witnesses or reliable evidence. Lots of leads followed up, but nothing solid ever came of them. One did have a sighting of a van, but the description was vague, and they had so many vehicles to follow up on that it wasn't of much use. And frankly, we don't even know if the van spotted was our van or not. Gilman has been coordinating with the local police departments to ensure families are being notified, so at least they will finally have an answer."

"Not much consolation."

"No, but it's something for them."

David looked at the photos inside each folder, pictures of sweet, innocent boys who should have had carefree childhoods ahead of them. He closed the files and placed his hand on them. After a few minutes of silent prayer, he slid them back across the table. "Okay, update me on the female."

Agent Gonzalez opened a thicker folder. "Female extracted from grave number two has been positively identified as Bethany Ann Andrews. Born in Morristown, Tennessee. History of petty crimes as a juvenile. Reported as a runaway three separate times. No father listed on birth certificate. Her stepfather has a lengthy record for assaults and drug possession. Mother has a record for drug possession and prostitution. The last contact either had with our subject was shortly before Bethany's eighteenth birthday, when she left the house for Nashville to be a star."

Gilman picked up the story. "About a month after she left home, she was arrested by Knoxville PD for prostitution and drug possession. A few weeks later, she was arrested a second time. She was convicted on both and sentenced to community service and a rehab program. I spoke to her probation officer, who said he thought she was going to be one of the few to turn things around. She was passing her drug tests and had enrolled for classes at Pellissippi Community College in Knoxville. And then she started missing her appointments with him. He guessed she had skipped town and reported it. The court issued the standard bench warrant, but it shows as never served because she never crossed anyone's radar."

"So she disappeared without a trace?"

"Not exactly. I called a Knoxville vice detective I know, and he dug through the old records. Turns out about six weeks after the warrant was issued for Bethany, a former coworker was arrested in a prostitution sting. The detective on the case thought to ask her about Bethany's whereabouts. She claimed the last time she saw her, Bethany was getting into a van with a guy. Said she remembered it because Bethany had told her she was out of the life."

"A van?"

"Even better. The notes describe a two-tone van with North Carolina tags, exact plate unknown. She gave a description of what Bethany was wearing, right down to the navy-blue book bag she was carrying." Gilman pointed his pen toward a stack of plastic evidence bags.

"Okay, I get what you're saying. Bethany Ann is last seen in Knoxville, carrying a blue book bag just like the one we found, climbing into a van resembling McGregor's." David stood and walked over to the timeline written on the whiteboard. He tapped the board with his hand and spun around. "But this is saying she was kidnapped six months *before* I last saw Rick."

"Yep, I pulled the reports to make sure we had the dates right. You wrote him a ticket for running a stop sign."

"I remember it clear as a bell. Mark had blown himself up in that stupid meth lab. I figured I would find drugs, put Dad in jail, and finally make detective, but I searched the van, and it was clean. Let him go with just the ticket." David stared at the board. "So we're saying she was kidnapped six months before I stopped Rick, and she was killed two years after Rick killed. That means she was alive and being held hostage the night I stopped him."

Agent Gonzalez said, "Yes. The forensics are clear."

"But Rick would have known about the house, so where was Matt hiding her from him?"

Gilman answered. "We don't think Matt was hiding her."

David spun around. "Rick knew she was kidnapped?"

"More than that." Gilman gestured at his notes. "The eyewitness describes the driver of the van as a white male in his fifties or sixties."

"What?" David sat down hard in his chair and cradled his head in his hands. "But why would Rick kidnap her? And if he did, for whatever reason, why would Matt keep her alive for so long after he killed Rick? Unless you think they kidnapped her together?"

David stood and paced the room. "What was her cause of death? Was she killed violently like Rick?"

Gilman pulled out the autopsy report. "No. She appears to have died from malnutrition and illness. Simply put, she was in such a weakened state, a flu virus could easily have killed her. Tissue samples may ultimately answer exactly what, but we don't have a specific cause yet. Unlike the other victims, she doesn't appear to have met a specifically violent end."

"So whether Matt knew or didn't know Rick kidnapped her at the beginning, he didn't treat her as violently as the others. And he kept her alive for another couple of years." He turned to Roxanne. "The profilers must be having a field day. What're their thoughts?"

Roxanne folded her hands. "They suggested her different treatment was because he viewed her differently, maybe simply because she was a woman and he couldn't bring himself to murder her. Remember, he didn't have a lot of experience with women in general." She turned back to the table and read from a file. "Matt's mother died of a drug overdose when Matt was two. Mark's mother left when he was an infant and never returned. We found she died of cancer, years ago in Texas. No sign she ever made any attempt to contact the McGregors after she left, so they may never have known. Rick had a number of girlfriends over the intervening years, but no one special and no indication another woman ever lived in the house long-term, based on neighbor interviews, though everyone is fairly isolated up there."

"So… Bethany was Rick's idea of a girlfriend? He just kidnapped a prostitute because he was lonely?"

"Can't answer that, but it might explain Matt's behavior toward her after Rick was murdered. In his own sick, twisted way, he might have perceived her as a maternal figure even though she was younger. Or maybe he thought of her as a sister."

David snorted. "So loving he let her starve to death rather than beat her or club her with an ax."

Roxanne shrugged. "The worst part is that Rick may have inadvertently taught his son how to satisfy his cravings. He may have given Matt the idea of kidnapping and holding boys at the house."

"What a sick family." David looked out the window at Main Street below him. "Okay. Let's move on for now while I try to puzzle this one out. You said we had four new IDs today. What's the last one?"

From behind him came the sound of shuffling folders and then Roxanne's quiet voice. "You're going to want to sit down for this one."

48

Heather stood in the driveway with her arms crossed, staring in the direction the boys had gone. Since Jaxon's return, she had been reluctant to leave him alone. She had dropped in his room night and day at the hospital. And since he had been home, she had been taking vacation days to be near, but had decided to go back to work that night and trust he would be okay. Sure, Connor would be around much of the time she wasn't, but he had been with him back on that fateful day too.

That was the problem. It wasn't fair—she knew it wasn't fair—but a small part of her had always struggled with the fact that Connor had left Jaxon alone that day. What an awful thing to think. Her eldest had been all of nine years old. Nine.

But he was still as carefree as ever, easygoing, devil-may-care, doing what fit him. It could happen again. They could get separated riding bikes. Or Connor could run into some friends, some older guys who didn't want to hang around a damaged sixteen-year-old.

Stop it.

"Well, I better be going." Harold jangled his car keys in his hands and turned toward his car.

"Wait." She didn't want to be alone. When he turned back, she asked, "Why don't you join us for dinner?"

Harold looked stunned and stuttered a reply. "I'd like that. I mean, if you want me here."

"As much as it scares me for him to leave the house, you're right about the bicycle. He needs the exercise as he rebuilds his strength. And he needs to play like a kid should." She turned and squeezed his elbow. "And he needs his dad around some. Both of them do. So maybe a family dinner sometimes would be good."

He smiled and nodded. "Excellent. I'll run to Abe's Market and get what you need. Just give me a list, 'cause I'm a little rusty in the non-frozen-dinner department."

"It's not like I don't have a zillion casseroles in there."

"Ugh. I'll go grab some burgers and grill them up."

She smiled. "Okay. I've got some baked beans. Maybe I'll make my potato salad."

Harold smacked his lips and made her laugh. After his car disappeared around the corner, she went back into the house and turned the TV and Xbox off, silencing the incessant music of the video game the boys had been playing before Harold had arrived. She picked up their drink glasses, wiped up water rings, and gathered chip bags. Long experience told her the snacks wouldn't dampen their appetites, at least if Connor's teenage years were any sign of Jaxon's. As skinny as her youngest was, he needed to eat.

She rinsed the dishes in the sink and stacked them in the drainer to dry. She walked back across the den and looked out the window, telling herself to relax and not worry that they hadn't reappeared. There was plenty of time before sundown and dinner. They were together. She needed to trust that Connor would keep him safe.

She straightened up the rest of the room before pausing, realizing she wasn't cleaning the house for herself. She wanted the house to look neat for Harold's return. After all those years of being disappointed and angry with him and his failings, she surprised herself, knowing she still had feelings for him. "Don't get ahead of yourself," she whispered then laughed. *But still,* she thought as she walked past a mirror, *some clean clothes won't hurt.*

She walked down the hall to her room to change but paused at the boys' room and pushed open the door. Connor's side of the room held the typical festive teenage decorations—posters, comic books, and games—but Jaxon's remained mostly bare. They had replaced his cartoonish bedspread with a simple gray cover from the consignment store. His first morning waking in the house, he had tried to straighten the bed, but it had been a jumbled mess. Connor had shown him how, an amusing event since her eldest rarely bothered to make his own bed.

Some new clothes—well, new to him clothes, donations gathered by a local church as the word of his return crept out —hung in the closet. A set of *Harry Potter* books—also a donation—lined the bookshelf. He had already read the first couple, as enamored with the story as any other normal teenager. She was worried they would be too dark with the children of the series under constant threat, but he found them entertaining and fun. She had promised to take him to the local library and get a card so he could check out more books. He was as voracious a reader as he had been at six. It was the one thing that hadn't changed about him, a comforting similarity contrasting with all of his changes.

On the desk corner nearest his bed sat the third book in the Potter series, a bookmark marking the halfway point of the book. She shuddered at the title, *The Prisoner of Azkaban,* but Jaxon hadn't been bothered at all. Instead, he enjoyed escaping into the story. She accepted anything that gave him that relief.

Holding the book in her hand, she sat on the edge of the bed and looked around. If the boys had grown up together, they probably would have been arguing for their own space, for rooms of their own. Just weeks before, Connor had been talking about his need to save enough money and find some roommates so he could afford to rent an apartment or trailer to call his own. Much to her relief, that talk had disappeared. It would come back. She wasn't naive, and she wanted him to go out on his own, to find his own life. She just wasn't in a hurry for it.

Jaxon was home. Soon enough, the room would become more decorated, messier, and more homelike. He would settle in and become increasingly normal. And sooner or later, they would argue about something. He was a teenager, after all.

They'd have to figure out school. Since he barely had seen the inside of a classroom, she didn't have a clue how it would work. But he was smart. He loved reading and had taught himself so many words through the games he and Kevin had played with the dictionary. Anything beyond basic math, however, eluded him. He needed tutors and private instruction, but she couldn't afford that. Teachers had already been in touch, volunteering their time, but it bothered her not to pay people.

But the town had rallied. Her church had come through with the clothes and books. Her hairdresser had come to the hospital and cut his hair for free. Her coworkers at the hospital had even raised a collection, giving her a wad of cash to get him whatever he needed. They didn't make any more money than she did but had been ridiculously generous, just like they always were when a coworker got sick or had a death in the family or any other trial of life.

And everywhere she went in town, people would stop her

and ask how he was doing. How could they help? Casseroles? Cut the grass? Drive him to doctor's appointments?

She ran her hand along his pillow, breathing deeply to inhale his scent. Yes, she was embarrassed to need the handouts, but she did need them. Her son needed them. He needed every break, every gift he could get, to make up for all the horrible things that had happened.

With the pillow squeezed against her chest, she looked over at Connor's bed. Since the return, he'd been acting like the man she wanted him to be. He had never appeared to be in a rush to grow up. Even getting a steady job had been a big deal. She had to trust him to look after Jaxon. After everything that had happened, he wouldn't be careless.

Her ex-husband was trying so hard to be a father. Her friends, neighbors, and even strangers in town were being so generous and kind.

For the first time in over a decade, since before Harold started having all of his issues when Jaxon was still an infant, she felt like all the pieces were falling into place, all because her youngest son was home, sleeping in his own bed every night.

The room blurred as tears of happiness filled her eyes. After years of struggle, life was finally smiling at her.

She had to admit, that scared her. Life had a way of throwing curve balls.

49

David took a seat in the chair at the end of the table, the coffee in his cup sloshing as his hands shook. "I'm sitting. What could possibly be any worse?"

Agent Gonzalez started to open a new folder but stopped. He folded his hands and looked up. "We received positive identification on the teen male this afternoon. In truth, we got it this morning, but I made them recheck. It didn't make sense."

David leaned forward with his forearms on the table. The hesitancy from the confident agent unnerved him. His nerves were tingling. "Out with it."

"The boy in that grave has been positively identified as Jaxon Lathan, the son of Harold and Heather Lathan and the brother of Connor Lathan."

Outside the window, a car drove down Main Street with its radio up loud. The bass notes rattled the window panes. David stared at the agent, disbelief numbing him. "That can't be."

"That's why I requested an extra review. The DNA has confirmed it beyond a shadow of a doubt."

David leaned back, the chair creaking under him. "But the kid… I looked at him myself. He looks just like Jaxon."

Roxanne nodded. "I know. I saw him. He looks like an older version of Jaxon. But you said yourself he was different. We all commented on how different he was. We just chalked it up to the experience."

"But his parents… and his brother… they…"

"Did the same thing you did."

"What? Saw a boy who resembled their son and said it was him?"

Roxanne slowly shook her head. "Saw a boy who they were told was their son and then looked at him and agreed. The power of suggestion is strong, especially since they've been wanting it to be true for ten years. They saw the differences. Mentioned them. Just like we did. But they accepted them because they wanted to. It made their nightmare end."

David hung his head. "And now I've got to restart their nightmare."

"Their nightmare was not knowing. Now, they'll know. But it's going to be one helluva jolt."

He slammed his fist down on the table. "We really do have Brian Rini all over again, don't we? Some impostor wandered in and claimed he's been held captive all these years."

He pushed away from the table and marched over to the window. He imagined the agony of telling Heather and the confrontation with Jaxon or whoever he was. But the vision crumbled as he thought through the boy's story. "But he's not like Rini, is he? That guy deliberately lied, and his story fell apart because he didn't have any real details to prove he was Timmothy Pitzen. He acted suspicious from the beginning, refusing fingerprinting and DNA. And he had no specific knowledge of where he had been held or how he got away."

He turned to face them. "But Jaxon—this kid, whoever he is—was there. He had to have been there to give us such details. He led us to the house with his description. Has the damaged hands to prove he escaped by beating his way through a wooden door. None of us have any doubts he knew where the house was and what it looked like. He has the significant, deep wounds consistent with abuse. He was a victim. So why lie about who he is?"

Roxanne answered, "The profilers suggested two possibilities. One is simply that he wants to be Jaxon because wherever he came from is somewhere he doesn't want to go back to. Remember, all of the victims were kidnapped when they were left alone at a very young age. Some of them came from homes like Heather's, a working mom doing everything she can and being forced to leave her children alone because she doesn't have another choice. But some of them also came from homes where the parents never cared and were even abusive, like Bethany's. Maybe he listened to Jaxon's stories and wanted to be him."

"And he didn't think we would figure it out?"

"If we didn't have DNA science, we wouldn't have figured it out. He fooled you, fooled his brother, fooled even his mom. And remember he probably went there when he was five or six or seven, the same as all of the others, so he would have no reason to understand how DNA works."

David settled back into his chair. "You said two possibilities. One is he lied about being Jaxon to avoid going back where he came from. What's the other possibility?"

"That's the hard one. Maybe he genuinely doesn't know where he came from. Maybe he was taken so young, he doesn't have a memory of before. If so, he embraced the only memory he has… his best friend's. Maybe he actually believes he's Jaxon Lathan."

"Lovely. So this poor kid is either from a place so bad he will do anything to avoid going back to it, or he's from a place he has no memories of. Either way, it's not good." He drummed his fingers. "Please tell me we're running his DNA."

Roxanne nodded. "We'd set it aside to run all of the others.

What was the point? But now it's the top of the list. They're working it as fast as they can."

David cradled his head in his hands. "In the meantime, what do I do with the kid? I've got to tell Heather what we know." He turned his focus to Gilman. "Track down the kid's psychiatrist. I need her quick. And that kid's gonna really need her."

50

H eather shushed Trigger when he sat up and woofed once, a surprised little chuff as if a squirrel had caught his attention.

Connor was in the middle of telling yet another slightly off-color joke he had heard at work. He held a half-eaten burger—his second—in his right hand and gestured with his left. Harold was dabbing his eyes with a napkin, his face red with merriment.

Jaxon chuckled, still too shy to laugh out loud and perhaps a little puzzled by the puns his brother used, but his eyes shimmered in the kitchen light, and his skin was taking on a healthy glow. He kept his voice low and quiet, deferential in so many ways, but he was talking more as his confidence continued to grow.

The scattered serving dishes on the table testified to how much of a celebratory meal it was. The potato-salad bowl had been emptied, the sides cleaned as if Trigger had licked them. The bowl of baked beans was nearly as empty with only a few bumps in the bottom. The platter that had held the burgers retained only a few scattered sesame seeds from the buns. Even her iced-tea pitcher sat only a quarter full, a sign that her fresh brew had been a hit with everyone.

Trigger stood and emitted a stronger warning bark. A pair of car doors closing in her driveway answered. Heather stood, already angry at the reporters who would have dared to come at dinnertime. She had warned them all to stay away. She told them she had no plans to talk to them. She wasn't going to sit down and cry in front of the cameras, no matter what big name wanted to interview them.

She thought she had gotten her point across the day before when she answered the door with a shotgun propped on her hip, to the horror of the reporter on the stoop and the hilarity of Connor, who rolled off the couch, chortling. When the reporter had tried to be offended by the greeting, Heather suggested he go explain to the sheriff and see how much sympathy he got. She didn't know if he did, because the last thing she saw was him slinking back to his news van.

Irritated by the interruption, she stood and waved at Connor to continue telling his stories while she chased away the visitor. Visions of telling a reporter to go to hell flashed across her mind as she strolled to the front door. She ripped it open, a hand held high to wag her lecture finger, but the anger drained when she saw the sheriff and psychiatrist outlined by the porch light.

After an uncomfortable pause, she gestured for them to come inside. The sheriff, however, took a quick look at the dinner table and stepped back into the darkness. With a wave of a hand, he invited her to join them outside.

Puzzled and worried, she grabbed a coat, slipped it over her shoulders, and stepped into the night, letting the screen door bang behind her. When she stood under the glowing front-porch light, David reached around her and pulled the main door shut, muffling the sounds of her happy family. Desperate to get back to the comfort of a few moments earlier, she demanded, "What's going on, Sheriff? They can hear anything you have to say."

"I'll come in and explain it to everyone, but I need to tell you first. I owe you that, Heather. And then Dr. Sorenson and I can help everyone else understand it too."

"Get to the point, Sheriff."

David looked at the psychiatrist and took a deep breath. "I really don't know how to say this other than to just do it. We confirmed that one of the bodies at the McGregor farm is Jaxon."

She shivered in the cold as a breeze rattled the leafless tree branches in the front yard. Her mind raced in confusion. "Sheriff, I've got some experience dealing with drunks, as you know, so let me be blunt right back at you. What the hell are you talking about?"

He pulled off his hat and squeezed it in his hands. "Heather, one of the bodies at the McGregor house has been positively identified as Jaxon."

She pulled the coat tightly around her, but it did nothing to ward off the chill deep in her bones. She turned her back to the sheriff and reached for the doorknob. "You're talking nonsense."

"Listen. Wait."

But momentum propelled her through the door. As she entered the den, Connor must have seen the look on her face, because he stopped mid-sentence, the laughter dying in his throat. Harold rose from his chair, but Jaxon—or whoever he was—looked down at the floor. She tried to prevent the sheriff from following her by pushing the door closed. "Go away, Sheriff. This is a family night. I will not have you messing that up."

He stopped the door with his foot as Harold strode toward them. "What's going on here?"

"Harold, I didn't know you would be here." David looked at the boys at the table and hesitated.

Heather didn't give him the chance. "The sheriff here is telling me that they positively identified Jaxon's body in a grave at the McGregor farm."

Harold paused mid-stride, confusion spreading across his face. He looked back over at Jaxon—or who they thought was Jaxon. His face darkened with realization, and he turned quickly back to Heather and reached for her. His effort to comfort her had the opposite effect, and she shook his hands off, screaming, "*No! No! No! That's not possible. He's sitting right here. My Jaxon's sitting right here. He came back. He came back to me. So don't tell me this.*"

She charged across the room, only slightly aware of the color draining out of Connor's face. She would comfort him soon enough, but her baby, her little boy, needed her. She reached to wrap her arms around Jaxon, but he flinched at the touch and recoiled in his chair. She ran her hands through his hair and begged him, "Tell them, Jaxon. Tell them who you are."

The boy's head rose slowly, inch by inch. Tears flowed down his face as he whispered something, too quietly for anyone else to hear. The words were muffled to Heather as the blood rushed through her ears and deafened her. Or maybe she heard it clearly but refused to accept it. Trembling, she leaned in until their faces were only inches apart and asked softly, "What did you say?"

He shifted his eyes with what appeared to be great effort and looked into hers as his head slowly shook back and forth. Dread filled her heart, and she resisted what she already knew deep inside. "Look at me, young man. Now tell me what you said."

The words slipped out, barely a breath of air but hammering her as if he had shouted them. "I'm sorry."

Her world froze. She was vaguely aware of Harold's hands on her elbows. Connor sat across the table from her, a horrified statue. The sheriff was little more than a distant shadow.

She sat down in the chair beside the boy and gathered his hands in her own. Dr. Sorenson settled in behind him and wrapped her arm around him.

Heather struggled to breathe, battling against the pain spreading in her chest and the thick fog clouding her mind. She wanted both to comfort the boy and to understand. When she finally got her voice working again, she asked quietly, "If you aren't Jaxon, who are you?"

He whispered, "I don't know."

The tears overflowed her eyes. "What do you mean 'I don't know?' You don't know your real name?"

"No."

She lowered her head and sniffed. "Do you know who your parents are?"

"No."

"Do you know where you're from?"

He hung his head. "No."

She struggled to ask what she needed to know. "Did you know Jaxon?"

He looked up at her, tears marring his face, and nodded.

"Is he... dead?"

He paused, glancing nervously around the room then back at her. His head dipped down then rose up in a slow, painful nod of agreement. His whispered answer seared her heart. "Yes."

Dazed and unsure what to do, she leaned forward and kissed his forehead. She leaned back, tucked his hair around his ear, and stood. She picked up the empty potato-salad dish and walked toward the sink. Three steps in, her world grayed, and the floor tilted. The bowl slipped from her hands and crashed to the floor, shattering and sending shards flying across the room. Her knees buckled, and she slumped to the floor. In her foggy state, she hadn't heard Connor and Harold approach, but she felt their hands on her back.

"Mom, you okay?"

"I'm…" *What? Dazed? Stunned?* None of the words fit. She was utterly and completely lost. Her Jaxon was gone. Her precious little boy was dead.

Out of the corner of her eye, she saw the boy she had thought was her son carefully place his napkin on his plate and stand on shaky legs. With the doctor's support, he stumbled across the room and out the front door.

51

I never meant to lie.

That snowy night when Deputy Patterson put me in the back of his car, I was scared, hungry, and tired. He asked me for a name. I gave him the only one I ever cared about, my best friend's.

After killing the hiker and beating Kevin, Matt had stormed up the steps and slammed the door closed. I lay on the floor with Kevin's hand in my own, watching him struggle to take his last breaths. I didn't let go after he stopped. I held his hand through the night and into the next day. His fingers stiffened and grew as cold as the room. His eyes clouded and stared into nothingness.

The room darkened as the sun set outside for the second time without my friend breathing. I finally let go of his hand and sat up with my back against that stone wall. I pushed the flap of skin hanging over my jaw and held it in place while I tied an old t-shirt around my head.

I awoke feverish and shaking the next morning. I licked water from the wall and crawled across the room for the meager supply of snacks we had hidden. And that's how I spent the next several days—staring at my friend as his body bloated, fighting off my own fever and infection that burned my face, and eating our snacks.

One morning—I have no idea how many days later—the door ripped open, and Matt stomped down the stairs. He pointed at the body and told me, "Drag Kevin upstairs."

I sat still, sure I was dying and not caring what Matt thought, and choked out the words. "His name was Jaxon."

Matt looked at me with his hands on his hips. "Kevin."

I shook my head, the pain flaring across my ear and deep into my brain. "Jaxon. With an X."

He raised his hand to slap me but stopped. I don't know why. We stared at each other like that for a long time, and then his hand fell to his side. "Fine. Whatever. Drag Jaxon upstairs. You've got to get this place ready for our next guest."

The rest of the day was simple enough. I dug two graves. The hiker went in one. Jaxon went in the other. And I went back downstairs with a bucket of food Matt gave me. Once the door was locked, I heard the van start up and leave.

A few days passed before the door opened again, and he shoved a sniveling little kid down those steps. "Take care of Steve for me, T-Dog, or you ain't gonna be lucky no more."

The door slammed shut, and the little kid sat up. He looked at me and said, "My name ain't Steve. It's Cody."

I looked at him and said, "Look, kid, you can tell me all about Cody and the things he used to do and the family he used to have, but here in this house, you're Steve."

I gave him a piece of moldy bread, and we ate in silence. He looked up at me and asked, "So what did you used to do before you came here?"

And so I told him about the mud pit I built with my brother, Connor.

So, yeah, I lied. The problem was I didn't know what I used to do *before*. I've never remembered.

After Cody died, I told the same story to the next kid. And the kid after that.

Forgive me, Jaxon. I never meant to steal your life. Giving your name to the deputy was a moment of panic, but when I met your mother and your brother and your father, I should've told them the truth. When they took me home, I should've told them.

But I didn't lie to Nurse Sheila. I really don't remember what my mother looks like. I don't remember a comfortable bed with pillows, a closet full of clothes, family meals, or a dog snoring in my bed. And the longer I had those things here, the more I didn't want to go back to the only *before* I've ever known, a cold stone cellar of loneliness.

I never meant to lie, but it was so much better than being Teddy.

52

Heather knocked gently on the closed bedroom door and waited for the muffled invitation before entering the boys'—*no, wait, it's just one again*—Connor's bedroom. He had swept up the broken pieces of the shattered serving bowl and washed the dirty dishes before retreating to his room.

He was sitting on his bed and leaning back against the wall, his eyes puffy and red. His arms were wrapped around his legs, his knees pulled up against his chest, looking much the same as she found him that day in the hospital after hearing that horrible story. Trigger lay beside him, his eyes locked on his master and a paw resting on his foot.

For a fleeting second, she started to tell him to get his shoes off the bed. Instead, she asked, "You okay?"

He shrugged, a barely perceptible movement. "I don't know. Sad, crushed at losing Jaxon all over again. And so pissed off at... whoever that is... for lying to us. How could he...? Why?" His head dropped as he buried his face against his knees, the tears flowing again. His shoulders shook with his sobs.

She sat on the bed beside him and wrapped him into her arms. His head fell against her shoulder as she patted his back.

She tried to remember when she had last held him like that —maybe the day in middle school when Cecilia had dumped him. She wasn't sure he had been as upset even then, so maybe it was even earlier when Duke died.

He raised his head and sniffled. "I keep thinking back to the day I first saw him in that hospital bed, looking so like Jaxon, and yet I was struck by how different he looked. I didn't believe he was back, couldn't believe it, but then I thought I was crazy not to accept it. I wonder…"

"Wonder if maybe you convinced yourself it was him because you wanted so badly for it to be true?"

"Yeah. I had doubts, you know, things weren't…" His voice faded away as he stared across the room at the empty bed.

She followed his gaze and felt the familiar ache of a lost child grow in her chest. Except, as it had to have been for him, it was familiar but different this time. Ten years ago had been a slow descent as hope faded with the passing of days and the years of no answers. But this time, the loss of Jaxon was like being shoved off a cliff. He was there. Then he was gone.

She whispered, "Me too."

He leaned back, his head thumping against the wall, and dragged a shirtsleeve across his nose. "I told myself it was because I was little when he left. That I didn't remember everything right."

Heather plucked at the covers, her hands shaking. "I convinced myself it was the change of so many years. He had grown up so much. But"—she let out a long breath, her voice growing quieter—"shouldn't a mother know her own son?"

Connor's strong arms wrapped around her and squeezed, his warmth comforting her. She had come into his room to support him, but he ended up giving her the pep talk. "We all fell for it. So many things were so close. We wanted it too bad."

She kissed his forehead. "Close, but not quite. That's what bugs me. He was always close but not quite. Like those eyes. Jaxon's eyes were crystal blue, shiny and bright. This"—she paused, searching for the right word—"*kid's* eyes were blue, but faded, dull, almost gray."

"I figured it was the stuff he'd seen and done. That that *man* had taken the brightness away."

Heather sniffled and nodded. "I did the same."

"And french fries. How could he not remember how awesome fries are?"

"Because he ate garbage for all those years." She shrugged. "At least that's what I told myself."

"It's when he met Trigger that made me wonder the most."

The dog whined at the mention of his name.

Connor rubbed the top of his head, stroking his ears between his long fingers. "It was like he'd never seen a dog, was scared of it. I thought, had he forgotten Duke? I mean, Duke slept in his bed as much as mine, so how could he'd have forgotten that? But then he came around real quick, and Trigger liked him, so I accepted it."

She ran her own fingers through the dog's fur, meeting her son's on the dog's neck. "Trigger's a good judge of character— you saw how he reacted to the sheriff's arrival tonight. I don't care much for that guy, either, so you're used to trusting his judgment."

Connor lifted the dog's head and kissed his nose. Trigger's tail thumped the bed in response. "That's the thing I'm sitting here trying to figure out. I mean, Trigger never met Jaxon, not the real one, so he didn't have any reason to be suspicious. But at the same time, he always liked… whoever. So if he's bad, why didn't Trigger tell us?"

"Because I'm not sure he is bad, just… confused." Heather ran her hand through her son's hair. He had never had the classic pretty-boy look. With his reddish hair and freckles, she thought he looked strong and ruggedly handsome, even if she was a biased judge. The stubble on his chin called for a razor, but his cheeks were smooth. She was struck again by how much of a man he was becoming. "He hurt me—hurt us—but still, it's hard to be mad at him, isn't it?"

Connor nodded, keeping his eyes downcast. "Weird, isn't it? I'm mad at him for lying, but I'm also worried about him. And what's going to happen to him."

She squeezed his shoulders. "They'll find his parents through that DNA testing, just like they figured out that Kevin was really Jaxon that way. Somewhere out there, he's got people who miss him like we miss Jaxon, right?"

"Yeah." His hand ran down the side of the dog's body in slow strokes as she waited for him to say more. He looked up at her with glassy eyes. "But what if they don't?"

She hesitated. The same horrible idea had been pestering her own thoughts. "They will, Con."

Several times, he opened his mouth, hesitated, and closed it, only to start again. Finally, he blurted out, "Would you be mad… if I checked in on him? Just to make sure he's okay."

"The doctors may not want us to see him. They might think we'll confuse him more." She smiled. "But I had already thought I might try to sneak up during my break tonight."

He nodded with her. "You aren't mad at him?"

She thought about it for a moment. "A little, I guess, but not really. More hurt and confused. I don't understand why he would lie about being Jaxon. I want to help him, but I don't know what's the right thing to do, for him or for you."

He looked up quizzically. "For me?"

"Sure. I'm worried about you. We have to bury your brother—your real one—and that's a big load."

"I know. It's just…" He looked down at Trigger as his hand continued to stroke the dog. He spoke softly, "I think I have to see him. Just to make sure he's okay."

She looked across the room at the vacant bed, its covers neatly tucked and the pillow fluffed. The bookshelf was devoid of the children's toys from the past, but the Harry Potter books remained. She struggled with her own feelings of anger toward the impostor, worry about the boy who had been in their family for a few days, and overwhelming grief for her real son. After so many years, she was finally going to bury Jaxon. Her youngest son was gone, as he had been for years. The last week of emotional rollercoaster—the last decade of it—would be buried along with him. They could finally properly mourn his loss.

But her oldest son was still there, hurting but alive. He was no longer a little boy, any more than the long-lost Jaxon was. But his little brother would never grow up, and he was rapidly becoming a man.

No, he *was* a man. And he wanted to do the right thing, comfort someone he didn't know even though it hurt him to do so. If that's what it took for him to heal, then so be it.

"I trust your judgment." she whispered. "Besides, he needs his books. Why don't you take them to him?"

53

"What's going to happen to me?"

The small voice trembled. David glanced into the rearview mirror at his passenger gazing forlornly at the passing houses. He gestured with his head toward the psychiatrist in the passenger seat. "For tonight, we're going back to the hospital. Dr. Sorenson has things arranged and will be with you in the morning as we figure things out."

David slowed the SUV to a stop at an intersection. A traffic light hanging from a line swung in the wind. The voice came from behind him. "I never meant to hurt them."

"I know, son. And they know it too. The news was a big shock to them, but they'll be okay. They're strong people."

The boy looked relieved and turned his attention back out the window. David tried to imagine what he was thinking as he stared at the lights glowing inside the houses they passed. He had spent the evening having a family dinner, eating good food, and laughing at jokes. The kid hadn't done something like that in years. He'd gotten a taste of the life the rest of them already knew, and in a flash, it was all gone again.

"If we could find your family, we could get everything

moving much faster. If I knew your real name, we could make that happen." He paused and thought, *I'll make sure it really is your name this time.*

The kid appeared deep in thought then slowly shook his head. "I really don't know."

"You don't remember your real name?"

The boy shook his head. He looked tired and resigned to being lost.

The glow of lights from the hospital was visible ahead, so David slowed the car to give them more time to talk. "Let's try this. Matt called Jaxon Kevin, right? What did he call you?"

"Teddy."

"Did he change your name when you got there like he did Jaxon's?"

"I guess so. He changed everybody's name."

"Okay, so let's call you Teddy until we figure anything out. Is that okay?"

The boy chewed on his fingernail before answering. "How about Theo? I don't want to think about *him* all the time."

"It doesn't even have to be Theo. Whatever you want it to be."

The boy sat in silence as they passed a streetlight then looked up. "Theo is okay."

David agreed. They needed to call him something other than "the boy." "Theo it is. But only until we figure out your real name. Deal?"

"Deal."

He was building some rapport and wished he had more time to work with it. He turned the car to drive down some residential streets before arriving at the hospital. "Okay, Theo, what can you tell me at all about before you went to Matt's? Do you remember anything about your parents? Or the town you were in? Brothers or sisters?"

Theo cocked his head and stared at the ceiling in concentration. After a minute of silence, his chin dropped in defeat. "Sorry. Nothing."

Disappointed, David decided to focus on as short of a period of time as possible. "How about the day he took you? Were you at a playground or park like Jaxon? Did he do the lost-dog routine?"

"I've always assumed so, because he did it so much. All the kids talked about it. I don't remember that day at all. It's like I blocked it out." He sat still for a moment then asked, "How would that help if I remembered how he did it?"

"We can compare what you know to reports of missing children. It helps narrow it down." David decided to focus his search in a different way—on the when. "You said he brought Jaxon after you were already there. Are you sure you were there before him?"

"I was there. I remember when Matt brought him. The other boy there at the time was older—maybe eight or nine. Kevin—I mean Jaxon—was more my age."

"Good. That helps a lot because now we know to look at missing-children reports prior to that date. By having a smaller pool of possibilities, the DNA matching can go much faster."

Theo nodded, continuing to chew on his lip as he processed the information. "What if we can't find a match?"

Dr. Sorenson glanced over at David as he gripped the steering wheel. They had discussed earlier how upsetting the evening's events could be for a teenager going through a lot of trauma. At the time of that conversation, David had been more concerned with the emotional impact to the Lathans, but now he wanted to not upset the boy any more than needed. "Let's not worry about what-ifs right now. Let's focus on finding you in the database."

"But it's possible I'm not there, right? You said that was true of some of the other boys."

David hesitated. "Well, yes, particularly older cases,

because not everybody was as rigorous about submissions as they are now."

"And since I was taken before Jaxon, I'm an older case?"

"Yes, it's possible you aren't in the database at all. But most are. Let's stay positive."

After a few more blocks of silence, David turned back toward the hospital but continued to drive slowly. His patience was rewarded when the voice piped up again. "You said it was possible some of the boys were never reported missing at all? What if I wasn't?"

"Let's not get ahead of ourselves, okay, Theo?"

"But it's possible."

Hesitating, David decided he had to answer to keep the trust going. "Yeah, it's possible. That happens sometimes, especially if the home isn't particularly stable or—"

Theo finished the thought. "Or if they didn't care I was gone."

David turned into the hospital entrance. "Possible, yes, but not likely. Let's stay positive."

"But if that's true, it would explain why I can't remember before. Because maybe I don't want to. I mean, what if they, like, gave me to him? It's possible, right?"

David parked the SUV and shut off the engine. Before opening the door, he looked into the darkened backseat. "One step at a time, Theo, okay? Can you trust me on that?"

When the boy nodded, David stepped out of the car and opened the back door. He draped his arm over the boy's shoulder and escorted him into the hospital with Dr. Sorenson in tow.

54

As small as Millerton Community Hospital was, the staff all knew each other. The nurse at the duty station on the fifth floor looked surprised when Heather stepped off the elevator. She was sure that word had floated around quickly about the deception, just as she had learned via the active rumor mill that the boy was now being called Theo. The nurse offered quiet condolences before a patient-call button interrupted their conversation. With a roll of her eyes, the nurse went into a patient's room, leaving Heather alone.

She padded quietly to the end of the hall and slipped into the room before anyone else noticed. Without the glow of monitors, only the night-light shining through the partially open bathroom door and the natural light through the window provided any illumination. Heather could make out the tray table pushed up against one wall and an empty visitor's chair. She sidled up to the edge of the bed and stared at the huddled form under the blankets, his open eyes glistening in the dim light as he stared back.

"I'm sorry," he whispered.

She blinked back the threatened tears. "I know, honey."

"I didn't mean to hurt anyone."

"We're hurting, but it's not because of you. We're hurting because we know my son is gone. We loved him."

"So did I." Those gray eyes blinked, and Theo shifted his gaze to the window. His tongue flicked out and ran across his lips. "I'm alive because of him. I would have never made it all those years without him."

She struggled with her emotions. She knew she would spend part of the next day at the mortuary, planning a service. Connor had promised to go with her and help figure out the arrangements. No nineteen-year-old should ever have to plan his little brother's funeral, but she needed his strength to get through it. And the boy sitting in front of her reminded her with his very presence of that pain.

But at the same time, she wanted to wrap her arms around him, pull him tightly against her, and kiss away that tear rolling down his face.

Her son was gone. This boy was there. The answer was that simple.

She reached out and held him as he cried. Once his tears dried up, she lowered his head to the pillow and pulled the sheet over his chest.

"I want to talk to you about Connor."

The sides of the boy's mouth turned up slightly. "I can see why Jaxon liked him so much. He's a good brother."

"Yeah. He's a great brother. I wish he had gotten more time to be one." She looked away to avoid making eye contact. "He'll probably visit you tomorrow. I'm not sure if that's good for him or not, but I think he will, anyway."

"You don't want him to see me?"

"It's not that. I'm not mad at you, Theo." She hesitated. "It's that I'm not sure he should. I'm not sure it's good for you, either. But I also don't know if it's bad for you." She smoothed his hair with her hand. "He's old enough to make his own decisions, and you've certainly earned the right to make your own decisions. I think maybe he needs to see you, needs to hear things."

"Needs to hear things?"

"I think he needs to know more about what happened to his brother while he was with you… there."

He studied his scarred hands. "Do you want to know more?"

"No." She wiped the sweat from her hands across her scrubs. "I want to remember Jaxon as a happy little kid, not how things were there. Does that make sense?"

"I understand." He nodded. "He was happy before. That's why I knew so much about you and Connor. He talked all the time about how great you were."

The room blurred as her eyes watered, and she fought against the tears. She resolved she wasn't going to cry in front of him again. He didn't need her tears. "I worked too much. I should have been there more. Loved him more."

Theo sat up in the bed and focused on her. "I lived because he was there for me, but he lived because he knew you loved him. He never doubted that, not once, not on the darkest day. He always thought you or Con would save him. Or maybe his soldier dad would bust down the door. You may not want to know anything else that happened there, but you should know that."

She bowed her head and let the tears flow despite her earlier efforts to hide them. She hadn't realized how much she had needed to hear that, but she felt tension slip out of her. When she felt steady again, she lifted her head and smiled at him. "Good luck to you, Theo. I mean that."

She turned to leave but stopped with her hand on the door handle when his voice reached her. "I am sorry. For lying, yeah, but for losing Jaxon too. I wish none of it had ever happened."

"Me too," she whispered and left the room.

55

David sipped a cup of mediocre coffee and scanned the notes on the whiteboards in the task-force room. Roxanne summarized the latest lab results. "Two more victims identified, both within the same two-hundred-mile radius that appeared to be Matthew McGregor's hunting ground. That brings us to ten of the fourteen young boys' bodies identified. Four to go."

He leaned back in the chair and sighed. The feeling of missed opportunities gripped him again. "If only I had figured out it was Matt McGregor back then. I can't believe I looked him in the eyes and didn't figure it out."

"And how would you have figured that out back then?"

"I knew he was messing with little boys."

"Boy. Singular. You knew he had touched one kid when he was a teenager. You didn't even know the details because no one ever made a report about it. You just followed up on it because you heard about it. You knew nothing else, and yet you checked on him. And at the same time, how many other convicted molesters did you talk to? A dozen? Two dozen?"

"But all those boys..."

She placed her hand on the stack of folders indicating Matt McGregor's victims. "Crossing state lines, keeping his abductions spread months apart, never doing anything dramatic. Each case, on its own, appears to be a situation of a child wandering off and becoming lost or a victim of a parental dispute. Even those considered abductions were never connected."

David shook his head. "Wattsville sits on a state line. Thanks to the interstate, he could reach seven different states in two hours or less. What I know about the guy says he wasn't particularly smart. I think he just ran on pure instinct and was lucky." He pulled his legal pad toward him. "Which brings me to the thing that's still keeping me up all night. I've been trying to figure out why Jaxon and Theo were allowed to mature into teenagers. In fact, if Theo's story about the hiker is accurate, and all the forensics say it is, then Jaxon, aka Kevin, would have kept living except for violating the rules. All of the other boys died much younger."

"Just luck, maybe, though I don't know if that's good luck or bad."

"I think it's more than that. All the other boys had one other thing in common. They were all either older or younger than Jaxon and Theo. Only those two are the same age. And they were near instant friends from the time Jaxon arrived, and their bond only grew over the years."

Roxanne nodded. "Right. We think they were allowed to live so long because they were friends."

"But see, I'm beginning to think that's not quite right. I read and reread the psychiatrist's reports last night. I don't think they lived so long because they were friends. I think Jaxon lived so long because he was Theo's friend."

Roxanne sat back in her chair and chewed her pen. "That would have made Theo more important to Matthew than Jaxon."

"Exactly. It clicked for me when I noticed an interesting anomaly in our interviews with Theo, when he describes the fear the various boys felt about being summoned upstairs."

"Of course. That must have been awful. The things that pervert did to them."

"Exactly, except his description is always in third person. They felt this. He felt that. He never says 'I.'" David flipped to a highlighted section in a pad of notes. "The psychiatrist working with him thinks he doesn't use 'I' because he was never the target. He never describes being touched. Not one single time. Dr. Sorenson thinks he may never have been molested."

"Maybe he just buried the memories."

David nodded. "Certainly possible, but isn't it strange that he doesn't have a problem remembering all the other horrible things that happened? He often describes being summoned upstairs, but he always seemed to assume Matt had some task for him to do so he didn't feel the same fears. Awful, heinous tasks like burying bodies or washing blood out of the van, true, but he also never mentions any other boy ever being invited outside to do tasks like he did."

"Was Jaxon the same way?"

"I wish that were true, but no. Theo remembers clearly consoling Jaxon after molestation episodes. They were less frequent as he was older, and especially if other, younger victims were with them at a given time, but Jaxon was not spared."

"So Theo wasn't molested. And Jaxon, who was molested, was allowed to live longer because he was friends with Theo. What makes Theo so special?" Roxanne started and sat up. "You're not suggesting—"

The sheriff nodded. "Bethany Ann Andrews. The prostitute."

"You think she's Theo's mother?"

"It fits and would explain why Theo can't remember a before. Maybe he didn't have a before. Rick meets a prostitute and maybe falls for her, or maybe he pays her to move in with him, or maybe he does kidnap her—who knows? He was seen picking her up in Knoxville. If Theo is the same age as Jaxon —and we all think he is because the timing is about right— Rick McGregor gets Bethany Ann pregnant and has a third son, Theo."

"So you think Matt and Theo are half brothers?"

"And a half brother to Mark. Same father. Three different mothers." David leaned back in his chair. "So I started thinking, maybe Matt killed his father precisely because Bethany was pregnant. Or maybe after the child was born. Either way, now he needs to keep her around to raise the kid. By the time she died, he had grown attached."

"So attached he left the kid in a basement and beat him."

"I didn't say he was normal."

Roxanne tsked. "That poor kid. Can you imagine the horror of finding out that maniac is your brother?"

David leaned back in his chair. "We'll know soon enough. Get your lab to test his DNA against Rick's and Bethany's. Since it's a simple yes-or-no question, we'll have an answer quick."

56

Connor strode down the hospital hallway, averting his eyes from the glances of the nurses working at the central station. Trigger, adorned in his purloined service-dog vest, walked beside him with his head held high.

In his earlier visits, he had worried someone might challenge Trigger's right to be there. He wasn't a service dog, and people knew it.

But now he worried about his own right to visit. Maybe Theo didn't want to see him, or maybe there was a rule against it. They weren't related, at least not anymore.

He realized he liked it better when he did things without thinking about the consequences. Thinking about what could go wrong was exhausting.

With a trembling hand, he knocked on the door and waited for the mumbled reply. He pushed the latch and stuck his head through the crack on the door. "Mind if I come in for a minute?"

Whatever hesitance Connor was feeling wasn't shared by the dog. Trigger let loose a soft chuff, forced open the door with his body, and scrambled across the linoleum floor. His claws clattered on the slick surface, and he launched himself through the air, landing with an enthusiastic bounce on the bed. The dog's squeaks of delight and Theo's giggles filled the room as Connor let the door click shut behind him. He set the stack of Harry Potter books on the bed and settled into the empty visitor's chair. Trigger's obvious delight—that sweeping tail threatened to clear the tray table of its water glass and pitcher—made Connor smile despite the violation he had felt since the revelation of the previous night.

Once the dog settled on the bed, still jubilant in the reunion but calmer, Connor cleared his throat. "I debated all night whether I should come. I didn't know if you would want to see me."

The smile faded from Theo's face, and he wouldn't meet Connor's eyes. "I'm glad you did. I wanted to say… I'm sorry. I should never…"

Connor waved the apology away with a swoop of his hand. "I think I kinda get it. Why you didn't tell us you weren't him. I mean, if you had told us, we probably wouldn't have gotten to know you. And we wouldn't have taken you home."

The bed squeaked as Trigger pawed at the boy's hand to continue petting him. Theo turned his head toward the dog, his eyes glistening. "It's the first place I've ever been I didn't want to leave."

Connor cupped his hands behind his head, looked up at the ceiling, and exhaled. "I get it. And I'm glad you were there. It was fun, hanging out."

Theo nodded. "I liked it too."

They sat in an uncomfortable silence, only the noise of the dog's panting in the room. Connor leaned forward. "Can you tell me something?"

"Sure."

"What was he like? My brother. Tell me something good about him."

Theo thought for a minute and then looked at the pile of books. "Did you know he taught me how to read?"

Connor sat up in shock. "He did?"

"Yeah. Most of the kids were so little they could only sound out a few words. I don't think I knew any at all. But Jaxon loved to read. We had a few old books lying around, and he read them all to me. He would read until it got too dark to see. And then he would tell me the stories of books he had read before."

"That sounds like Jax."

"So, anyway, one of the books we had was that dictionary. I don't remember who brought it or anything, but it was always there. And Jaxon liked to flip through it and learn new words, so one day he started showing me how words worked. He invented the dictionary game to teach me how to read. He would look up a word and have me sound it out. We kept trying harder and harder words, and we had to try and figure out what they meant without looking at the definition."

"So he taught you Harry Potter?"

Theo shook his head. "No. We didn't have those. I think he would have liked them. But I know I can read 'em because he showed me how."

"That's cool." Connor shifted in his chair. Something had kept him up all night, and he had to ask. "The story about Kevin being beaten for calling out to the hitchhiker. Was that true?"

The boy buried his face into the dog's neck, his shoulders shuddering. He sniffled and answered, his voice muffled in the fur. "Yes. Everything I told you was true. Except my name."

"So Kevin was Jaxon?" He could barely bring himself to say it. "That means you saw that man beat my brother to death?"

"Yes."

The room blurred as tears of anguish filled his eyes. His

chest ached, as if he was drowning in a sea of pain. He struggled to breathe, each intake of air hitching against the sobs trying to escape. Jaxon had been beaten to death because he had ridden off with his friends rather than watch his little brother.

Theo sighed. "I wanted to stop him, but he would have done the same thing to me."

"I get it."

"He was my best friend. I loved him. Like a"—Theo took in a deep breath, his own words slurred with emotion—"like a brother. If I could have stopped it…"

Connor rose to his feet and stumbled toward the bed. He reached out for the younger boy's hand, his fingers wrapping around his wrist. "I'm glad he had you as a friend. I can't imagine how horrible it would've been alone there."

Theo looked up, their eyes meeting. "It was awful alone. Once he was gone, I wanted to die too."

Connor wrapped his arms around the boy, drawing them chest to chest, where they consoled each other. Trigger wriggled between them, alternately licking their faces clear of the flowing tears. "I'm glad you didn't."

57

The number of agents had dwindled to only a couple, the buzz in the large room muted. Excess computer equipment had been packed into boxes and stacked along the wall, waiting for movers to carry them down the steps and load them into trucks. The case files were moving back to the sheriff's office.

David sat at the conference table with his coffee cup in hand and the DNA results for Theo in the other. Ever since the confirmation had come in, he had been horrified how right his conclusion had been. And how wrong.

He looked at Roxanne. "Thanks for your help. We'd be waiting for months for the state labs to get all these tests done."

She looked glumly at the board. One more child victim's name had been filled in. Three question marks remained. "We'll keep trying, but sometimes those identifications never happen. John Wayne Gacy killed thirty-three young men, but six of the recovered bodies were never identified. Some took years to be."

"But the science is better today, right?"

"True, but if a kid was never reported missing, we wouldn't

have any dental records or DNA to match to. No matter how good the science gets, it's tough to find something without data."

David gripped the coffee cup in his hands and studied the rippling surface. "The new one is the same as the general pattern among the others?"

"Yes. He disappeared while riding his bike alone in a vacant field. It was just down from his house, so his mom felt safe. She was working two jobs and took a nap on the couch. When she woke up, he was gone. A canvass of the area didn't turn up anything suspicious. No unusual cars, a man they had never seen before, or anything else like that."

Lieutenant Gilman spoke up. "Knowing the connection now, we asked the investigators to go back through the notes. During a search of buildings in the area, they discovered one neighbor had what appeared to be fresh moonshine—several cases of it—though no evidence of a still. They destroyed it and let the owner off with a warning."

David sighed. "Let me guess. A delivery from Matt?"

"A local investigator went back out to ask. The man who'd had it in a storage building is now deceased, but his son owns the farm today. Says he didn't know anything specific about it, but he also said his dad and grandfather both swore McGregor Lightning was the best around."

David settled the coffee cup on the table and folded his hands. "So we think he delivered the 'shine and then spotted the kid?"

"Best we can tell, he didn't target the boy in advance, but he fit the target profile."

"Another clue, though."

"No reason for their detective to make a connection. The farmer clammed up when they found the 'shine, so they assumed he had a still hidden somewhere. They had bigger issues so didn't search too hard for it. And they never suspected a delivery."

"If only Matt's name had come up. If only I had questioned him harder the first time around. If only I had known about the other boy Buck knew about... I'll always wonder."

Roxanne nodded. "Won't we all, but 'if onlies' will kill you."

David had given the same lecture to dozens of cops over the years. Don't sweat every little mistake, because we all make them. But he didn't think he would ever be able to go to sleep without wondering what he could have done differently.

He focused on the test results in front of him. "These are the DNA results for Theo."

Roxanne replied. "Just as you thought, Bethany is the boy's mother.

Gilman chimed in. "I've searched for surviving relatives. Bethany's mother is dead—cancer. We did find her natural father, not that it will do any good. He is serving two consecutive life sentences in Arkansas. He robbed a convenience store, and the clerk decided to fight back. The clerk and a customer were killed. No other relatives on that side. A smattering of cousins, Bethany's stepfather, who didn't sound like a winner in the first place, and not much else. We don't have much hope to find him a home on that side."

"And certainly not on the McGregor side, either." David drummed his fingers on the table. "This whole case. I get close, but I never quite get it right."

Roxanne leaned forward. "Your idea to test Rick for paternity got us there, though."

"Yeah, but *grandfather*? Damn it. I have to tell that kid his father is his worst nightmare."

They sat in silence as a mover rolled a hand truck of boxes past them.

Gilman said, "I don't get why Matt McGregor would have gotten her pregnant."

David grimaced. "Just a theory, but I called the profilers with Roxanne, and they think it's as good a guess as any. Buck gave us the clue."

"What clue?"

"Nobody needed to worry, because Rick was gonna cure Matt good. Fix him once and for all. So in Rick's screwed-up parenting, he kidnapped a prostitute for his son. Not just kidnapped her, but forced his son to have sex with her. Probably watched him to make sure he really did it. Otherwise, how would he know?"

"That is really twisted." The paper clip Gilman was twisting snapped in his fingers. "And Rick really thought that would cure him?"

"If you have a better theory, we're all ears. But we know Rick kidnapped her, and we know Matt impregnated her."

Roxanne looked out the window. "Can you imagine how the dynamics of that house changed dramatically when Bethany found herself pregnant?"

David grimaced. "And even more so when Theo was born."

Gilman piped up. "Because it'd been a long time since the McGregor house had a crying baby?"

"Not just the fact they had a baby." David's eyes grew sad. "A male baby. Rick may have realized that rather than curing his son, he had brought temptation right inside the house. We'll never know for sure, but we could certainly see Rick and Matt fighting over what to do with the kid. Best guess is Rick was murdered over it. It's as good a theory as we have. It would have taken a fairly strong trigger to both commit your first murder and for the victim to be your own father."

"But he let Bethany live?"

"He didn't hate her for any reason and was probably

ambivalent about her. He needed her to care for and raise the boy. And remember, he didn't directly murder her, not in the same sense as his father, but rather she died of malnutrition. Depraved indifference may qualify for murder in a courtroom, but he didn't physically kill her in the way he killed the others."

Gilman leaned back as if in shock. "So Bethany dies, and Matt is now all alone with his son, a little boy no one even knows about. Why go get other boys, risk getting caught, when he had what he needed at home?"

David pushed his chair back and stood up. He slammed his hands into his pockets and walked over to the window, staring down at the nearly empty street below. "Because this monster, this despicable, disgusting monster, had the slightest conscience. The kidnappings didn't start until Theo was three or four. With Matt's age preference, the temptation must have been powerful, but he couldn't bring himself to touch his own son."

Gilman shook his head. "You're saying he beat the kid, but he wouldn't stoop to molesting him?"

"In this monster's mind, beatings were normal. He was beaten as a kid, right? But desires were different. He needed other outlets for that, but he knew bad things would happen if he got caught again, so he targeted boys who were all alone, defenseless, and kept them."

"And he made Theo live with them, down in that basement."

"Think of Matt's life as a child. He was raised to do his father's bidding and haul moonshine up and down cellar steps. When he was old enough to drive, he delivered the liquor and drugs and did chores around the house. Probably maintained the still, because he was making and delivering it after his father died. So now, he has his own son and raises him to take care of the new family business—the ones he brings home. He can teach them the rules. To do that, he has to live with them, but he's also let out of the basement for other 'chores' like digging a grave or chopping wood."

"Holy crap." Gilman rested his face in his hands. "And Jaxon?"

"Just a kid like all of the others, except he and Theo were the same age. They hit it off, becoming friends, and Matt, in his own demented way, wanted his son to have a friend."

"What a sick son of a bitch."

"No arguments from me." David leaned his head against the window, the cool glass calming his fraying nerves. "And now, I get to go sit down with this kid and his psychiatrist and help him understand that his tormentor was also his father."

Roxanne walked up beside him and put a hand on his shoulder. "All you can do is tell him the truth."

David turned to her. "The truth is that the day I talked to Matt McGregor, I didn't just miss that he had kidnapped Jaxon Lathan. I missed that he had his own son locked in a dungeon. How do I live with that?"

58

My name is Ted McGregor.

After all these years of not knowing my real name, I know who I am.

I don't like it.

My father is a serial killer. I dug their graves.

Am I like him?

Heredity—the transmission of the sum of the characteristics and potentialities genetically derived from one's ancestors to descendant through the genes.

Dr. Sorenson said not to worry. We could discuss it in our sessions. Besides, she said, I don't think like him.

But I do.

Patricide—one who murders his own father.

My father killed his father, and I would kill mine if I weren't too late. He murdered my best friend. Jaxon deserved to go home. And they deserved to have him home. Instead, they are burying him tomorrow.

And then they will go home and rebuild their lives.

But where do I go? Do I crawl back into that basement? Back to my family home? To my only home?

I'm Ted McGregor.

Please forgive me.

59

"I don't know, Connor." Heather stood in their small den, looking out the front window.

"But he was Jaxon's friend. He deserves to be at his funeral."

She gestured out the window at the crowd of reporters in the street. "But they'll be all over him. It's bad enough for us, but he's so fragile."

Connor slumped in the chair. "Broken, maybe, but fragile? That kid ain't fragile at all."

Heather turned away from the window and sighed. She had to bury her youngest son in a day. She had been preparing herself for the funeral for a decade, but it had always been an abstract thought, not a looming event. A week before, she'd had the brief luxury of thinking her youngest was alive, but reality had come crashing down.

Most of the town wanted to turn out to support them. People, total strangers, followed the news stories and were expected to travel from far away. The church service would be small, an event where they could control who entered, but the burial itself would be at the cemetery where anyone could visit.

The police expected hundreds, maybe thousands of mourners to line the curb to show their respects.

The intense media pressure had faded for a while but came back with a fierceness when they discovered Jaxon was in fact dead, not alive. And with the revelation of the mysterious boy's true identity, the coverage had taken on a frenzied pitch. Security officers at the hospital had already caught three reporters trying to sneak up to his room, including a photographer for a tabloid, who was trying for exclusive pictures.

Out in the open of the cemetery, he would be targeted by their long-range lenses. Their presence was too much for her, and she was already trying to protect Connor from it. She had no idea how Theo would handle the pressure. The media would focus on it—*The boy who lied—film at eleven*—and the gawkers would post their morbid videos of him on YouTube and Facebook.

And wouldn't they just love to have photos of him sitting with the family?

She had sat in Theo's room last night, talking about it. He hadn't argued with her and had accepted her suggestion that he shouldn't be there, but that bothered her more. He accepted her decision simply because he had never in his life had the permission to say no. He didn't understand that it was an option to stand up for what he wanted.

She sat down opposite Connor. "The truth is... I don't have a clue what the right thing to do is. If it was just us and not all of that media horde—"

"Then he would be there with us."

She folded her hands and stared at them. "Yes."

"And let's say that all along he had told us he was Theo. We would still want him to be there to say goodbye, right? Because he was Jaxon's friend."

"Yes."

He leaned forward. "Then that's the right thing."

"But don't we owe it to him to protect him from them?" She waved her hand toward the mob outside.

Connor replied quietly. "For the few nights he was here, I lay in bed at night and listened to him snore. I mean, that kid can really snore like a freaking freight train. I even asked one of the docs about it, and he said it's probably 'cause that monster broke his nose so many times."

"I know. I could hear it in my room."

"For the last two nights, I haven't had to put up with that snore. You would think I could sleep, but I don't. It's too quiet. And it made me wonder how many nights Jaxon fell asleep comforted by that crazy snore, knowing his friend was close."

Heather wiped away a tear.

Connor sniffled and continued. "The thing is, Jaxon was in Theo's life for more years than he was in ours. I think it's only fair he gets to say goodbye like we do. I don't know how, but I'm going to make sure he can be there."

Heather stood and glared out the window. "Then let's figure it out."

60

Connor rapped his knuckles on the door and pushed it open. The hospital room was dark, the lights off, and the window shades drawn. He could see Theo lying in the bed, motionless under the covers.

It's like he's crept back down those stairs into the basement and given up.

He waited for an acknowledgment, a hello, a "go the hell away," but nothing was coming. *Fine*, he thought as he hung the bag of clothes he carried on the hook on the back of the door. *I'll show him how annoying big brothers can be.*

He took two steps across the small room and whipped open the blinds, letting a burst of sunshine flood the room. The boy on the bed flopped his arm over his face and scrunched it up against the blast of light with a groan. Connor turned and grinned. With a singsong voice, he chanted, "Come on, sleepy-head, we've got to get you ready."

He said nothing for seconds and then mumbled a reply. "For what?"

"Jaxon's funeral. You've got to dress up and go be miserable with the rest of us. It's what adults do."

"I'm not going."

"Oh yes, you are. And don't tell me you don't have clothes because I even went by the Goodwill and bought you some." He slipped the plastic cover off the hanging clothes. "A pair of slacks, a white shirt, a sport coat that isn't hideous—well, not totally—and a tie. And, yeah, you've gotta wear a tie, but you're gonna look slick, dude."

The boy peeked from under his arm at the clothes before squeezing his eyes shut again. "I told you, I can't go."

"Yeah, okay, the sport coat probably is a reject from a TV weatherman, but it's what you get for leaving the shopping to me. Every girlfriend I've ever had told me I dress like crap, and some of them wore hiking boots more than I do."

"The coat's fine, but I can't go."

"And why not?"

"Didn't they tell you who I am?"

"Yeah, sure, you're Theo. Now get out of bed." He clapped his hands for emphasis.

"McGregor. Ted McGregor. How can I go to Jaxon's funeral when the filthy scum who killed him is my father?" He turned his back toward Connor. "You must hate me."

"Hate you?" Connor sat on the bed and rested his hand on the boy's shoulder, feeling him flinch at the touch. "I hate Matt McGregor. 'Filthy scum' doesn't come close to describing what I think of him. I can teach you a whole list of vocabulary words to describe him that probably weren't in your dictionary. But here's the thing—you aren't him."

The mumbled reply sounded resigned. "How do you know? I mean, it's genetics, right? I might turn out like him."

"Sit up. Look at me."

Theo refused to roll over, so Connor stood and grabbed the controls dangling off the rails. He pressed a button, and the mechanical whir filled the air as the head of the bed began elevating. When it became impossible to continue lying down, the younger boy sat up and faced his visitor. The covers dropped off his shoulders and to his waist, revealing the patchwork of scars and fading bruises on his chest. Connor pointed at them. "You think you're going to turn into a monster who can do that?"

Theo pulled the sheet up to his chest, hiding the marks as best he could. "It's possible."

"Yeah, it's possible, genetics or not. It's also possible you could take all the crap that happened to you and use it to help others who've been through things like it."

"But…"

"You know my father, right?"

"Yeah, of course."

"A recovering alcoholic and drug addict. Never showed up for anything on time, and that was when he got there at all. When my little brother disappeared, that man was so high he didn't come down for days. He didn't even know Jax was missing. Do you think I'm like that?"

The answer was quiet. "No."

"It's not like half my friends at school weren't smoking weed or going to keggers on the weekend. They gave me tons of grief for not joining in. I went to the parties and had fun, but I wouldn't touch that stuff. You know why? Because I decided the one thing I never wanted to be in life was my father, some guy too high to show up when his kids needed him. Some idiot who would rather hang out with other druggies than his own wife and family."

Theo's eyes grew wide. "I thought you liked him."

"I do. Now. Sober. Showing up when he tells me he's going to. He made mistakes—tons of 'em—but he's different now. I'm not going to screw up like he did." Connor gripped Theo's wrist in his hand and beamed his prankster smile. "I'm going to screw up in totally new ways."

Theo couldn't help a slight grin at Connor's patter, but he shook his head in resistance. "You're stronger than me."

"Are you freaking kidding me? You're way stronger than me. You survived all those years in that place. I never would've made it." He sat down on the side of the bed and draped his arm over Theo's shoulder. "Besides, if it's genetics, maybe you'll be more like your mom."

"Oh, great, a prostitute."

"Sheriff Newman told me all about her, and you know what I see? A really strong woman you should be totally proud of."

Theo turned his head, an eyebrow raised as if he was confused.

Connor continued, "She's being held by those whack jobs and finds herself pregnant. So she gives birth—no hospital, no drugs, no doctor, nothing, but she does it anyway. And then she takes care of you—nurses you, feeds you, takes care of you when you're sick, all while she's growing weaker. You're alive because of her."

"Yeah, okay, but I meant before that."

"Before? Just proves how smart she was."

"Smart? How do you figure that?"

"Think about it. You ever see Matt with books? Any books in the house at all?"

Theo thought about it. "An old Bible was all I ever saw, but don't think he ever touched it. I don't think he could read."

"But you had books."

"Not from him. The other kids must've had 'em when he took them."

"Yeah, sure, little kids' books. I can see some kid sitting around a park in the summer with a book in his hands, because that's the kind of thing Jaxon would've done. And then when Matt entices the kid into his van, the books come along."

Theo shrugged, so Connor continued. "But a dictionary? Even Jaxon wasn't enough of a bookworm to take a dictionary to a park or while he was out playing. So if it wasn't one of the kids', then it had to be hers."

"Why would she...?"

"She was enrolling in a community college, right? They found her knapsack. The dictionary you used had the mark of a used bookstore in Knoxville, so it makes sense it was in her book bag. She was trying to make a life for herself, despite all the crap that had happened to her. You know how much strength that takes? How smart she must've been? I'm thinking you're more like her."

After a quick squeeze of the boy's shoulders, Connor stood. "See, I think you're wicked smart when it comes to words. You know more dictionary definitions than I ever will. But who you become, who you are... that takes a lot more than just genes. I know that, and I got a C in biology. Barely."

Connor started laying clothes across the foot of the bed, smoothing wrinkles as he went. When he looked up expectantly, Theo said, "I still can't go."

"Why not?"

"You don't need a reminder of *him* there."

Connor stopped and stared. "It's Jaxon's *funeral*. The whole thing is a reminder of him, that he killed him. We'll be thinking of *that monster* the whole time."

Theo hung his head. "I'll just make it worse."

"Don't you get it?" Connor leaned across the bed and stared directly into the boy's eyes. "When I look at you, I think of Jaxon's friend, a really strong guy who survived all that crap and made my brother's time there bearable. Frankly, you're probably the one decent thing that comes from Matt McGregor's existence. So yeah, I want you there. And you're going even if I have to drag you in that silly hospital gown with your skinny ass flapping in the breeze."

He stood and lifted the sport coat, studying the checked pattern of bright colors. "So get out of that bed and into the shower, because we've got to get you into this monkey suit. We're gonna need something to put a smile on people's faces."

61

Heather sat rigidly in a folding chair, staring at the simple casket adorned with flowers. A strip of fake grass masked the pile of dirt that soon would be shoveled into the hole. Her son had spent years underground in a cold stone cellar, had been buried unceremoniously in an unmarked grave, and was about to be buried for the third time in his all-too-short life.

She couldn't bear to look at the coffin any longer and closed her eyes. In the movies, mourners at funerals always huddled under umbrellas in a steady rain. They clutched their overcoats tightly against the wind, their breath forming clouds in the cold air. The thick skies blocked the light of the sun. Shadows danced among the drifting fog. The weather was as miserable as the crowd.

Not Jaxon's funeral, she thought as she looked around. A crystal-clear blue sky was marred only by wisps of light clouds. A single jet contrail crossed overhead. The brilliant sun warmed the earth, the snow a distant memory. Birds sang from the trees as they built their nests. A flock of geese flew in formation over the gathering, honking as they returned north. Squirrels scampered among the tombstones.

The warmth of the day made her black dress itchy and uncomfortable. She fidgeted in her seat, impatient to race home so she could change into the comfort of jeans and a sweatshirt.

The minister uttered the cliché "God works in mysterious ways." She bit her lip to keep from screaming. With a gloved hand, she wiped sweat from her forehead. Her dark sunglasses hid her puffy eyes as she scanned the cemetery, desperate to focus on anything other than the casket containing her son's skeletal remains.

Connor had worked his magic. He'd reached out to his friends from high school and people he worked with to get the word out through social media. The older generations picked up the message and spread it at Abe's Market and other gathering spots.

The message was succinct: protect the family.

Instead of crowding the cemetery, the townspeople lined the streets. Boy Scouts in uniform stood at attention beside members of the VFW. Families congregated on the sidewalk. They stood quietly as the small funeral procession passed, hands over their hearts and tears in their eyes. And as the hearse turned into the cemetery, the people stepped across the entrance and blocked the TV vans and others from following.

A group of motorcycle riders, accustomed to mounting their Harleys to show respect at veterans' funerals or Toys for Tots charity rides, formed an intimidating barrier and shepherded the press into a parking lot across the street. American flags flapped in the wind and blocked the views. Photographers tried to aim their long-lens cameras in the family's direction to catch glimpses, but a collection of wreaths had been strategically placed around the small group of mourners. Volunteers, mostly off-duty sheriff's deputies and volunteer firefighters, patrolled the perimeter, discouraging unscrupulous media members or curiosity seekers from getting closer. The end result was that almost no photos of the family and Theo would be taken at the funeral.

The few-dozen mourners standing about the family—the closest friends, coworkers, Nurse Sheila, and others from the medical team—were safe to honor the lost boy.

Harold squeezed her left hand. She suspected he was doing more than communicating his comfort to her—he was seeking comfort himself. His hand quivered in hers, probably a sign of how badly he craved a drank.

Connor sat to her right, squirming in a suit two sizes too small. He had bought it for the senior formal a year before, scrimping together savings to buy it off the rack of the consignment store only to be dumped by his girlfriend two nights before the big event. It had been small for him then, but factory work had developed his muscles since. She had tried to convince him to wear more casual clothes, or at least leave the too-tight coat at home. "No one will care," she'd implored.

"I care," he'd said. He wanted to pay respects to his little brother. To do that properly, he needed to be in a suit. Even if it didn't fit. A couple of hours of discomfort was nothing compared to what his brother had suffered.

He had brought Theo into their house earlier that morning, decked out in the new-to-him suit. The sport coat was beyond hideous, nearly clown-like, but it was clothing Connor had bought with his own savings, such a thoughtful act in itself. When she had returned from fetching her keys from her bedroom, she walked in to find Connor tying Theo's tie, teaching him how to create a Windsor knot. He was patient and caring, as if he had absolutely nothing better to do than help a boy learn something he'd never had to learn before.

Now, Theo sat beside Connor, tears streaming down his face as he witnessed the second burial of his friend, which was being done with love and respect instead of some callous tossing of dirt on top of a lifeless body. Connor's arm was draped over the back of the boy's chair, his hand gently placed on his shoulder.

She watched them out of the corner of her eye, the two leaning on each other as they struggled through the emotional day.

When she had gone into the kitchen that morning, tired from a long night at work and already exhausted by the demands of the coming day, Connor had greeted her with a full breakfast: strong hot coffee, scrambled eggs, grits, bacon, and biscuits. She wasn't sure how much was his doing and how much might have come from Abe's Market, but it was a thoughtful gesture.

But she also knew in a glance that he wanted something— something big. She savored the food and waited for him to work up the nerve. When he finally did, his proposal hadn't shocked her. She had even considered it herself.

She looked at the two boys and debated whether she could do it.

62

———————

C onnor stood close by the casket as the few mourners stopped and offered their condolences after the funeral. He received the usual comments—how tall he was, how he must be surrounded by girlfriends, was he thinking of college, my, how grown up he was. He thought of them as the inane things adults said to kids, though he thought of himself less and less as a kid. He smiled as best he could, always unsure how to react to comments like those but determined to muddle his way through.

Through every hug and pinch on the cheek, he kept Theo close. Nurse Sheila wrapped the younger boy in a giant bear hug. Dr. Sorenson asked him how he was holding up. The others were kind to him but seemed to struggle with what to say or how to react. The awkwardness was apparent—even what to call him seemed difficult, though everyone knew his name, thanks to the explosion of media coverage.

After several painful minutes, the crowd dwindled to the few of them standing around Heather—the family, the sheriff, and the FBI agent. Connor watched his mother carefully, looking for signs she had considered their conversation. He knew the ask was big, but he hadn't made it lightly. When she approached Theo, Connor held his breath.

She took the younger boy's hands in her own. "Jaxon would appreciate that you were here for him."

"Thank you for letting me, ma'am. I know I'm not… the easiest person to see."

She nodded and reached out to sweep his hair off his forehead. Her fingers slid down the side of his face and lingered over the scar, tracing its line. "I caught up with Dr. Sorenson this morning before leaving work. She showed me their plan for your continued medical care and the counseling you're going to need."

She dropped her hand to his shoulder and squeezed it. "And that's not all. You'll need to work through the schooling you've missed, so that's going to mean specialized classes and lots of self-directed learning."

"Connor's told me that I've got a ton to learn."

"You'll have a lot of decisions to make. I know it would be hard to stay here. You might be better off somewhere else in the state. Away from all this madness." She swept her arm around the cemetery in the direction of the cordoned press.

"I know. A social worker came by this morning and told me about a boys' home down near Raleigh. She said fewer people would know, but some still would."

"I've thought that too. But all this attention will die down some day."

"She said I could change my name if I wanted."

"You could. You could get away from it all."

Heather hesitated and looked again at Connor. He nodded at her, more convinced than ever that what he wanted to do was the right thing. The sides of her mouth turned up in a small grin, an acknowledgment that he had won.

She turned back to Theo. "We've been talking, Connor and I. You need more than counseling and teachers, more than a roof and food. It's up to you, because, well, if you did what we're thinking, you'd be right here, where everyone knows. And they won't forget. Small towns don't forget things."

Connor draped his arm over the boy's shoulder. Heather clasped Theo's hands in her own. "Why don't you come home with us? We're not the perfect family, not by a long shot, and you'd have to carry your own weight with chores and walking the dog and stuff like that, but we do have a bed and a place at the table."

"But…" The boy looked wildly from face to face.

Connor squeezed him in a hug. "And we've gotta do something about that awful snoring of yours if we're gonna share a room."

Theo's face reddened as tears welled up in his eyes. "But if I'm there, you'll be reminded of Jaxon every day."

"Hon, I never want to forget him. He was the dearest, sweetest little boy." She reached out and squeezed Connor's hand. "Well, one of the two sweetest little boys."

"No, I mean, not just of him, of what I did, of that man, of…"

She wrapped her hand around the back of his neck. "You're not him. Never have been. Never will be. Whether you decide to come live with us or not, I never want you to think otherwise. Do you hear me?"

His words were choked in reply. "Yes, ma'am."

"Good. You take all the time you want to decide, but whenever you're ready—"

"I don't need time. Yes. Please. Yes."

She pulled him toward her, her arms cocooning him against her chest. Connor wrapped his own arms around both of them.

63

David pushed open the door of Sammy's Pub, the only true bar in Miller County. As sheriff, he only went in there to break up a fight or to find a patron who had failed to show up for court, but he wasn't on duty. He came only in search of a stool and a drink.

Roxanne had left, the last of the FBI agents to pack up her gear and move on to their next case. David had gone home to his apartment, but it felt empty and unwelcoming. He had called to chat with his kids, but his ex-wife said they were out and wouldn't be back until late. Needing to do something, he decided to go to his office and catch up on the paperwork that had piled up, but when he stood over his desk, he didn't have the heart. All he could see in his mind was a row of photos of little boys who would never grow up.

He locked his gun and badge in the desk and drove to the pub. Sammy stood behind the bar and watched him settle in, a slightly surprised look on his normally stoic face. With a shrug, he tossed a towel over his shoulder and took David's drink order. Seconds later, a shot of whiskey and a frosted mug of beer were placed on the counter. David lifted the shot glass and was studying the dark liquid inside when a voice behind him interrupted his thoughts.

"Last person I expected to see in here."

David turned as Harold Lathan settled onto the stool beside him. "I could say the same for you."

Sammy set a club soda with a lime twist down in front of Harold. He picked up the drink and nodded at the bartender. "Oh, it's the one bar a recovering alcoholic like me can feel quite comfortable in. Sammy would never, ever, serve me any alcohol, no matter how much I begged. If I'm gonna fall off the wagon, I'm gonna have to do it in the next county."

The bartender leaned back against the mirrors behind him, arms crossed as he surveyed the crowd. David tossed back the shot of whiskey, felt it burn down his throat, and chased it with a swallow of ice-cold beer.

"You know, Sheriff," Harold said as he swirled his drink with a plastic straw, "you're not going to find any answers in there. Trust me. I know. I spent half my life searching the bottom of a glass."

"Not looking for answers. Just saying goodbye to my career."

"Oh? Not running for reelection this fall?"

David snickered and traced his finger through the ice sliding down the side of the beer glass. "Even if I ran, I wouldn't win. The biggest criminal in Miller County history operated with impunity while I looked the other way. The voters won't forget that."

The answer was as frosty as the beer mug. "Since I was the one you were looking at while he was getting away with his garbage, I can see where some people might be disappointed."

"Touché." David raised the glass toward Harold in a mock toast then drained it. "You may not believe this, but I'm truly sorry about that. I blew it."

David motioned for refills. After Sammy set the drinks down, Harold asked, "Curious, Sheriff, how many registered sex offenders are there in Miller County?"

"One hundred eighty-two."

"You don't need to look that up."

"Nope. I know it."

"And how many of them did you talk to when Jaxon disappeared?"

"Not all of them because some of the offenses had nothing to do with little boys."

"But all of them that did."

"Yeah."

Harold sipped his club soda. "And was Matt McGregor on that list?"

"No. Should have been, but no."

"But you went and talked to him anyway?"

"Yeah."

Harold set his drink down on the bar. "Here's the thing, Sheriff. I've learned a lot over the years. One of those things is that my boy, Connor, is a pretty smart kid."

"He is."

"And he convinced his mother to take an orphan under her wing. Not just any orphan, but the son of the man who killed her son. That's some serious compassion."

David ran his finger along the rim of the refilled whiskey glass, already thinking of how good it was going to feel going inside him. "It's the only real hope that kid has."

"He doesn't get that compassion from me. That's all his mom. It's the same compassion she shows me, despite all the ways I've failed her over the years."

"People can change. She knows you're one of them."

"I'm not sure the sheriff I knew a few weeks ago would've been able to understand that."

David ran his hand over the stubble on his chin. "No, I

don't think I could have. This whole mess has been humbling. I've got my own mistakes to atone for."

"Exactly." Harold stopped stirring his drink and set the straw on the counter. He picked up the glass and stared at it. "That's why you've earned my vote for the first time ever."

"But—"

"Don't worry, Sheriff. I've done my time. I can vote again."

"That's not what I meant."

Harold laughed. "I've always said what we need in Miller County is a sheriff who has both compassion and toughness. In my life, I've certainly needed both. You've always had the toughness, and as much as you might think I hate you, I actually admire that part. I deserved to be arrested and punished." He sipped his drink. "But the compassion? That was lacking. You always seemed too worried about playing to the law-and-order crowd's votes. But now, I think maybe this whole mess might just make you a better sheriff for it."

David shrugged. "Even if you're right, that law-and-order crowd outvotes everyone here in Miller County."

Harold stood and threw some cash on the bar. "Maybe so. But you'll never know unless you run. I'm thinking some of that law-and-order crowd has their own issues to deal with. In the privacy of the voting booth, they might give you a chance."

David listened to the bar door squeak open and closed behind him. He stared at the drinks on the bar, running his hand over them. *To have another drink or not. To run for reelection or not.*

Odds were good that he would lose the election. He deserved to. But he used to love law enforcement because it meant seeking out the truth, protecting the innocent, and punishing the guilty. Maybe he needed to get back to seeking truth and stop worrying so much about votes.

"You're right, Harold," he mumbled. "I'll never know unless I run."

He pushed back the stool, opened his wallet, and threw money in front of the full glasses. Sammy, arms still crossed, nodded as the sheriff walked out the door.

64

I'm lying in bed with Trigger's head resting on my bare chest, his warm breath pushing across my skin. The bruises continue to fade, but the scars will remain forever.

Connor is across the room, snuggled under his blankets, the rhythm of his breathing telling me he is deeply asleep.

The room is dark. Only a few shadows from outside dance across the walls. He offers every night to leave a light on in case I'm afraid of the dark, but I assure him that darkness doesn't scare me at all. It's familiar in an almost comforting way. What lurked in the dark back there terrorized me, but it no longer lives.

No more pretending. No lies. I am who I am, and they accept me for it anyway. We don't talk a lot about it, but we don't have any more secrets.

Instead, we talk about their jobs and how hard they work and how much money they take out for taxes and insurance and how so little is left over to pay the bills. Despite that, they like what they do and are eager to work. I offer to get a job and help, but they say I need to focus on me first.

I'll be going to counseling a couple of days a week. The

other days, I'll be tutored by teachers at the school and will work toward getting my GED. School doesn't make sense for me since I missed so much, but they are confident they can get me caught up so I can get my diploma.

The weirdest discussion of all is that I don't exist, at least not legally. I have no birth certificate or any records at all. The courts will solve that and make me legal, but I have to decide what name to use. Heather assured me I can use Theo McGregor if I want—it's the name that has always belonged to me—but the sheriff suggested I might want to use something else. I can have a new name to go with my new family.

When we discussed it, Connor opened his mouth to say something, but I kicked him under the table. I knew what he wanted to say because we talked about it at night, but Heather wasn't ready for that yet.

I want it to be her idea. And if she doesn't get there, that's okay too. I won't ask. But I hope she will.

I've only had one brother in my life, the boy I spent years of darkness with. I wish he had been able to escape with me, because he was the best friend I ever had. And I think his brother will end up the second-best friend I've ever had, and he will end up like a brother too.

It's funny. Back there, names never meant a whole lot. We barely even acknowledged our real ones. But out here, names are important. Names are for remembering. Names are for honoring.

Brothers should have the same last name. I hope someday that will be true.

D.K. WALL NEWSLETTER

If you enjoyed *Jaxon with an X*, please subscribe to my monthly newsletter to learn about upcoming projects and to receive FREE subscriber-only bonus stories.

If you decide it's not for you, simply unsubscribe. No questions. No fuss.

dkwall.com/subscribe

ACKNOWLEDGMENTS

About 4 a.m. one wintry morning, a coyote loped along the side of Interstate 40 through the Pigeon River Gorge, unperturbed by my passing car. His gait was purposeful and intent.

Where was he going? Where had he come from? Where was his pack?

I gripped the steering wheel and focused on the dark road, worried I would round a bend and discover a rockslide covering the lane. It happens more than you want to know in the mountains of Western North Carolina.

That chance encounter evolved in my mind to form the opening chapters of *Jaxon With An X*—a child, equally focused, stumbling through the snow.

Where was he going? Where had he come from? Where was his pack?

I can't explain the creative process any better than that.

The publishing process, however, is much clearer thanks to an amazing team who helps me cross the finish line.

Once again, I had the pleasure of working with Lynn McNamee's Red Adept Editing team as we took Jaxon from drafts to book.

Content Editor Angie Lovell's probing and thought-provoking questions shaped the characters and tightened the story. She gets the pleasure of asking me why a character does what he or she does.

Line Editor Kate Birdsall and Proofreader Kristina Baker have the unenviable task of challenging sentence structure and my somewhat creative uses of commas.

The cover artwork is the creation of the incredibly talented Glendon Haddix of Streetlight Graphics. His ability to capture the loneliness and journey facing young Jaxon astounds me.

A mighty team of advanced readers devoured the book and offered their encouragement and error-catching eagle eyes. The story is richer because of their efforts.

My head cheerleader Todd Fulbright asks me every day how my stories are coming together and is my sounding board for thoughts. When I get stuck, we can bounce the ideas around until he helps me see the path forward. He's already seen the outline for my next book and asks me daily how it's coming.

And finally, dear reader, I thank you as well. I appreciate the emails and notes, the subscribers to my newsletter, the commenters on my stories, and the friends on social media. Your encouragement and kind words motivate me every day to sit down and write.

D.K. Wall

ABOUT THE AUTHOR

D.K. has lived his entire life in the Carolinas and Tennessee—from the highest elevations of the Great Smoky Mountains near Maggie Valley to the industrial towns of Gastonia and Hickory, the cities of Charlotte and Nashville, and the coastal salt marsh of Murrells Inlet.

Over the years, he's watched the textile and furniture industries wither and the banking and service industries explode, changing the face of the region. He uses his love of storytelling to share tales about the people and places affected.

Today he's married and living in Asheville. Surrounded by his family of rescued Siberian Huskies known as *The Thundering Herd*, D.K. is hard at work on his next novel.

For more information and to enjoy his short stories and photographs, please visit the author's website:

dkwall.com

ALSO BY D. K. WALL

The Lottery

Jaxon With An X

Liars' Table

Sour Notes

FOLLOW D.K. WALL ON SOCIAL MEDIA

facebook.com/DKWallAuthor

Printed in Great Britain
by Amazon

47266657R00189